FLYING CLOSE
TO THE
SUN

Lyndal Hennell

Published in Australia in 2021 by Lyndal Hennell

Website: www.lyndalhennell.com
Email: lyndalhennell@ozemail.com.au

ISBN 9780645261806 (paperback)

A catalogue record for this book is available from the National Library of Australia

Typesetting and cover design – Brisbane Self Publishing Service

Disclaimer
This is a work of fiction. Names, characters, places, incidents and events, other than those clearly in the public domain, are fictitious and any resemblance to actual persons, living or dead, is entirely coincidental.

This book is dedicated to best friends.

Distance and time cannot separate them.
Whenever they reconnect, all the weeks, months, or even years
just fade away, with shared laughter and memories.

Greek mythology, the Legend of Icarus

Icarus and his father, Daedalus, are imprisoned on the island of Crete by King Minos. To escape, Daedalus fashions two pairs of wings out of wax and feathers. Icarus soars high into the sky on his wings, excited by the thrill of flying. He ignores his father's warning and flies too close to the sun, which melts the wax. With no feathers left, Icarus is flapping only his bare arms. He falls into the sea and drowns.

1

Today

I have done this before. Violence. Death. Shock. Grief. A funeral. Repeat. This one is as bad as it can get. I am so tired of it all.

"I'm glad that's over." Luca's voice reflected his weariness.

I squeezed his hand. "Me, too."

His eyes glistened with unshed tears, and I could feel his anguish and pain. I shared it, but I held my emotions in check. It had been a tough day. A rough few days. The last year had been a nightmare, to be honest. Grief was not a new experience for us, and I had become numb to the loss. In trying to be strong for Luca today, I was not letting myself feel anything.

We stood in front of the funeral home, a small group of close friends, separate from the family. Less than ten people in total. That was all that was allowed. Our heads bowed as they wheeled the coffin by us to load into the hearse. It would be taken to the crematorium. There was no guard of honour; we could not draw any attention. A quiet, modest ceremony was our new normal. Everyone was silent, lost in their thoughts and memories.

I didn't want to look at the coffin, but it demanded notice regardless. It was a cool, light pine, polished to a shiny gloss, simple but classy. A wreath of roses perched on top. They had thought of everything. The elegant wooden box was a reminder that the person I had seen virtually every day for the last decade was suddenly gone. It was as if a part of me was gone too, and I would never get it back.

With the light draining from the day, we huddled together sharing the last of the sun's warmth. A lump rose in my throat as I took stock of these incredibly special people that I still had in my life. Fatigue and anguish were etched in their faces, and not just from recent events. Eyes darted from side to side, checking for danger, mine included. It was a force of habit. We were in a public place, quite exposed and it was getting late in the day. I was sure I could see the bulge of a handgun at Jackson's waist, and I knew Luca would at least have a knife strapped to his leg. Most of the girls were probably carrying pepper spray in their handbags. Self-protection was a fact of life now.

Memories flooded back. The love I felt from my friends was a comforting cocoon, though shadowed by today's sorrow. I mused over the relationships, the highs and the lows, and the journey we had shared. It was unfathomable that only a year ago the biggest problems we faced was whether we would have a date for school formal, or if we would pass a maths exam, or who was going to win the football final. Now, it was staying alive.

Our town was safer than a lot of others, but we were sensible to be wary. It was not so small that everybody knew each other, but small enough that strangers stood out.

Unfortunately, it was not only strangers we had to be afraid of. Only a few blocks made up the town centre, a light sprawl of commercial businesses and government buildings. One end was crowned by our landmark building, the old post office and courthouse, dating back to 1886. The looming clock tower was a permanent witness of change. Our indoor shopping plaza looked weary and almost abandoned, with its front windows mirroring the emptiness of the town. Pubs were littered with smashed glasses, footpath bars had broken stools and tables, while the cafés and restaurants were pad-locked shut, except for the courageous few. The funeral home stood forlornly at the other end of the main street. In the deepening hues of dusk, it reminded me of a ghost town.

When we were growing up it had been a safe town, friendly and welcoming, and one where parents had felt com-fortable letting their children play outside and walk to and from school. Walking the streets now was done cautiously, only during the daylight, and never alone. The wide roads that led off the town centre had once supported small-town traffic but today were mostly empty. They were lined with a jumble of brick and wooden houses, many of which were abandoned and falling into disrepair. There were broad foot-paths, but no pedestrians and the playgrounds were deserted and gloomy. It had a sad feel, yet also one of obstinate hope. That was what I wanted to anchor into, the promise of a better future, a safer time ahead.

It was not about the buildings and the roads though; my home was about this small group of close friends. Standing with me, supporting, loving, and protecting me. With so much loss, I was fortunate to have these brave, caring people beside me. Most of all, I knew I would not be here at all without my best friend, Sage.

I had not always lived in this town. When my mother had died, my father had wanted a fresh start. We had moved from Melbourne to this smaller regional community in south-eastern Victoria. That was when I met Sage, both of us eight years old. I was the new kid at school and Sage Ferry had been assigned as my buddy, my saviour, even then.

"Nova. Is that the name of a star?" she asked.

"It's when a star suddenly gets brighter," I replied. "Is Sage a plant?"

"Yeah." She laughed. "Stick together?"

"Like glue."

I joined her in laughter, as she swung her arm around my waist, leading me into the shared adventures that became our childhood memories. That was the start, as they say, of a beautiful friendship. We stuck together and I did shine brighter when I was around Sage. Braver and more confident than me, she was kind but fierce. She was the person I went to for advice and wisdom. Burning sage is used to purify the energy in a room, and she did that, too, restoring me, calming me.

Mia nudged me from behind and interrupted my silent reminiscing. "Hey BFF! You okay?" As she hugged me, I drew on her energy and love. "We'll get through this together."

I was not so sure. Cooper and Jackson shifted closer. I could feel their concern and their sorrow too.

"It was a nice service," Cooper said dutifully, pushing aside the hair that fell across his forehead.

He always knew the polite thing to say. His smile was kind, his presence constant and steady. I had missed that.

"Funerals are shit." That was Jackson's contribution.

He was less conventional than his twin, more passionate. His feelings were honest and deep. I had missed that, too.

"Especially this one." Mia was agreeing with them both.

"Yep." My voice caught in my throat, and I felt Mia's probing gaze.

Jackson watched me, too, and I sensed his analysis. He was searching for clues as to how I was handling this, and he was coming up blank. I was not just numb; I was hiding the darkness I had inside. Buried deep, a heavy weight, like a terrible secret.

My emotions should have been on overload, but I was still dazed. The trauma was too fresh. My insides had been wrung dry. There were flutters of confusion from my friends as they experienced my lack of pain, the absence of grief, my nothingness, but I was determined to stay strong. I had built a wall. This barrier held back a churning sea of sorrow, a violent storm inside, and the dark shadow I was hiding. It was difficult enough to feel other people's pain. If I let down my defences, I was worried my suppressed emotions would rip me apart.

That is what it is like being an empath.

2

A year ago

Year 12, senior year at high school. All previous years had led to this inevitable peak. Right from the start there was a kind of urgency about the year. I was expecting it to be eventful and interesting. Sure, I knew I would struggle with study loads and exams, but there was also the irresistible promise of excitement and fun.

"Stick together?" Sage asked as we walked through the school gates.

"Like glue," I promised, feeling confident that with her by my side I would get through whatever this year threw at me.

At seventeen, I was a high-achieving academic student and a fan of sci-fi and fantasy, much more nervous around people than I was with books and numbers. Tall and gangly, I had a loose-jointed clumsiness that resembled a new-born foal standing up for the first time. My lack of coordination meant I was unpopular in team sports and, other than walking or running for fitness, my preference was to avoid sports all together. Dull brown hair hung in straggling waves down my back, and usually I looked like I had just come in from a windstorm. I liked to think my green eyes glittered like emeralds, but Sage said they were the colour of grass. Grass is nice. I was inseparable from my four friends, Sage, Mia, Ava, and Imogen, but had never had a boyfriend. I was hoping that by some miracle that might change this year. The trouble was, I was socially awkward, and that was on a good day.

The first day of the school year dawned hot and sticky. February was promising a sweltering end to the summer. The red brick school buildings were stuffy and chaotic. Classrooms and corridors were crowded with students hustling and bustling, making noisy chatter and sharing their holiday adventures. With the lingering warm nights and long daylight hours, we were not quite ready to let go of the parties and our summer freedom. Friends greeted friends, while teachers tried to create order and make announcements. The roll was called, and the day began.

At the bell after morning break, I was still sorting my timetable and classroom route, and with my eyes on my schedule rather than where I was going, I ran headlong into Cooper. It was like bouncing off a bus. I managed to keep a grasp on my laptop, but my books and papers tumbled from my arms to spread all over the floor.

"Oops, sorry," I stuttered, and knew my cheeks were flushed with colour.

As we both bent to pick up my things, our heads met with a crash. I saw stars. He had a hard head.

"Sorry," I repeated.

I swayed a little as I stood up, and awkwardly clutched at my books, saving them from another spill. Cooper just laughed and rubbed his head where we had made contact.

His tawny blonde hair was dishevelled, and he swept it back off his face, revealing twinkling brown eyes clearly amused at my discomfort.

"No problem. Hey, are you still up for some maths tutoring this year?" he asked.

"Umm, sure. Yes."

Last year, I had tutored Cooper a few times in the lead up to the exams. He had been dating my friend, Imogen. They went out for a month, which was Imogen's usual amount of time with the same guy. Cooper was still keen on her, but she had moved on. While discussing maths problems, we had commiserated about our unsuccessful love interests and become friends.

Lost in my thoughts, his voice brought me back to the present. "I'll message you."

He smiled, and it had just the right touch of intimacy. My knees wobbled a bit, and I felt a surge of heat in my cheeks again.

"Of course. Okay. Great. Yeah."

Shut up, Nova. I watched him walk away. With his long stride, shirt untucked, and strong, broad shoulders, he made even a school uniform look good. My friends, who had been watching, were waiting at the end of the hallway.

"So, Nova, what's going on with you and Cooper?" Mia asked. "I think he likes you."

"No, he just wants maths help. He still likes Imogen."

No way would he be interested in me.

"He's a really nice guy, but I just don't like him that way," Imogen said. "You should go for it."

"Do you still like Callum?" Ava wanted to know.

Callum was my first crush. He hardly knew I existed and was way out of my league.

"Well, there's no hope there," I admitted glumly.

"You deserve better anyway," Sage reassured me. "Callum may be cute, but you are far too good for the likes of him. Cooper, on the other hand, he could definitely be your type."

"What is my type?" To be honest, I was starting to think that if they were breathing and remotely interested in me that would do.

"Someone gorgeous and sexy that treats you with respect, and love, and worships the ground you walk on." Ava had a list. "And is an amazing kisser!"

Yep, that would be good too.

The following day, I ran into Cooper again. Late for class, we converged on the doorway at the same moment. This time I succeeded in keeping a hold on my books. His shoulders did not leave much room, but I managed to squirm around him, beating him into the room. Neither of us wanted to be the last one to sit down.

"Hey, that's cheating." He was laughing quietly, and his eyes danced.

I grinned back at him.

"Glad you could join us, Cooper." The teacher's voice dripped with sarcasm.

My grin changed to a smirk. I had escaped attention. Cooper shook his head at me, but I heard his breathless chuckle.

Friday afternoon, I slammed shut my locker door and turned into Cooper's solid chest. He was waiting for me.

"Hi, Nova." His voice was deep and silky.

"Hi." The air felt chilled as I stepped back from the warmth of his body.

I had to put some personal space between us, worried he would hear the racing drum of my heartbeat.

"So, maths tutoring?"

"Umm, sure, when?"

"After school next Wednesday? I want to get a start early this year and really do well."

I nodded. "Library?"

"Yeah, great, thanks." He swept the hair off his face and his eyes crinkled at the sides with his smile.

My knees felt weak, and my throat was dry. The whole week I had been circling him in a space-time continuum, and we kept colliding.

The first Saturday after school went back was the traditional girls' night at Mia's. The five of us settled in to watch *Grease*, knowing all the lyrics by heart. Singing aloud and dancing was compulsory. Having taken over the rumpus room at the back of the house, we had party food and drinks. In between off-key renditions of *Greased Lightnin'* and *You're the One that I Want*, we plied Mia with questions about the latest back-to-school gossip.

Although she did not stand out in academic or sporting circles, socially, Mia Taylor was at the centre of things. Her caring, kind-hearted nature meant everyone liked and trusted her. She knew all the school rumours. If you were interested in a guy or a girl, or wanted to know if someone liked you, Mia was the one to grill for information. If she did not already know, she would find out. Her deep blue eyes reflected a natural assurance, and when she smiled and laughed you could not help but join in. With her easy-going chatter, she filled in those awkward silences for me, never even seeming to notice them.

Halfway through the movie, we heard, "Sup, girls?" It was Mia's boyfriend, Kenji.

With the perfect amount of swagger to be both cool and charming, Kenji was gatecrashing our sleep-over with three of his mates. Cooper was one of them. While I struggled with the instant party, Mia delighted in it. She switched on some music and her dreadlocks swung from side to side as she danced about, refilling the snack trays. Imogen was unmistakably flirting with Liam, and Cooper dropped down next to me. I expected him to moan about Imogen and was surprised when he reached up to brush aside my hair. It was an intimate gesture. Mortified by the heat flooding my cheeks, I aimed for a smile, but suspected it came out as a nervous grimace. My hands spread out like starfish on my knees.

Ava must have messaged her girlfriend, Prisha, because she turned up a short time later. Prisha's long silky black hair hung down her back and her dark skin met with Ava's freckled complexion as they joined in a kiss. Ava's red curls shone in the light, a halo around their heads. They had been going out since last year when they worked on the *Save the Brumbies* campaign together. I smiled, sensing the love they shared.

"What are you so happy about?" Cooper had been watching me, while I had been observing my friends.

I shrugged, feeling caught out. "It's just good to see other people happy."

"Yeah, it is." His eyes never left my face.

"I really like your pyjamas." Cooper raised his eyebrows suggestively.

I was not sure if he was making fun of my *Harry Potter* T-shirt and shorts. Imogen and Sage wore skimpy singlet and shorts sets, and I suddenly felt like a twelve-year-old.

"Yeah, well, we weren't expecting company." I spoke sarcastically but felt the flush of warmth in my cheeks again.

It was mortifying, but I seemed to constantly blush around Cooper.

"No, I mean it. They suit you. I like Harry Potter," he said.

I was still not sure if Cooper was sincere or laughing at me. I kept my eyes lowered and frowned in concentration. Although I tried to think of something clever to say, my mind was a blank. When I looked up, his face had drawn closer to mine.

"Nova, you're funny."

"Am I?" I was worried that he meant funny strange.

He leaned in closer, too close, and I jerked backwards.

"I always feel comfortable around you."

That sounded like it was a good thing. "Oh, right."

He moved in again and I lowered my eyes but did not move back. I pressed down on my knees to try and stop their nervous jiggling.

"I've been thinking about something all week."

"Oh yeah?" I managed to make my voice sound casual, but I couldn't stop fidgeting.

"Nova, look up."

I did and he was awfully close. When he smiled, I felt the butterflies in my stomach doing somersaults. He was particularly good looking.

"You keep turning away."

"Sorry, I don't mean to."

"Can I kiss you?"

I was caught off guard. It was as if I had forgotten how to talk. He waited until I eventually nodded. This time when he leaned in, I did not back off or turn away.

It was my first real kiss, full on and open mouthed. I don't think time stopped, but my heart skipped a beat or two. His lips were soft and tender, and he tasted sweet and salty at the same time. The patchy stubble around his mouth and chin tickled my cheeks. We fit together like pieces of a puzzle, and the intensity surprised me. Breaking apart, I had to gulp in air, taking a moment to catch my breath. I shifted nervously, not knowing what to do with my hands. They looked conspicuous clasped on my lap, so I sat on them. Although I felt Cooper watching me, I avoided making eye contact. Looking around for Imogen, I could only see Sage, who was giving me a thumbs up, and Mia who was sending me air kisses. When I turned back to Cooper, his eyes were bottomless brown pools.

"Is everything alright?" he asked. "You look like you're wanting to escape."

His hand was moving up and down my arm, sending electric shocks through my body, while his other hand played with my hair. My mouth was dry. I nodded like an idiot.

"I'm fine," I managed to croak out.

I was not fine. A better description was terrified, or ecstatic, or confused, or all of them. I really had no idea.

"That was unexpected." He spoke quietly, just loud enough for me to hear. "In a good way."

A shiver ran down my spine and I knew I was sensing Cooper's uncertainty, but it was also something else. He was excited.

"For me, too," I said.

With an arm around my shoulders, he pulled me in closer, and we sat almost nose to nose. His contentment passed through me, a warm ocean wave, gentle and blissful. I felt his fingers on my arm, grazing across my bare skin. He talked effortlessly about school and football, and I relaxed to the smooth song of his voice. Pulling my hand to his mouth, his soft lips sprinkled kisses across my knuckles. I had no further interest in Callum or any other boy. It was all Cooper. I was falling, fast and hard.

Once Prisha and the boys left, we stayed up talking and analysing everything. That was our usual mode of operation after a party or night out. Tonight, Cooper and I were the main topic of conversation.

"Coop likes you, Nova." Mia was convinced. "You two looked good together."

The other girls nodded in agreement, my cheerleaders.

"Are you sure you are not interested in him?" I checked in with Imogen.

"Positive. He is much better with you, and Mia's right, you two looked happy."

"You had your eyes on Liam all night anyway, Imogen." Mia nudged her.

"Yeah, maybe I could see myself with him." Imogen laughed.

"And another poor guy comes under your spell!" Ava teased Imogen.

Sage turned back to me. "Nova, do you like Cooper?"

"Yeah … yeah, I think I do," I said.

Who was I kidding? I smiled internally; I liked him a lot.

Cooper Lewis was popular. Opening batsman for the cricket team in summer and captain of the football team in winter, he excelled at all sports. He was well liked and respected by teachers and students equally. His confidence made him seem like a player, but I knew from our conversations and the insecurity he had about Imogen that it was not the case. A genuinely friendly guy, his smile always hovered around his mouth. He was exactly that boy you are happy to take home to meet your father. It was evident that I had jumped in at the deep end and was way out of my depth.

I had always been hypersensitive to people's emotions and energy, taking them on as if they were mine, but I was also able to provide comfort and reassurance with a hug or a touch. When Kenji told Mia a few weeks ago that he did not want a girlfriend through senior year, I genuinely shared her devastation. While I gave her the hugs I knew she needed, I found myself listening to sad songs and holding back my own tears. Two days later, when Kenji told Mia that he could not cope without her and they made up, I walked around with her in a happiness bubble. Sometimes it was draining, absorbing people's emotions, swinging from a blissful high to a rock bottom low. When I was ready to explode, Sage helped me find my calm centre again. She knew just the words to reel me in, to soothe and restore me.

Now, it was my own feelings for Cooper that were creating an emotional whirlpool. I soared with the thrill and plunged with anxiety.

Like most high school senior girls, my priorities were my love-life, friends, and school, usually in that order. Beyond that, I didn't pay a whole lot of attention to what was going on in other parts of Australia, let alone the rest of the world. Yet, when my eyes scanned the news headlines on my phone, it was impossible to ignore the shocking reports of global violence.

Wild brawl in Bangkok leaves dozens dead, hundreds injured.

Doctors fear worst as emergency wards fill up with victims of violence in the UK.

Racial riots explode in Washington.

Increasing aggression on the streets in Buenos Aires.

Police unable to stem escalating violence in Paris.

Social media was saturated with staggering accounts of increasing aggression and random violence in the US, South America, Europe and across Asia. People were being attacked and killed, on their own and in crowds, in the streets and in their homes.

It was all a long way away. It was not happening in Australia. It seemed unreal.

Although the headlines gave me a niggling sense of foreboding, I pushed these concerns to the back of my mind. Instead, my thoughts were occupied by my first kiss. I caught myself smiling when I was alone, enjoying the warmth that spread when I thought about Cooper. The slight unease I felt, I just put down to falling in love.

I did not realise the world was about to go crazy.

3

Over the following week at school, I managed to spend quite a lot of time with Cooper. We sat together in maths and biology and had a tutoring session in the library. I tried not to worry about his feelings for Imogen, when he told me how easy I was to talk to or how funny I was. Mia organised a group to go to the movies on Friday night and there was a dance at the community hall on Saturday night. She made sure Cooper was going to both.

At the movie, we sat together, nudging elbows, and sharing popcorn.

In the community hall, it was hot and stuffy, and bodies bumped against each other in a badly choreographed dance. While Cooper moved with an effortless coordination, I shuffled and swayed and tripped over my own feet. In a break, outside, the cool night air was soft on my skin but the heat between us remained. He leaned in, touching his forehead against mine and all my senses were flooded with him. I lost myself in the depths of his twinkling eyes, tingled where his fingers rubbed on my palms, and listened to our breathing synchronise, just before we met in a giddy kiss.

On Monday, I drew a whole lot more attention at school and my heart sang when I overheard someone say, "she's with Cooper". When I was continually asked if I was going out with him, I fidgeted, stuttered, and began hiding in the bathrooms to escape the curiosity. Sage and Mia assured me Cooper was going to officially ask me to be his girlfriend. I was both doubtful and hopeful.

Wednesday after school in the library, I was tutoring him in maths. We sat at one of the quiet study tables, talking in whispers amid the muffled stillness.

"I can't concentrate on maths; it's too hard," Cooper moaned.

"Just look at the exercises we did in class." I kept my voice low.

"All I can remember about class is your legs."

"My what?"

"In class you showed me the hole in your tights. Now all I can think about is your legs. They're very sexy." Cooper's whisper was deep and husky as he moved his hand to rest on my knee, squeezing it gently.

I glanced up from my knee to meet his eyes. A deep brown with solemn intensity yet shining with sparks of dancing mischief. I had to turn away. My heart pounded and I hoped he couldn't hear it amidst the silence of the library. Cooper seemed to be waiting for me to speak but words failed me. Heat rose in my cheeks, spreading through my whole face. I shifted nervously on the hard plastic chair. It was easier to study the rows of neatly stacked books than it was to look at Cooper.

"Umm … sorry. Ahh … I don't know what to say," I eventually managed.

His hand reached for my face, gently turning me back to make eye contact.

"Nova, will you be my girlfriend?" Cooper grabbed my hand and squeezed it.

I lowered my eyes again. His smile was blinding.

"Are you … do you … girlfriend and boyfriend?" My words were a jumbled mess.

Cooper laughed and lifted my chin till our eyes met again. It was as if he could see straight into my heart.

"Yeah. I want us to be official. You to be my girlfriend. And me your boyfriend."

"Well. Yes. Okay. Yes." I almost shouted the last word.

He moved forward and I knew he was going to kiss me. I glanced about nervously looking for the librarian, but she was nowhere to be seen, so I leaned in to meet him. His head tilted to the left and mine to the right, yet our noses still bumped until our lips locked and the kiss found its natural rhythm.

Over the next two days at school, Cooper and I became an obvious couple. He would steal up behind me, his arms creeping around my ribs, hoping to catch me by surprise, but I had forewarning. I could sense him coming, his warmth shone like a beacon from a lighthouse.

Being in a relationship also meant my circle of friends grew larger and this was a real test for my social skills. Cooper and Jackson were twins, but they were as different as night and day and extremely competitive. Jackson was the moodier one. Although I had seen him around at school, I didn't know him well. He showed a scornful contempt for school and sport, in complete contrast to Cooper, yet I knew Jackson was naturally athletic and ranked among the academic high achievers. With his motorbike, black leather jacket and biker friends, he was considered one of the school rogues.

It was Friday and Cooper slouched beside my locker, trying to convince me to come to his football game on the weekend. Jackson came up behind me.

"So, Nova, I've always thought you seemed normal." His tone was teasing but his expression stayed serious. "Why on earth would you want to go out with my brother?"

Cooper shot him a look of irritation. "What do you want?"

"I want to steal Nova away, to save her from being bored to death by your football games." Jackson put his arm around my shoulders and raised his eyebrows at me.

Although not identical, they were physically very similar. Jackson's hair was longer, more of a chestnut brown, and his eyes were a dark cocoa colour, more brooding than warm. He pushed his hair off his face with the same gesture that I loved in Cooper. Shifting uncomfortably, I tried for a smile, but it felt forced and artificial.

"Piss off, Jack." Cooper shoved Jackson and pulled me into his arms.

Jackson wore a sulky expression, but I thought I detected a quiet laugh as he loped off.

"Just ignore him," Cooper said in a quick dismissal.

I had a feeling that would not be easy.

From the start of the school year, the teachers had emphasised that Year 12 was a pivotal year for our future career choices. They complained about our lack of attention in class and piled on more homework. We grumbled and protested and tried to balance the assessment workload with our social commitments. Despite this stress, school had been ordinary and safe. Until now.

Troy's face, usually lit with a friendly smile, scowled at me in confrontation. "I need you to do my maths homework, like you do for Coop."

"Troy, I don't do Coop's homework." I tried to step back but was confined by the lockers behind and Troy in front.

He was so close, his breath fanned across my face, and he snarled. *An actual snarl.*

The hallway was crowded with an ordered chaos of students, rummaging in lockers, and exchanging the last banter before the bell called us to class. With Troy's raised voice, a crowd began to form, eager for a distraction from classroom demands.

Cooper came to my rescue. "Troy, back off dude. What are you doing?"

Troy turned and punched him in the jaw. Cooper fell back against the eager crowd. It triggered an instant uproar. Boys and girls throwing punches, pushing, kicking, wrestling. An elbow in my face, a push to my stomach, I was shoved back into the lockers, unable to escape. The stress we had all been feeling had become a savage frustration, a bitter resentment, a blind rage. It was a gnawing hunger in my body, painful and demanding. I curled into a crouch, close to the floor.

With the click of heels, a teacher approaching, students scattered but I could still sense the lingering fury. Cooper pulled me to my feet, and I turned on him.

"This is all your fault." The anger I had absorbed needed an outlet.

"What? I didn't do anything." His voice was defensive, and I sensed his confusion.

I clenched my teeth and clumsily pushed against his chest with my fists, fighting against the bitterness trapped inside me. Cooper simply folded his arms around me, tight and protective.

"I got you." His voice was a whisper close to my ear. "Let's get out of here."

He led me outside into the parking lot, and safe in the bucket seats of his car, I felt the rage gradually draining away. Cooper absently rubbed his jaw, still red from Troy's punch.

"Why do you think it's all my fault?" His forehead was wrinkled in a frown and his voice was tentative.

"I don't. I'm so sorry." I knew the words sounded empty, insufficient.

"I've never seen Troy like that before. He is normally one of the cooler guys on the footy field. It was like he was possessed." Cooper eyed me warily, probably wondering the same about me.

While I could tell that Cooper was puzzled and hurt, I didn't know how to make him understand. There was still a sour taste in my mouth from the aggression I had felt in my classmates. To say it out loud would sound stupid. *I soak up the emotions of others and feel them like they are my own? Really?*

We sat in the car, holding hands, fingers entwined. The drone of voices and sounds from the school buildings washed over us, soothing with its familiarity.

Sage found us after the school bell. "Troy has been suspended. He threw a chair and stormed out of the principal's office. And there will be the usual tirade at assembly tomorrow about the **No Fighting** school policy." Pushing her hair out of her face, she peered at me through her glasses. "You okay?"

I nodded but felt her doubt when she hugged me. "Come on, let's go home."

Cooper had footy training, so we left him to get our bus. I explained to Sage that I had absorbed Troy's anger.

"Yeah well, you do that. But then you calm people down. Usually." She shrugged.

"This was rage like I've never felt before," I admitted. "It was overwhelming, scary."

"Let's go home and chill. I'll even let you watch Star Wars." She pointed two fingers towards her mouth, pretending to gag.

It was the perfect remedy. Sage got me, accepted me, and knew what I needed.

Summer was gradually fading, and the leaves were turning autumn shades of russet brown, red and yellow. Cooper and I were on a date in the National Park. We crossed a graceful wooden bridge to find a secluded spot at the foot of a small hill. The food was stacked neatly in a picnic basket, with bright plastic plates and colourful containers. I was sure his mother had packed it for him. Carefully setting up on a checked woollen blanket, Cooper spread out fresh sandwiches, a salad, and some fruit. His eyes sought mine for approval and his face lit up with a smile when I piled my plate high. After filling our stomachs, we lay back in a comfortable food coma.

Cooper propped himself up on his elbow to look at me. He reached over, pulled on my earlobe gently, and twirled strands of my hair between his fingers.

"Am I your first serious boyfriend?"

He watched my face. I felt my face burning as I lowered my eyes.

"Is it that obvious? I'm not very good at this."

Laughing, Cooper brought my face up so our eyes met. "No, I didn't mean that. I just wondered if it was always like this for you." He gestured back and forth from him to me.

"Like what?"

He shrugged and I sensed him searching for words. "I think about you all the time."

I twisted my fingers together and bit down on my bottom lip. It was clear to me that I was in love with him, but I didn't want to be the first to say those words and I did not want to seem needy or clingy. The silence grew as he waited for me to say something.

"Am I your first serious girlfriend?" I asked eventually.

"Yeah, you are. I've never felt this way about anyone before."

I raised my eyebrows in disbelief and choked back a nervous laugh.

"Don't look so surprised." Cooper's voice carried his hurt.

"Well, girls basically drool over you." I kept my voice light, but it was the truth.

His head shook in dismissal. "I guess I was waiting for someone really special."

Clear brown eyes, shining with affection, met mine. His expression was serious, demanding the same from me.

"Nova, I love being with you. I want to spend all my time with you."

"I love being with you too, Coop." I could admit to that.

This relationship had become intense, fast. The story of my life. Strong, deep emotions. When I committed to a friendship, I went all in. I loved with all my heart, and I seemed to draw the same devotion from my friends, or in this case, my boyfriend. That phrase … *my boyfriend* … still sounded a little strange in my head.

On the way home we witnessed a car accident. The light changed to green and the car at the front stalled. The driver behind blew their horn, accelerating to move around but slammed into the first car. Bolting out of their cars like bulls out of a gate at a rodeo, the drivers went head-to-head, screaming at each other. Their rage was an explosion. My chest tightened and it was hard to breathe. While Cooper and another bystander went to help, I remained in the car, immobilised. The raw aggression drenched me. Abuse was hurled around indiscriminately. Cooper kept his distance, shook his head at them and then came back to the car.

"You okay?" he asked.

I glanced at myself in the side mirror. My face was pale and washed out. My knees and hands were shaky. My breathing was still ragged.

"I'm fine," I said, to reassure myself as much as Cooper.

"There's nothing we can do. Let's go."

While he drove, Cooper continued to glance across at me. His concern was a tonic, soothing and strengthening. I made the effort to slow my breathing, and gradually, as we moved further away, the anger left me.

While I delighted in the joy of my new relationship, the hostility and aggression around the world was escalating. Australia showed a significant increase in violent crime, and it was hard to ignore the horror described on the radio and television.

Stabbing incident at local school, 16-year-old girl dead.

Mystery surrounds the discovery of a whole family found dead in their home.

More people missing, feared dead.

Is this violence an epidemic?

Gang violence and racial tensions in Melbourne reach an all-time high.

Crowd hysteria and aggression at the football.

In the bigger cities, people were looting stores, stealing cars, breaking into houses. There was robbery, aggravated assault, road rage, rape, and murder. It was in schools, in shopping centres, on the streets. I reflected on the incident at our school and the road rage that Cooper and I had witnessed. The violence was even in our peaceful town.

Odd twinges of fear and anger nagged at me. They were empathic echoes. I felt it as real pain. The dig of a needle into my skin, a twist of nausea in my stomach. Mostly distant, but strong. It was like I was coming down with a virus, yet I knew it was just my sensitivity on high alert, somehow being influenced by the violence.

I tried to ignore it.

4

Our relationship was getting serious. It was time to bring Cooper to meet my father, while he was home. When my mother had died from cancer, my father rose to the challenge of sole parenting. He was a research scientist in genetic engineering which seemed to involve more computer work than laboratory time. Initially, with our move to a regional town, he had worked a lot from home, especially after school hours. Recently, his job had become more demanding, and he was away two weeks of every month, working in different laboratories around the country. He had reluctantly decided I was old enough to manage without him and arranged for me to board with Sage's family, when he was gone. An older father, he was a quiet man, and happy with just my company. We did not do much socialising, which probably explained my lack of confidence with people. Our relationship, while not especially close, was characterised by fond snippets. Helping me with homework, singing aloud to songs on the car radio, eating burgers and chips on Friday nights, and watching sci-fi movies.

We had never discussed boys. It was best to jump right in.

"Dad, I've started going out with someone, and want to bring him over to meet you."

"But you're too young to be dating."

His face was tired, lined with years of worry and he rubbed at the tufts of grey-white hair around his balding scalp. Green eyes, just like mine, and usually sparkling with love, narrowed with disapproval. His forehead creased further in a frown.

"I'm seventeen! I'm a senior," I protested. "He's a really nice guy. Captain of the football team."

"You need to be concentrating on your studies."

"It's not going to affect my schoolwork. It's my first boy-friend and I want you to meet him."

He was old-fashioned and protective, but I had my argu-ments lined up, ready. After a small show of resistance, he gave in, as I knew he would, and so I arranged for Cooper to bring me home from school.

"Dad, this is Cooper." I made the introductions. "Be nice," I added in a low voice to my father.

My father gave me a patronising look, then turned to evaluate Cooper. They shook hands.

"Hello, Mr Wilson." Cooper was relaxed and friendly. "Thanks for having me over. You have an amazing daughter. She's helping me to improve my maths grade."

My father smiled at me proudly. *Way to go, Cooper.*

"I hear you play football."

They launched into a conversation about the latest foot-ball teams and results. I sighed with relief as they settled in with the ease of people that had known each other longer.

"Would you like a beer?" my father asked Cooper.

"Thanks, but no, we are going to do some study and I have to drive home."

Another point to Cooper, Mr Responsible. My father winked at me.

"I'll leave you kids to it, then."

It was that easy. Even my cat, Thomasina rubbed up against Cooper's legs.

Despite Cooper's declarations, I was the queen of self-doubt and being a girlfriend was not easy. He was busy with the football season just starting and parties after every game. His teammates demanded his attention, running a play-by-play analysis of the game they had just won or lost. It could take all night. The girls were like moths to a flame.

Imogen did not help. She gravitated to Cooper when she was between boyfriends. He enjoyed the attention. Imogen Baker was hard to compete with. School captain, a high achiever, oldest in a big family, she always got what she wanted. Of medium height and build, her light brown hair was worn in a bob. None of her features were particularly outstanding, but in a room of people she stood out like the only one in colour. Her self-possession and air of aloofness made her more desirable. Guys wanted to date her, and girls wanted to be her. She and Cooper made an attractive couple and I honestly believed he still had feelings for her. When I tried to talk to him about it, he accused me of being jealous. I was.

My insecurity found some refuge in a developing friendship with Jackson. He was surprisingly easy to be with. I did not have my licence, so he would borrow Cooper's car and take me to watch Cooper's football games. His quick, dry humour made fun of everyone, including himself. Hours would pass and our conversations flowed effortlessly, sometimes serious and probing, but more often light and teasing.

A few weeks after Cooper and I started dating there was the usual post-football match gathering at the club. The music was loud, drinks were flowing, and everyone was celebrating the win. Cooper was drunk and he and Imogen were flirting. Fighting back tears, I looked for Sage to take me home. As I walked out the front of the club, I found Jackson instead. A crowd of his friends slouched over their bikes. They managed to pull off the look perfectly, cool with a hint of menace. Jackson saw me and came over.

"You okay?" he asked.

I wiped at my eyes, brushing away the threatening tears. "Yeah, I just want to go home. Have you seen Sage?"

"No, but I'll take you. Is Coop being a jerk again?"

"Yeah." A noise escaped from my mouth, half laugh, half cry.

"Come on."

He put his arm around me and shuffled me over to his motorbike. It was a solid machine, and the paintwork and chrome gleamed. Obviously well looked after.

"On that?" I was horrified. "My dad will kill me."

"I promise I'll be really careful with you." His dark brown eyes twinkled with a dare as he pushed his hair off his face, with the same gesture Cooper used. "Come on. You'll love it."

I shrugged. *Why not!* He helped me into his leather jacket and strapped the helmet onto my head. The jacket was soft, well-worn, and smelt like fresh air, an afternoon in the country. I was not sure if it was a leather smell or a Jackson one.

The engine was powerful and loud. The bitumen stretched beneath us, and although I knew Jackson was keeping well under the speed limit, my knees almost skimmed the ground as we took the corners. My heart was a jackhammer. Arms hugged tightly around Jackson's waist, I rested my helmeted head on his back. Without his jacket, I could feel the rippling muscles of his stomach and his back through the light shirt. There was a heat between us. He looked over his shoulder at me a couple of times and grinned.

"You okay?" He shouted above the noise of the bike.

"Go faster!" I urged, accustomed now to the throb of the bike and revelling in the danger.

His shoulders shook in silent laughter, and he threw the throttle wider. It was thrilling and horrifying at the same time. I was home all too quickly. Rigid after the nervous excitement, I could not get off the bike, and I could not let go of Jackson. It was suddenly quiet when he cut the engine, except for my breathing, which was fast and loud.

"Umm, I'm happy just sitting here," he said, laughing again. "But I'm not sure Coop would like it."

"I don't really care what he thinks at the moment," I retorted, but I did loosen my grip around his waist.

"Thanks for the lift," I said, climbing off the bike.

My arms hung awkwardly at my sides, like spaghetti. I avoided meeting his eyes.

"No problem. You feeling better?"

"Yeah, I'm fine. That was the coolest thing I've ever done."

"You need to get out more." He laughed and I joined him.

"Do you want to come in?"

He shook his head. "Maybe another time."

I handed him back his helmet and started to take off his jacket.

"Keep it. Bring it to me on Monday at school. I don't need it. You really warmed me up, you were hanging on so tight." His tone was flirtatious.

I could not help the laugh that escaped my lips and punched him playfully on the arm. He climbed back on the bike, revved the engine, and took off with a screech.

"Show off," I said quietly to the empty space he had vacated.

Climbing into bed, I saw a message from Cooper.

Where are you?

So, he had realised I was not there.

I'm home

Why did you leave?

I wasn't feeling well

Ok. I'll call you in the morning X

Cooper turned up on my doorstep early the next morning, with some ragged flowers and apologies. Our home was an old cottage, crooked and crumbling. The front path wound through overgrown but blooming garden beds and an arched trellis of climbing roses. I was fairly sure the flowers had been picked from my own yard.

"Sorry about last night. I know I was a dick. Imogen and I were just flirting. I'm not interested in her."

He was genuinely remorseful; I could feel it. Jackson had probably said something.

"Nova, I care about you. So much that it scares me a little. It has happened so quickly, and I worry that we're getting too serious. I think about a future with you, but we are still young. Sometimes I feel like I need to pull back a bit." He spoke as if he had rehearsed the words.

Cooper's earnest face melted my heart. I could sense his strong feelings for me, but there was also a lump in my throat, his words were a reluctant assurance. My mind clouded with confusion.

"I can't work out if you're saying you want to be with me or you want to break up," I said quietly.

"I definitely want to be with you." He reached to hold my hand and rubbed my palm with his thumb in that special way we shared. "Forget it. I'm an idiot. Just forgive me."

I did. I was in love with him. My heart raced both with exhilaration but also a level of anxiety. I tried to convince myself that I was overreacting to Cooper and Imogen. Yet, I still felt pangs of dread, and sometimes a darker rage. I was not always sure the anger was even mine or anything to do with my feelings about Cooper. When I was like this, I needed Sage.

Sage Ferry had a presence that drew people to her. She was petite, but fiery, assertive, and vibrant. Her eyes were a sapphire blue, and up close it was like looking into the depths of an ocean. She wore glasses that suggested wisdom beyond her teenage years. Locking those astute eyes onto me now, she listened as I poured out my confusion. Although she gave her advice freely, it was her mere presence that helped me. Our friendship was true and strong. Sage challenged me as often as she sympathised, but she was always on my side. She had been dating Luca seriously since last year, so was my expert on boys and relationships. My emotional balance returned over shared laughter as she drew out the details about Cooper and my ride home with Jackson.

"It's not like you to be angry at anyone. Let it go. Coop is a dick, but I do think he cares about you." She always got straight to the point. "But Nova, it's not good to get too close to Jack."

"What do you mean?"

"I know you, Nova. You're falling for both of them."

"No. Don't be crazy."

"I don't think I'm the crazy one." As she raised her eyebrows, I felt her shrewd assessment.

"Stick together?" I asked sheepishly.

"Like glue."

I knew I could always rely on that.

5

Sage, Luca, Cooper, and I were at the matinee session of the movies. As we came out of the theatre, we found ourselves on the edge of a brawl in the lobby of the cinema complex. The fury and violence rolling off the young men was a physical blow to my stomach. Strangers were punching and kicking each other as if in a combat zone. Anger rose like steam building to a boil. Even though bruised and winded, they continued to swipe at each other. Fists connected with faces; bright crimson blood splattered on the dull grey carpet. As we tried to squeeze past, one of the guys lunged at us. His eyes burned red, glazed, incensed. He growled as his fist shot out, a king-hit to the back of Cooper's head, who dropped like a sack of potatoes. Luca stepped between Cooper and the fight, but the aggressors were already making their exit to the sound of the police sirens. Cooper had a cut over his eye, where his head had connected with the floor. Blood drizzled down his cheek leaving a shiny trail. He had not lost consciousness but was groggy. I hoped an ambulance was on its way.

Because it was a head injury, Cooper was taken to the hospital and his father, a doctor, wanted him to stay overnight for observation. Luca took me up and I was able to see Cooper for a few minutes.

It was a large regional hospital, white walls, large windows, long corridors, and an overwhelming scent of antiseptic. Jackson was there but moved to the hallway so I could go in. Cooper was limited to one visitor, and only fifteen minutes.

The room was spacious, modern, and sterile. His hospital bed was raised slightly at the head. Cooper gave me a watery smile as he reached for my hand.

"Being close to you always makes me feel better." It came out in a croaky whisper.

"Are you sure you're okay?"

I was worried. He didn't look good. His eye had closed over with swelling, a developing purple-brown bruise the only spot of colour on his otherwise deathly pale complexion.

"Yeah, I'll be fine."

He did seem to brighten up with me being there. We sat quietly holding hands for a few minutes. I concentrated on sending my love and compassion through our connection.

"I'll miss Ava's 18th tonight," he said suddenly.

The planning for her birthday party had been going on for weeks.

"It won't be any fun without you," I said, squeezing his hand gently.

"Make sure you miss me. Behave yourself; don't flirt with anyone."

I poked out my tongue and shook my head in mock annoyance.

Jackson walked in, with his impeccable timing. "I'll look after her. Time's up."

Cooper tried to glare at him out of his one good eye. "Leave her alone."

I could sense the annoyance from Cooper. He did not trust Jackson with me. There was something else; he was not quite sure about me.

"Bro, don't you trust me?" Jackson teased. "Or is it Nova you don't trust? She can't resist my charm."

Cooper's pallid face turned thunderous.

"I'll be fine. I promise. And I'll be thinking of you all night." I kissed him gently on the lips, in reassurance.

Cooper locked his arms around my back, trying to pull me onto the bed beside him. I knew he was doing it because of Jackson's barb.

"I don't think that's a good idea." I laughed and squirmed carefully out of his grasp.

I blew him an air kiss and then I dragged Jackson by his shirt sleeve out the door.

"Jack, stop teasing him. He's injured."

"Who says I'm teasing?"

Jackson draped his arm around my shoulder. "Do you need an escort to the party?"

"Definitely not. I'll go with Sage."

I untangled myself and pushed him away, but I could not help laughing with him.

The party was strange without Cooper, as we had become such an established pair. The music was loud and over its roar was the hazy chatter of friends. Lights flashed, photos were taken, speeches and toasts were made to Ava. We danced, we laughed, and we danced some more. Cooper's football friends hung around me, unnecessary bodyguards, and I knew he had sent out a message. A few times, I noticed Jackson watching me and when we made eye contact, he sent me a conspiratorial wink. It was not until the end of the night that he approached.

"Can I give you a lift home on the bike?" he asked. "I bought an extra jacket and helmet."

"I'm at Sage's place at the moment."

"That's cool." He smiled as he gestured towards Cooper's football friends. "You'll have to escape those goons. I'll wait for you outside."

I knew Sage was going back to Luca's place so it would save them dropping me off, and besides, I could not resist another ride on the bike. But, when I told her, she exploded.

"What part of don't get too close to Jack, did you not understand?"

"It's nothing! The bike is just so much fun."

"And what about Coop?"

"What? There is nothing going on with Jack. Surely I can trust Coop's brother?"

"Nova, you can be so naïve." Sage glared at me, and I glared back. "Message me when you get home." She gave me reluctant permission to go.

Jackson gave me a helmet and the soft leather jacket I wore last time. I hugged it to my face and drew a deep breath, inhaling the same outdoor smell. This got a laugh from Jackson who shook his head at me. He wore a black aviator jacket tonight, with skinny black jeans. I was not going to admit how good he looked.

"Did Sage give you a hard time?"

"No," I lied. "She just doesn't want me to end up as road carnage."

The bike ride was just as glorious as I remembered. I watched the road pass underneath while the vibration of the motor was a pleasant shudder through my body. Jackson's body was a buffer for the wind, but it still made its way down my sleeves, crisp and fresh. A small laugh escaped my lips.

"You seemed more relaxed," Jackson said, on arrival at the house. "I was actually able to breathe this time, because you weren't crushing my ribs."

"Ha, ha, ha." But I did feel more relaxed. "Why doesn't Coop ride a bike?"

"He's not cool enough." Jackson's eyes sparkled. "Are you going to invite me in tonight?"

"Ahh, it's not my home. I don't … well I am here a lot. And they wouldn't mind. But. It's not … umm. Better not." My disjointed sentences tumbled out like random letters in Scrabble when you fail to make a coherent word.

Sage's warning was still ringing in my head, and I wasn't sure how Cooper would react. Jackson sat on his motorbike silently, his eyes narrowed, and his forehead wrinkled in a pensive frown.

"Night then." I turned towards the front door.

"You know, you deserve someone better than him." His comment stopped me in my tracks. "He's too boring for you."

"What, do I need someone more exciting like you?" I asked, coating my words with heavy sarcasm.

"Oh no." His laugh was slow and deliberate, but his eyes were still serious and intense. "You deserve someone far better than me. You're special, Nova. You're passionate and exciting. You are really intuitive, and you're so easy to be around. You make people want to be better somehow."

I had a sense of being challenged and cherished at the same time, vulnerable yet safe.

"Are you sure you haven't been drinking?" I felt the all too familiar heat in my cheeks and sought to hide my embarrassment with a joke.

"Not a drop. I would never when I was hoping to bring you home."

I still didn't know how to handle this, so I stood there, looking at the ground, arms clasped clumsily behind my back. The silence hung between us awkwardly.

"Night, beautiful." Jackson said at last and started up the bike.

Its roar was deafening.

"Night." I croaked back.

These Lewis boys did my head in. Butterflies swarmed in my stomach and my heart thumped. I was a push-bike that had been enjoying a smooth ride but had suddenly veered off the track and now the ground was rocky and unpredictable, yet exciting at the same time.

The next day Cooper was out of hospital. The bruise on his eye had started to yellow and the colour had returned to his cheeks; he was on the mend. A mound of pillows propped him up, confined to his own bed, under his mother's watchful eye. Teasing me gently about flirting with other guys at the party, he said he had heard reports about me.

"Did you have spies watching me?" I was indignant. "Don't you trust me?"

I was sitting on the side of his bed. He reached for my hands.

"Of course, I do. It's the other guys I don't trust."

"Pfft!" I shook my head and frowned in pretence of annoyance.

Cooper pulled me closer and kissed me. My nose bumped his clumsily, until I relaxed under his gentle guidance. His lips brushed against mine softly at first, playful, and then he pressed harder, and we melted together.

"Nova, I know we're young, and we haven't been going out that long, but I think I'm in love with you." His voice was breathless too, so at least it was not just me.

"I think I'm in love with you too, Coop."

It was easy to say. *I did love him.* I had known it for weeks. I wasn't going to let Jackson's taunts confuse me.

After the brawl at the cinemas and the incident with Troy, I had been combing the news reports. Violent crime was spreading, everywhere. Overseas governments had implemented curfews and lockdown procedures to keep people safe. Isolation was considered the best safety measure. The World Cup football competition had been suspended, as had American football and baseball, due to crowd rioting.

The Australian government had not yet taken extreme measures but were encouraging people to stay at home, especially at night. Police officers worked overtime, and hospital staff were complaining about the increase in emergency admissions. Overseas travel was severely limited, as we closed our international borders, even to our neighbours, New Zealand. Interstate travel was restricted to work and emergencies.

Blame was thrown around and the media sensationalised the conspiracy theories.

Computer games causing the violence on our streets.

Anti-vaxxers blame the vaccines.

Mobile phone towers make people angry.

Food additives create aggression.

Scientists were blaming genetics, specifically something called the warrior gene.

The warrior gene makes violent criminals.

The warrior gene is bringing the world to its knees.

It was difficult to know the truth from the conspiracies.

As my father was a genetic scientist, it seemed logical to talk to him about it. Even when he was away, we spoke daily. He had always been reluctant to talk about his work and I knew some of it was top secret government research. I expected him to laugh at the theories, but his avoidance seemed to be more deliberate, and I had the sense that he was hiding something.

"We'll talk about it when I get home." I had to be content with his promise.

6

On Friday night, one of my favourite bands was playing in Melbourne at the Music Bowl. Mia had organised tickets for a group of us. Leaving straight after school, it was just over two hours on the train. The seats were worn and dirty, the air was stale, and the carriage was crowded, but we managed to stay together, and it felt safe. I had changed into tight jeans, a black lace singlet and an olive-green suede jacket. I knew I looked good when Cooper winked at me, and Jackson raised his eyebrows in approval. Excitement spread as the tracks sped past.

The Music Bowl throbbed with loud music and strobe lights. Packed in like sardines, the crowd swayed and pulsed. Songs blasted from the speakers, and screaming voices sang along. Smoke machines blanketed the crowd in a hazy mist. Fists pumped the air, phones captured memories to post on social media, everyone's attention was transfixed on the stage. The music reached its peak, before slowing for the end during the obligatory encore. Our voices hoarse, legs aching from dancing, we were fulfilled and ready for home.

Around the back of the bowl's canopy, we found ourselves hemmed in by the limousine leaving with the band. The crowd rushed at the car, with an aggressive energy. Not just excitement, but fury. A surge forward, a stampede of people, wildebeest blindly following one another in a wake of fatuous destruction. They pinned us against the security railings. The air was punctured by shrieks. A guy with a shaved head and neck tattoos was yelling nonsense, waving his arms around. A freckled girl howled, her eyes as wide as dinnerplates, red-faced, frenetic. My terror was reflected in Mia's face and fingers of panic encircled my throat. I lifted my head, fighting to breathe the air above the squash of bodies. Suddenly beside me, Mia went limp, slipping into the mass. I struggled to hold her up.

"Mia, Mia!" The throng of people muffled my voice. "Help!"

We were sinking below the crush of an avalanche, suffocating and deadly. The crowd's frenzy was hard and unforgiving. A bomb exploded in my brain as I took on all their emotions, simultaneously frozen and frenzied.

"We've got her." I heard as I felt other arms taking Mia.

Jackson was beside me, his eyes wild. "Hang on to me."

He was making space by pushing people away. His fear was a deluge of ice down my back and added to my emotional overload. Then everything went black.

I came to, lying on my back, the grass beneath me cold and spiky. Cooper stood over me, his eyes crinkled with worry. Mia, at my side, smiled weakly, and I felt her relief. Sage hovered behind her, concerned and protective. I tried to lift myself but fell back again, feeling queasy.

"Take it easy," Cooper said.

"What happened?"

"You both fainted. Kenji and Jackson got you out." Cooper was apologetic. "I couldn't get to you. We have to wait here for the paramedics."

I reached for his hand and clutched Mia's with my other. The fear was slowly draining away.

"Thank you." I turned to Jackson, but he just shrugged.

"I couldn't let you get trampled." He winked at me.

"That was crazy." Cooper's voice was frustrated. "What is wrong with people?"

The paramedics cleared us to go home, with someone to watch us overnight. On the train, Mia rehashed what had happened, while I sat quietly, glad to be leaving the city. We were tired and it would be a late night by the time we got home. Cooper had his arm protectively around my shoulders. Jackson kept glancing at me. I sensed their concern, and Cooper's guilt that his brother had been the one to carry me out. My stomach was still churning, my head ached, my legs felt weak. The emotions I had felt from the crowd were alarming. They had been angry and vindictive. It did not make sense after such a great concert.

On Saturday night, Cooper's parents were away, and he invited a few friends over for pizza and beer. Mrs Lewis kept an immaculate house and we sat around the lounge room, wary of making a mess. A classic, French Chaise lounge and two comfortable armchairs surrounded a polished wooden coffee table. While Cooper, Luca and Kenji sat on the thick, hand-woven rug playing video games, Sage, Mia, and I perched on chairs, a little afraid we would stain or crease the luxurious butterscotch velvet upholstery.

"Apparently Troy is not coming back to school. He has been a real nightmare for his parents, and I heard he punched his dad. His parents are going to send him to a boarding school in Melbourne," Mia told us.

"We'll have to replace him on the team." Football was always high on Cooper's list of priorities. "He never used to be like that at all. It's weird."

I felt the concern swell in the room. We all liked Troy.

"It is weird." I shivered with the memory of his aggression.

The pizzas arrived and with them came Jackson and one of his biker friends, Han. Initially I sensed some wariness of Han from the others. He was a big, solid guy, and with his black leathers and foreboding expression he was a little frightening. Yet, I could sense that underneath that tough exterior he was kind and gentle, and I was usually accurate in the feelings I had about people. It was like looking through a smudged window that suddenly became clear. Jackson winked at me when he recognised the effort I was making to engage with Han and the others joined in. They helped devour the pizza and added to the laughter and chatter.

Just before midnight, Alexander, the twin's older brother, arrived home, drunk, loud, and abusive.

"Shit! What are you lot doing here? Cooper, do Mum and Dad know you're having a party?"

"They know I'm having some friends over; it's hardly a party."

"Yeah, well you're making a bloody mess."

"Settle down, Alex," said Jackson.

"Piss off. It's time you all went home. This is my house."

Alexander had been leaning against the chaise sofa and when he took a step, he staggered and reached out to steady himself with his hand on my back. His irritation and aggression scorched me like a flame, and I flinched.

"What's your problem, Nova?" Alexander shoved at me, knocking me to the floor.

"Alex, leave her alone." Cooper faced up to his big brother.

"Who do you think you are, you little shit?" Alexander swung a punch, but his balance was unstable, and he stumbled to one side.

Cooper caught the fist easily in his hand, but Alexander pitched forward, falling against Cooper who struggled to support his brother's weight. Jackson rose to help his twin. Alexander had found a solid footing and his anger grew. It felt senseless and raw. He shoved his brothers away, turning back to me. His grip on my wrist was strong and firm, and I could not pull it free. My arm was twisted behind my back, and I bent forward in pain. With his other hand, Alexander reached for Sage and grabbed a handful of her hair, pulling her towards us. Sage gave a cry of pain. It became a scramble of bodies. Kenji had put Mia behind him, and Luca was climbing over them to get to Sage. My heart raced as the adrenaline rose in the room, and my stomach churned with the emotions spilling from my friends. Fear, frustration, and fury. The anger continued to grow; it was a bushfire being fanned.

"Shit, Alex, stop it." Cooper's voice was both embarrassed and furious.

Cooper's fist sunk into Alexander's stomach, forcing him to release Sage and I. Alexander doubled over in pain, sucking in loud shallow breaths. Cooper took the opportunity to hold him in a head lock, while Alexander continued to struggle and curse. Sage and I had moved to safety where

Luca had a protective arm around each of us. I concentrated on breathing slowly, calmly.

"Come on, Alex. Let's go upstairs." Cooper was still angry. "Nova, Sage, are you okay?"

"Fine." Sage rubbed her scalp but smiled weakly.

Cooper turned to me and I nodded, though my arm felt like it had been hyper-extended. He looked relieved.

"Geez, Alex, you're a dick." Cooper held Alexander by one arm and Jackson was on his other side while they marched him up the stairs, ignoring the tirade of his colourful abuse.

"Well, that was fun." Han gave a deep chuckle, lightening the tension.

The night was over, and we cleaned up, preparing to leave, waiting for Cooper to re-appear. I felt the atmosphere in the room return to a level of calm, but the ease was gone.

"I'm so sorry everyone. He's drunk, but he's not normally like that," Cooper apologised.

Jackson had remained upstairs, and I guessed he was putting Alexander to bed.

"Nova, are you sure you're okay? Sage?"

Cooper clearly felt responsible for his brother's hostility, and we hastened to reassure him. I pressed my palm to his and we intertwined fingers while I tried to send him comfort.

Alexander could be sarcastic and even condescending at times, but this was another level of aggression. Like Troy, it was out of character, and it was frightening. The brutality was in our homes now, amongst people we knew.

I chalked up the recent incidents of violence, with mounting uncertainty. The cinema brawl, the concert chaos, the skirmish at school, and Alexander's outburst. The anger rested in the pit of my stomach, in my clenched fists, all over my body. It did not make sense and I wanted to talk it through with my father. I was trying to connect the dots, but I could not make out the final picture.

7

A comfortable warmth tingled through my body; my father was due home today. I had missed him. The school day dragged, but I worked on curbing my impatience by mentally planning our week together. Just before lunch, Sage and I were called up out of class, to the office. That was never a good thing.

"Do you know what we have done?" Sage whispered to me, both curious and anxious.

I shook my head; I had no idea. The administration office was noisy with phones ringing and people talking. The Deputy Principal stood waiting, his hands clenched behind his back. With our arrival, an artificial smile left his face as quickly as it had arrived. By his side was Sage's mother, Mrs Ferry, and her face was drawn in a frown.

"Mum, what's going on?" Sage asked in a low voice.

"Just wait, I'll explain at home." Her mother spoke kindly, but with an abrupt pause in the background noise, her voice was unnaturally loud.

She looked at me, then looked away again quickly, and nodded at the Deputy. He had not said a word. Sage and I exchanged a frightened glance.

No one spoke on the way home. My stomach was churning as I sensed a deep sorrow in Mrs Ferry. We followed her into the lounge room where family photos cluttered the mantelpiece above the fireplace. It was my second home, but everything felt strange and cold. She took a deep breath and gestured for us to sit down. Although the couch was comfortable and well-worn, I sat clumsily balanced on the edge.

"Is it Dad?" I asked, somehow already knowing.

Mrs Ferry studied my face, her eyes shining with concern, her mouth uncharacteristically grim. She took another deep breath.

"Nova, there's been a tragedy. Your dad ... was at the airport. He was shot. I am so sorry. He didn't make it. They tried. He ... passed away. I'm so, so sorry."

Her words came out in stilted sentences and sailed past me like arrows being shot in slow motion. I didn't want to register the meaning of those words. Then the impact of Sage's shock slammed into me, and it was a boulder pushing me off balance. It was as if the earth dropped beneath me, drawing me into a black abyss. I felt a single tear spill onto my cheek and tasted the saltiness when it reached my lips. Another tear followed and reached my chin, hanging for a second before it dropped to my shirt. I looked down to see a tiny damp spot. Then they overflowed, silent but savage as my heart wept.

8

The next week blurred. A fog descended. Words came at me in misted speech bubbles. Mr and Mrs Ferry looked after the funeral arrangements. They contacted an uncle I hardly knew, that lived overseas. He would not be able to come for the service. There were legal matters to organise. My father had left arrangements for his property and money to go into a trust, which would look after me, until I was legally an adult. I just nodded and waited for the intermittent flashes of clarity. Sage was like a sunflower, breaking through the gloom, bringing me warmth and light. At other times I felt the sharp needle of pain, twisting my guts and sucking the air from my lungs. These moments made me savour the lethargic numbness and dense fog when it returned. I barely responded to visitors; it was too much effort. Thomasina, my cat, seemed to sense my distress and spent a lot of time in my lap. She was more comfort than anyone.

The police incident report swirled in my head, jumbled up with conversations I had overheard. My father had flown into Melbourne airport and been shot in the carpark. Two bullets to his chest and he had died instantly. The gunman had got away and the police were still investigating. There were so many violent crimes these days that this was just added to their list. I thought I should be feeling angry, but I just had a hollow disbelief that it had even happened. I still expected him to walk in the door.

The day of the funeral came. The rain was relentless, the wind bitterly cold. My body moved on autopilot, dressing myself, walking, sitting, standing. The coffin rested solemnly at the front, demanding attention that my father would have hated. A small congregation listened to the moving speeches. Dad had been a generous, kind friend, a conscientious employee and was valued for his contribution to the local community. Sage had helped collate a photo slideshow. Soulful music brought the gathering to tears. Although surrounded by people, I felt alone. Only seventeen and both my parents were gone.

Outside the funeral home, I waited for the hearse to pass. Sheltering under an umbrella, watching the trees bend in the wind. The lawn was perfectly manicured, and the flower beds ordered and neat. It was all a bit too formal.

"I don't have anyone anymore." I whispered to myself, quietly but aloud.

"You have me." Sage had heard me.

"And me." Chimed in Mia, Ava, and Imogen in succession.

They pulled me in for a group hug.

"Can I join in?" Cooper put his arms around all of us, then reached for my hand.

The warmth of their love was comforting, but the bite of grief was stronger.

I said appropriate polite words of thanks as people shuffled past, Sage's parents at each of my elbows.

Jackson did not say anything, just hugged me tight, wincing as if his ribs hurt. His hands rubbed my back, transmitting his sympathy and concern. I saw that his face was bruised and scratched, and I had a vague recollection of Sage telling me he had been in a motorbike accident a few days ago.

"Are you okay?" I managed.

Jackson nodded, giving me a half-hearted smile.

"When do you feel like you'll be back at school?" Cooper had hung back while the others drifted away.

"Tomorrow."

His concern made me want to reassure him, but I still felt wretched. I heard my father telling me to keep living my life. Maybe school would help the healing.

When tomorrow dawned, I changed my mind. The sympathy from everyone was a heavy burden I was not ready to carry. Mrs Ferry suggested another couple of days off. By Thursday night, I decided I had grieved enough. There were only three weeks until the end of term and I had a lot of catching up to do. I just had to get through one day and then it was the weekend.

Friday morning, I rose, making the motions of getting ready for school. A light breakfast of toast and juice, then slipping into my school uniform. Mr and Mrs Ferry had both left for work when the doorbell rang. Puzzled as to who it could be at this early hour, I opened the door wide. Jackson stood there, in his jeans, aviator jacket and with two bike helmets in his hand.

"I thought you might want to ditch today and just get out of town for a bit." He watched my face for a reaction. "Or I can just take you to school if you prefer?" There was his usual grin.

Sage looked at me. I shrugged and raised my eyebrows at her in a non-verbal question.

"Just go," Sage said. "You need to."

"Should I?" I wanted further reassurance from Sage.

She hugged me. "Go get changed."

She pushed me back towards the bedroom. I changed into jeans and a T-shirt, with a jumper, and boots.

"Get your swimsuit too," Jackson called out.

I wondered where we were going. It was autumn, cloudy and cold. I threw shorts, another shirt, sandals, swimsuit, and towel into a small backpack. Sage and Jackson were talking quietly. She was giving him instructions about looking after me, and he was answering her just as seriously.

"Message me when you get there and then when you are heading home too," Sage ordered, mothering me.

Jackson had a jacket for me, the same one I had worn before, which I had started to claim some ownership on. I strapped on my helmet, climbed on the motorbike, and wound my arms around his waist.

"Be careful with her." Sage frowned at Jackson, then she looked at me and grinned. "Have fun!"

9

Once we hit the highway the wind roared, and the motor-bike sang. The quicker we went the more stable I felt. It was a combination of elation and fear, pleasure and anxiety. The Lewis family owned a holiday house, down on the southern coast, at a tiny little place called Woodside Beach. It was just over an hour's drive. I was almost sad when we arrived.

The beach house was lovely. A quaint white seaside cottage externally weathered by the wind and salt spray. Internally, it was modern and spacious, beautifully decorated with polished wooden floors, giant scatter rugs and comfortable bright furniture. Colourful prints adorned the walls, idyllic photographs of the beach behind. Down the hall I could see four bedrooms, while we stood in a huge open space which was a combined lounge, kitchen, and dining area.

I messaged Sage that we had arrived safely. After some consideration, I messaged Cooper and got a *WTF* in reply.

"Did you tell Coop what you were planning today?" I asked Jackson.

"Well, I told him he should bring you up here for the day. He said he couldn't miss school, so I said I would," Jackson admitted, his tone carrying a little guilt. "But I don't think he really believed me. Have you told him?"

"Yeah. He's not very happy."

"Meh. He'll get over it. Just pull the sympathy card on him." Jackson shrugged.

"You're awful." I couldn't help laughing and it felt good, cathartic.

I needed this, and Jackson knew that in some way that Cooper did not.

"What do you want to do first?" Jackson asked. "Something to eat. A walk. A swim. Or we can just sit here for a bit."

"Umm … let's go for a walk. I'd like to see the beach."

A warm tingle ran down my spine. Jackson was easy to be around. We kicked off our shoes and changed. I couldn't help but admire his casual, relaxed look, with black patterned shorts, a pale blue T-shirt, and a light grey hoodie. My denim shorts brought out the goosebumps on my legs, so I kept on my jumper. The sun struggled to find space between the clouds, but the rain was clearing.

A white rickety wooden fence enclosed a small back-yard, and a gate opened onto the beach. It was only a couple of minutes to cross the dunes and I could feel the fine sand between my toes. My heart skipped. It felt like I was opening an old familiar box of happy feelings that had been locked away. I needed to dust them off.

"Let's run!" I took off, getting a head start before Jackson had a chance to react.

We moved down to the tide line and jogged on the wet sand. Running on sand was a challenge for my coordina-tion and I stumbled like a drunken sailor, yet each step was a release of the heaviness I had been storing in my body.

Jackson hardly broke a sweat. His graceful long strides kept pace easily with my staggered running. Eventually, I collapsed onto the sand, puffing and gasping. Jackson dropped beside me.

"You okay?" He seemed genuinely concerned.

"Yeah fine." I giggled. "Obviously not very fit."

I felt my heart lighten with simple pleasure, dusting off another emotion I had stored away. Jackson laughed that easy laugh of his and put his hand over mine on the sand.

We just sat looking out to sea. It was quiet and peaceful. Jackson's contentment sifted through me. The beach stretched endlessly in both directions, deserted except for us. Rolling sand dunes, with short, tufted grass, all but blocked the houses from view. The pristine white sand led down to gentle waves. An odd shell or bit of driftwood blotted the otherwise clean and pure landscape.

Swimming in the freezing cold sea revived me further. We splashed in the small waves, shivering, pushing each other under. For lunch, we had hot chips on the beach, smeared with tomato sauce, and relished their sweet and salty tang. Afterwards, we took a leisurely walk down to some flat coffee-coloured rocks. The brown slabs clustered to create tiny rock pools, waves breaking over them, littering broken shells and strands of seaweed.

"We better head back," I said finally, pointing at the rain clouds gathering on the horizon.

Our phones had been left at the house while we went swimming and they had been flooded with missed calls and messages from Sage and Cooper.

Ring me urgently.

It's crazy here. There has been a big brawl in town.

The highways are closed from 5pm.

YOU NEED TO COME HOME NOW OR YOU WON'T BE ABLE TO GET BACK.

Are you ok?

Jackson had similar messages from his parents. He rang his father to get a clearer story. Gangs from Melbourne had come into our town with weapons and there had been a huge brawl in the main street, with dozens injured. The mayor was closing the highways to stop any more people arriving from the city. We could probably get through but there was a possibility of violence at the barricade. Jackson's father suggested we stay put at the beach house, safe, and come back in the morning.

"Just be careful," Sage told me when I rang.

I could hear the worry in her voice.

"I'll be fine. It's probably just as well with the wet roads. The house is amazing, and it's right on the beach."

"Now you are making me wish I was there."

"I wish you were. It's going to be a little weird, just me and Jackson." I lowered my voice for the last part.

"Yeah, I can imagine. Behave yourselves."

"Yeah, yeah. He's Coop's brother."

"Yeah, I know. I'm not sure that makes a difference. He likes you, Nova."

"We are just friends," I said firmly.

My call with Cooper was a lot worse.

"I can't believe you went with him, and now you're spending the night with him."

I could almost taste his fury coming through the phone.

"It's Jack, your brother. He did a nice thing. You could have brought me. You know how I've been feeling, and it's been great to clear my head and get away for the day. I didn't know this brawl was going to happen." I couldn't help my defensive retort.

"Do you have feelings for Jack?"

"Of course not. He's your brother and my friend. I'm in love with you, Coop." I changed my tone, keeping my voice even and calm.

Why did everyone think I had feelings for Jackson? Did I?

Cooper also rang Jackson, and I could hear Jackson telling him that he should have more trust in his girlfriend.

"Stop teasing," I mouthed.

He shrugged. "Don't be a jerk, Coop." Jackson ended the call abruptly.

After these calls, my heart felt heavy again and a level of gloom had returned. It weighed on Jackson too.

I puzzled over the violence in town that had created this situation. "Do you think something has caused all of the violence? This town brawl, at school, the concert, and all the news reports. My Dad …" I choked on the last words, unable to finish.

I felt Jackson's concern and affection shoot across the room to me. We were standing on opposite sides of the kitchen bench, and he reached for my hand. His hand was warm and comforting.

"You mean like the warrior gene or vaccines or something?" he asked gently.

"Well, I don't really know what to believe. But the world is becoming angrier and more violent. I can feel it." I paused to take a deep breath. "I wanted to ask Dad about it, but I never got the chance. He works … worked in genetic research." I paused again to swallow the lump that had formed in my throat. "I don't really know what he was working on, and it probably sounds stupid but sometimes I even wonder if he was killed because of his work."

Jackson was silent. He didn't laugh at me or dismiss my concerns. His hand was still warm on mine and his sympathy flowed through it. I also sensed his frustration and some fear which matched my own. It sat heavily, a stone in my stomach.

"I really don't know, Nova. I'm sorry you never got to ask him." His compassion was a warm coat on a cold day. "Have you talked to the police?"

"They think it was just another random act of violence. And there have clearly been a lot of them." I shrugged. "They are probably right."

"Maybe. I guess you have to leave it up to them." He squeezed my hand, and then gestured at his face. "Did Sage tell you what happened to me?"

The bruising was fading to yellow, and the cuts had almost healed. I had noticed more bruising around his ribs too.

"She did, but I'm not sure I really took it in."

He squeezed my hand again.

"It was crazy. I pulled up beside a car at the lights, and the guy started yelling at me for no reason. I laughed at him and gave him the finger." He paused, looking sheepish. "Then he gets out of his car, drags me off the bike and starts laying into me. He pulled off my helmet and was punching me in the head. His eyes looked crazy. Bloodshot and bulging. I managed to push him off and he fell back on his arse. To be honest I just wanted to get out of there, so I took off and left him sitting on the road, shouting after me."

"That's awful. Were you badly hurt?"

"Just some bruises and wounded dignity. He was like fifty. I should have been able to take him easily. But you are right. The world is becoming angrier. I don't know why."

I sighed, my mind still struggling to understand these acts of violence. After a few minutes of silence, Jackson grinned at me.

"I have a plan," he said. "Will you just go along with me?"

I nodded.

Jackson pulled me into the lounge room and patted the couch. "Sit your butt down here."

He shuffled through Netflix for the Zombie apocalypse movies. That was Jackson's sense of humour. I relaxed in the ease of his friendship, and we returned to our usual light banter.

Cooper's bedroom was roomy and sparsely furnished. A large glass sliding door opened out onto a patio and the backyard. Jackson's room was across the hall. Although tired after the day on the beach, I couldn't sleep. I had messaged Cooper again, but he had not replied. Thoughts tumbled around in my head, the violence in town, my father's murder, Jackson's attack. I fluffed the pillows and tossed around on the bed. With no street noise and only the gentle background of breaking waves, the quiet was unnerving. I must have drifted off but was pulled from sleep by noises from the house next door. Doors slammed and voices raised in anger. I crept out of bed and across the hall. The floor was cold under my bare feet. Goosebumps spread over my arms and legs. Jackson's door was open, revealing a room identical to Coopers. In the pale moonlight I could see the whites of his eyes. He was awake.

"Are you okay?" he asked.

"I can't sleep. I heard a noise."

"Yeah, same." He flipped back the bed covers on the opposite side of his queen-size bed. "Come on, climb in."

"I can't." I looked at him dubiously.

"I won't touch you," he said solemnly. "It's probably the only way either of us will get any sleep."

Climbing into his bed, I was careful not to make contact. There was a good deal of space between us but regardless I lay there stiff and rigid, not game to move. My mind returned to Cooper's words and before I could stop myself, I blurted out what had been running riot inside my head.

"Coop thinks I'm into you."

"Yeah? And what do you think?" His voice was deep and sombre, and his eyes were large black pits in the semi-darkness.

"I don't know. I don't know how I feel."

There, that was the truth. I was in love with Cooper. But Jackson really got me in a way Cooper didn't. Like bringing me here and listening to my stupid fears. It had helped.

"Well, I guess you need to work it out." This time his voice was flippant.

"You're not interested in me." It wasn't a question, but my voice rose at the end of the sentence as if it was.

"Really? Then why do I hang around you so much? Why do I try so hard to make you smile?" The last part was said quietly, as if he was asking himself.

"Jack, I ..." But words failed me.

Jackson's frustration twisted through me like a knife. My head felt fuzzy and dense.

"You're my brother's girlfriend," he said at last.

"Yeah I am. And I love Cooper."

"I know you do." His voice softened, and I felt his weariness. "Let's just go to sleep."

He turned over, facing away. Neither of us said anything else. It was warm and cosy under the bed covers. Eventually I heard loud, regular breathing. My thoughts kept me awake a while longer.

I was not sure what I had gotten myself into.

10

I woke to my phone ringing.

"Nova, I have to tell you something." It was Sage, her voice was strange.

"What's going on?"

"I'll just say it straight," she paused, "Cooper hooked up with Imogen last night."

Silence. I didn't know what to say.

"Mia and I both saw them, and they left the pub together." Her words came out in reluctant bites.

"Okay, right." The calm voice did not sound like mine.

Jackson glanced over at me and raised his eyebrows in a question.

"Nova, are you okay?" Sage asked.

When I did not answer she continued. "He's a complete shit for doing this to you. I can't believe it. And I can't believe Imogen could be such a bitch. It's like she just wants what she can't have."

Sage was babbling now, and I tuned out. I felt like my face was collapsing, a balloon deflating. Beside me, Jackson reached for my phone. He had a conversation with Sage and hung up. My body sagged when he pulled me into a hug. I was aware of him speaking, but my ears had stopped hearing sounds.

"I need to be alone," I said.

Inside the walls were closing in on me, so I went out to the patio. My stomach churned, threatening to vomit. With my head between my knees, I counted breaths until the nausea subsided. It was as if I had been hit with a sledgehammer. My thoughts were fractured, unable to form into anything coherent, so I put my head in my hands and sobbed as if it was the end of the world.

Eventually, I became aware of Jackson beside me.

"Will you come back inside?" His voice was gentle, pleading. "It's cold out here."

I gripped the wooden arms of the patio chair trying to draw on its strength. A deep breath flooded my lungs with the chilly air. I stood and followed him inside.

"Nova, he's a jerk." He rubbed my back. "What can I do?"

"Nothing. I should never have come down here," I said.

I knew I had hurt him. Jackson just nodded and went to get our things organised. We rode back to town without speaking. The highway was open, and we were not stopped. I hardly thought about the brawl from yesterday, but I did notice the police cars on the outskirts of town. Instead, my head swam with the meaning of Cooper's betrayal. While the sun was warm on my back and my jacket was snug, I shivered.

Cooper sat on the bonnet of his car, waiting outside Sage's house. The thunderous look he directed at Jackson transformed to one of love and welcome for me. Jackson kept a neutral face and just helped me off the bike. He took my backpack through to Sage who was standing on the door-step, and I heard them murmur to each other. Cooper looked between us hesitantly and I felt his uncertainty, but I could not sense any guilt or deception.

"Are you okay?" he asked.

"We need to talk," I said. "Wait here."

He moved in to kiss me, but I brushed past him.

"Do you want me to say anything?" Sage asked.

"No, I got this." My voice was steady. "Can you two wait inside?"

Hidden within a bike helmet, I'd had time to compose myself. Cooper leaned back against his car waiting for me. His smile was friendly and confident, but I could feel an underlying apprehension.

"I missed you last night."

"Did you?" My tone was cold and hollow.

That is when I felt it, his shame.

"How could you? You and Imogen." I blurted it out.

"What are you talking about?" He kept his face com-posed but my stomach twisted, and I knew it was from the tension he was hiding.

"I know you hooked up with Imogen."

"I didn't." Cooper's shoulders hunched and he pushed his hands deep into the pockets of his jeans.

"Don't lie to me Coop. I know you did. At the pub. And then you left the pub together, so who knows what happened then."

He opened then shut his mouth without saying anything. I wrung my hands together and ran my tongue over my lips. My mouth was dry.

"You did, didn't you?" I wanted him to admit it.

Cooper shifted his weight from one foot to the other. "Who told you that?"

"It doesn't matter. You cheated on me. You're not over her."

"That's not true. I don't care about her. She was just here. And you weren't. You were off with my brother. I don't know what you two were doing."

Cooper took his hands from his pockets and folded his arms across his chest in a barrier of protection.

"I didn't do anything with Jack." I was quietly lethal.

Although I recognised the double standard, I was not going to share the blame. I had gone with Jack, but as a friend. Cooper and Imogen had history and that made this whole situation worse. The betrayal soaked through my bones, feeling heavy and oppressive.

"But you went with him. Why did you go?" He was on the defensive.

"I don't know. Because he asked. As a friend."

Although I felt his glare, I stared at the ground, silently counting the blades of grass on the nature strip to keep myself steady. The lawn was a mix of green and brown, struggling to stay alive in the lower temperatures.

"Did you sleep with her?" I had to ask but I wasn't sure I wanted to know.

"No. We just kissed and fooled around a bit." His voice was pitched high, and the sentence came out in a rush, like he was trying to get it over with quickly. "I'm sorry, Nova. I'm an idiot. I was angry with you. I was drunk."

His eyes were begging for forgiveness, and his arms now hung limply at his sides. It seemed as if he wanted to reach out for me but had decided against it. I wasn't sure if he was telling the truth about not sleeping with Imogen, and then

I wasn't sure if it mattered anyway. It was still a betrayal. I wrapped my arms around myself in a hug.

"And does that make it okay?" My voice was harsh in my ears and Cooper flinched.

"No, of course not. But it didn't mean anything."

My feet kicked against the footpath edge, restless and fidgety. "Coop, this hurts too much. I don't want to be with you anymore."

It was a decision I had made on the ride back. My thoughts still raced about in my head. I was scared that I was overreacting. I would probably regret it later. But the trust was gone. Yes, I had gone with Jackson, but Cooper and Imogen had taken things to another level. Breaking up seemed like the best solution. Rip the band aid off quickly.

"Are you breaking up with me? That's not fair. I was stupid, but you went with Jack. I want to be with you, Nova. I'm in love with you." His voice was a whine.

"I thought we had something special, but I guess not. Don't make this harder."

I stumbled as I turned away and both Sage and Jackson appeared, each grabbing an arm. They had obviously been listening from inside the house. Cooper turned on Sage.

"Did you tell her? It's none of your business. Now look what you've done." Cooper's lips thinned into a tight line, and he spat his words out as if they were something distasteful.

"This is all your fault." He looked to Jackson. "You took her up there. You wanted to split us up."

Jackson punched him. It was a dull thud and Cooper staggered backwards, his hand to his cheek. I moved towards him, instinctively wanting to help him, still loving him, but Sage grabbed my arm.

"No, you don't," she said. "He deserved that."

She pulled me away. I was not crying, yet, but my heart throbbed in pain, as much as I imagined Cooper's face did. We moved inside to the roar of Jackson's motorbike leaving. Over my shoulder, I saw Cooper was rubbing the side of his face and looking after me.

For the rest of the weekend, I was in turmoil. I could not turn my emotions down. Betrayal hurts like nothing else. A knife twisting slowly, ruthlessly. Grief over my father resurfaced and engulfed me. My head hurt, my body was heavy and tired. A shadow descended. The relief I usually felt in Sage's presence could not penetrate the blackness. Rage was building from the pits of this darkness and was fuelled by the angry world around me. It tasted bitter in my mouth, making it hard to swallow.

"I need to find Imogen." I told Sage, as we walked into school on Monday.

"Nova, are you okay?" Sage had rarely seen me angry, and I could tell she was surprised. "Maybe you shouldn't be here."

"I'll be fine," I reassured her. "I won't lose it."

We found Imogen and I did lose it, a bit.

"Imogen, you are my friend. How could you do this?" My voice was louder than I had intended, my tone scathing.

"Cooper said you had gone off with Jackson," she said weakly.

At least she didn't try to deny it. My anger still boiled, and it felt like there was steam rising all around me.

"I wouldn't do that. And I didn't think you were that sort of person either," I said.

"There were two of us, you know. It's not just me to blame." Imogen glared at Cooper, who had just arrived on the scene.

"Don't worry, I do blame both of you."

"Nova, calm down," Cooper said.

Didn't he know you never tell a woman to calm down? I flashed him a venomous look. Cooper raised his eyebrows and seemed surprised at my anger too, but he stood his ground.

"I don't care about Imogen. She doesn't mean anything to me." His eyes stayed on my face, and he did not even glance at Imogen.

"Thanks very much." Imogen spat the words at Cooper.

The air was charged with our emotions. I let them pulse through me, then took a deep breath, held it, and let it out. My fury went with it. There was nothing more to say. A small crowd had formed around us. My cheeks burned as I sensed their curiosity. This was juicy gossip. I bowed my head, avoiding their eyes and walked away. Sage followed me loyally.

"Stick together?" I needed her today.

"Like glue," Sage promised.

Sage, Mia, and Ava stayed close all day. I had schoolwork to catch up on after my two-week absence and I let that occupy my mind. Cooper avoided me, and Imogen went home, sick. Jackson winked at me whenever we crossed paths. At the end of the day, he waited for me at the school gates.

"Do you want me to hit him again?" His voice was light and teasing.

I laughed. It felt good.

"I wouldn't mind, to be honest, but probably better not."

"Well, let me know if you change your mind."

He loped off, and my gaze followed him. I bet it was awkward in their house.

Classes and a heavy schedule of missed homework kept me busy all week. If I was not in the library at lunchtimes, Sage and I joined Mia and Ava in one of the science rooms that no one ever used. The weather was turning colder, and it was good to be inside. Imogen was conveniently busy with school captain tasks. I moved seats in the classes I shared with Cooper and made it clear I did not want to talk. Both Imogen and Cooper had sent me several messages apologising, but Sage would not let me reply.

Once the anger had drained away, my heart was an aching hollow. I sobbed to break-up songs until I was left parched and sore, finding far more songs about love lost than love found. Sage and I ate ice-cream, the standard break-up comfort food.

Meanwhile, the world kept circling the sun, and it continued to get angrier and more violent.

11

Violence was spreading in Australia. The radio and television channels streamed story after story with gruesome details.

Inner city shooting result of gang war. Several killed.
Security concerns on public transport. Avoid travelling alone.
Riots in schools. Keep children at home.
Looting in shopping centres. Staff are afraid.
Racial violence in friendly neighbourhoods.
The warrior gene – dangerous DNA.

Then the worst of all – *Prime Minister killed in violent attack.*

Our federal government was in chaos. The Deputy Prime Minister had stepped up, but he had been whisked off to a safe location. State governments were adopting the same practices as the UK and USA, enforcing social isolation, and increasing police presence, hoping to prevent further escalation of the widespread hostility. Sports, concerts, and all large crowd events were cancelled to avoid mob violence. Lockout laws came in for all restaurants, pubs, and clubs.

Schools were closing for the Easter holidays a week early, and exams were being postponed. I wouldn't have to face Cooper or Imogen for three weeks. We went into lock-down and only left the house for work, for shopping, and for limited exercise.

Sage had a part-time cashier job at the supermarket, and I scored some afternoon and night shifts to help with stacking the shelves. People were stockpiling food and essential items to avoid leaving their homes. The shelves emptied as quickly as we were filling them. Anger and resentment flared when things ran out and people were abusive and aggressive. Dealing with the customers had become a daunting role and I worked with my jaw clenched, my muscles tensed. I was a coiled spring only just kept under control, but at least I was busy.

Mobile phone coverage was becoming increasingly unpredictable as communication transmission towers were targeted by fanatics and blamed for the increase in anger and violence. We were often left with no signal, no wi-fi. It made staying in contact with people even harder.

Mia and Ava visited us. I had insisted they not take sides, but mentally put my fingers in my ears when Imogen's name came up. When Luca dropped by every day, his and Sage's efforts to include me just created greater exclusion. My heart ached with betrayal, yet I missed Cooper. Jackson advised that Cooper was miserable too, and I was secretly pleased.

Exercise helped, and I ran until exhausted and slick with perspiration. Online yoga and meditation calmed and centred me.

It was mid-April, Easter weekend. Two weeks into isolation, and we were going stir-crazy. Mia planned a small gathering at her home. Cooper was not going. I was ready to party. My body craved some fun, a release.

We dressed up. Sage was stunning in black jeans and a red long-sleeved silk top. Her blonde silky hair cascaded over her shoulders, shimmering as she walked with the natural elegance of a dancer. I wore tight blue jeans, a long black shirt, and my favourite ankle boots. My hair resisted any styling, so I just went with a carefree, messy look. Our glamour added to the excited buzz I felt.

Resentment stabbed briefly when Imogen arrived, with Liam. I suspected he was just for show. She looked amazing, as always, in fitted leggings and an animal print jumper. Everyone had made an effort after two weeks in lockdown.

"I hope it's okay with you that I came tonight." Imogen was trying hard.

I almost choked on my tongue trying to be civil and polite. "Sure, of course. We're still friends. I just need a bit more time."

I did want to get past it. Imogen had always been one of my best friends. It was not easy though.

"I'm so sorry it happened. I didn't mean to hurt you."

I nodded, fidgeted, and made an excuse to move away. I could only handle so much awkward conversation.

We drank shots and danced. Mia's long flowing, floral dress, with her Doc Martens, suited her zany dance moves. Ava had a more classic style, with white T-shirt, faded jeans and black boots. She had the dance coordination of a natural athlete. Prisha was never far from her side, and they made adoring eyes at each other. The music was loud, the bass thumped, and the alcohol made my skin tingle. There was a fuzzy chatter of talk and laughter. The air was cosy with friendship. Jackson arrived, very sexy, all in black. We avoided each other for a while, but I felt his eyes on me. The alcohol gave me a comfortable buzz and when the music slowed, I grabbed his hand and pulled him out onto the patio. I was sweating from dancing and the cool night brushed across my glistening skin.

"I'm glad you came," I said.

"Me too. It's good to get out, isn't it?" His tone was polite, starched.

I laughed at him and nodded. He grinned back.

"You look good." He was still uncharacteristically formal. "Great actually," he added.

"You too. Very sexy." Although alcohol had clearly loosened my tongue, I still felt the familiar heat flood my cheeks.

He raised his eyebrows. "Nova, are you flirting with me?"

"You wish." I choked on a giggle.

"This is weird. You not being my brother's girlfriend anymore. It suits you."

I fluttered my eyelashes at him and bumped my hip to his. His laugh vibrated between us, creating a comfortable rhythm.

"I'm here for you, Nova, if there is anything you need. You know that." He had turned serious again.

"Like punching Coop?" I joked.

"If you want me to," he said. "He deserved it."

"Stop being so serious."

It was a playful scold and his mouth spread in a wide smile.

We danced and Jackson's arms were strong, keeping us both balanced, while his eyes had a playful twinkle. The party went on into the night. Two weeks in isolation and now we could not stand still. Mia tossed us all out at midnight.

Sage was going home with Luca. Jackson offered to split his ride-share car with me. Sitting close, in the darkness of the back seat, his arm rested across my shoulders, warm and comforting. My head was snug against his chest. He smiled down at me, tender, and kind. His lips fluttered across my hair. I reached up for him, pulling his mouth to mine in a kiss, demanding a response. I got one. Sparks flew. His lips were not gentle anymore, they were scorching and insistent. I was reluctant to pull away, but I had to.

"I feel sick," I moaned.

"I don't normally have that effect on girls." His voice was light with laughter.

"It's not you; it's the alcohol." I groaned again, waves of nausea rocking me.

"Just pull over here." Jackson instructed the driver and hauled me out of the car.

I vomited. In some bushes, bent over like a pretzel. Jackson held back my hair and it was humiliating. The cold air helped as we trudged the rest of the way home. I held a finger to my lips, not wanting to wake Mr and Mrs Ferry as we went inside.

After I cleaned myself up, Jackson sat with me on the bed. I could feel his affection drawing me like an oasis in a desert.

"Thanks, Jack. You're really nice."

"You're nice too." He chuckled.

"Why do things have to be so complicated?"

"Like what?"

"Like Cooper."

He shrugged. "Yeah. And you. And me." He kissed the top of my head.

"It's not fair."

"No, it's not." His voice was distant, as if he was not even talking to me.

I shuddered, suddenly exhausted. Tears leaked from my eyes. He pulled me against his chest. It was warm and solid. Dawn was creeping through the curtains when I felt the cold left by Jackson moving away, going home.

12

Ava had left Mia's party with Prisha, who lived around the corner. Rather than wait for a ride-share car, they had walked. From Prisha's house, Ava had decided to run home. Fit and fast, Ava Chapman was a sprinter. She had known it was a risk on the streets at night, but it was less than a kilometre and she had done it a hundred times. Tall and slender, with short red curly hair, and vivid green eyes, Ava was a natural beauty and hard to miss.

That night she was attacked and raped.

I heard the story from her the following day.

Ava noticed the two guys, early twenties, hanging around on the corner. She crossed the road to avoid them. They saw her, yelled out, and jogged in pursuit.

"Hey gorgeous, wait for us." One of them called to her.

"I like redheads. I bet you're a wildcat." The other shouted after her.

Ava kept sprinting and did not answer. She thought she could outrun them, as she did most of the boys at school.

The taller of the two was faster. With an almost unnatural speed, he caught up and tackled her from behind. Ava went down hard, face first. He held her down. Puffing announced the arrival of the second man. She would have easily outrun him. With her arm twisted behind her back she was dragged to her feet. They were brutal and rough. Her arm was stretched to breaking point. A shirt was shoved into her mouth. It was hard to breathe, and she could not scream. Her jeans snagged on bushes as they pulled her off the footpath, into someone's yard. A large overgrown hedge blocked them from the road. It was secluded and private.

They raped her.

Ava fought. Wriggling. Punching. Kicking. They took turns to restrain her. She could not be sure who was who, or even when they changed places. One merged into the other. A malevolent glint in his eyes, the smell of sweating desire. She heard whispering, without listening to what was said. Soft hands stroked her, then pinched her when she struggled. She cringed as if brushed with smooth snakeskin. Her clothes ripped, her body tore. Eventually she lay still. Shutting her eyes, she prayed for it to be over. Laughter floated above her. She wondered if there were people in the house nearby, sleeping or watching late-night TV. No one came to help her.

Ava must have lost consciousness because she woke up lying on the grass. Battered. Bruised. Bloody. The mouth gag was gone. Her hand came away from her face marked with dried blood. The taste of metal was in her mouth, unmistakably more blood. Her clothes hardly covered her. Thankfully, she still had her phone. She dialled her father.

At the hospital she was examined, and they called in the rape crisis counsellors. She had to submit to a rape kit before they cleaned her up. The police took her statement. Finally, she was given some sedatives and she slept.

In a small-town news travels fast. Mia heard about Ava being in hospital and rang Sage and me. We went up on Easter Sunday morning.

Bruises covered her arms. Her eyes were haunted, hinting at the atrocity. Her curls were flat, and her freckles stood out in the paleness of her face. She reached for my hand, clutching it tight. Her story was hard to hear, harder to tell. She was reciting it verbatim now. Ava was strong and fearless, but I could not imagine how anyone could recover from this.

Ava's rape hit me like a bulldozer. My body shook as I absorbed her emotions as if they were mine. The fear was an icy grip squeezing my throat. Shame lay heavy across my shoulders. And the violation made me cringe and shudder with revulsion.

The world had become an extremely dangerous place.

13

I was a chaotic mess. Exams were scheduled as soon as we returned to school, and it was difficult to study in preparation. My emotions were all over the place, up, down, flat, and numb. There was the overwhelming concern I had for Ava and lingering grief for my father. My issues with Cooper and confusion over the kiss I shared with Jackson seemed petty, considering what was happening around us.

Cooper messaged me after hearing about Ava and wanted to meet. It was time.

He took me up to the national park. Although it was still open for exercise, lockdown meant it was deserted. There was an autumn chill in the air as we wandered slowly along a carpeted path of mud and fallen leaves. We had shared our horror about Ava's rape in the car on the way, but now were both silent.

"Nova, will you forgive me about Imogen? Can we try again?" Cooper asked eventually, his voice soft and persuasive.

"I want to. But it still hurts, Coop. I don't want to be in a relationship where I'm always wondering if you'll hook up with Imogen when I'm not there."

"I miss you so much. I've never felt like this about anyone else." His voice rang with sincerity. "I know I hurt you. I was drunk and angry at you not being here. It's no excuse, but it won't ever happen again. I promise. I honestly don't care about Imogen."

I kept walking, watching the ground in front of me, where a weak sun shone between the trees and wove a broken pattern on the dirt. It was easier if I didn't look at his face while I searched for the right words.

"I need to tell you something before you hear it from someone else. After Mia's party, I kissed Jackson."

"I already know. He told me."

"He would!" I sighed in exasperation.

"Was it to get back at me?"

"Yeah. Maybe. I don't know."

He shrugged in dismissal. "Nova, I want you back. I love you." His eyes were wide and unflinching. "Do you love me?"

He stopped walking and tugged on my hand to hold me beside him. I could tell he was a little afraid to hear my answer. There was a warmth around my heart, and I wasn't sure if it was my love for Cooper or his for me. I wondered if it mattered. With a few deep breaths, I felt the cold air whisper through my lungs, carrying a light fragrance of damp earth and wet grass. It helped clear my head. I wanted to be happy. I had been happy with Cooper. He was a safe place in this dangerous world.

"Coop, I do love you." I was as sure as I could be.

I felt the relief flood his heart. He brushed the hair back from the side of my neck, then leaned in to kiss me on the little dent of my collar bone. His lips fluttered on my skin, tickling like feathers. Goosebumps rose all over and I shiv-ered, not with cold but with longing. He stroked my face and scattered little kisses over my cheeks and finally on my lips. It was sweet and rich, like strawberries and chocolate.

"Can we try again? Will you be my girlfriend?" Cooper's voice was a soft murmur against my cheek.

"Yeah, I will. I want to try again, too." I had made my decision.

The sun seemed suddenly brighter, the grass greener, the day warmer. Despite everything else, this was right.

I knew, however, that I had to address things with Jackson before I saw him at school.

Jackson's bedroom was untidy. There was hardly a space on the floor that was not covered by books, clothes, or shoes.

I took a deep breath. "Hey. I need to tell you Coop and I are back together." It came out in a rush.

"No kidding." His voice was loaded with a heavy sarcasm. "He already told me."

I wondered if they relished showing off to each other or genuinely talked.

"Yeah." I paused. "Look, thank you for taking care of me after Mia's."

Jackson waited. His hand moved up to push his hair from his eyes.

"About the kiss. I really care about you …" I left the sentence hanging.

"But you care about Coop more." His bitter tone was a dart to my chest.

"Sorry." I didn't know what else to say.

He studied me for a moment, then grinned with his usual arrogant cheekiness. "I bet our kiss was better than anything you've had with Coop."

I shook my head. "You're an arsehole!" But I laughed.

I still felt the draw of Jackson's magnetism. These Lewis boys were easy to love. I remembered Sage's advice. *I was with Cooper. And I was just friends with Jackson. Period.*

Afraid that they would not be able to contain the increasing violence that had become the norm in classrooms and playgrounds, schools and colleges across the state, with the support of the government, made the decision to close and move instead to online learning for term two. Our senior exams were still scheduled for the first week back, at school, but with tight security. The mood around the school was miserable. Ava's rape still hung between us. There was a natural exam-anxiety, but an additional discomfort, a feeling that the world was no longer familiar or safe. Teachers were silent and severe; students were grim-faced and grieving.

Cooper came out of each exam, pale and complaining of abdominal pains, convinced he would not pass and worrying he had an ulcer. I spent so much time trying to comfort him, the butterflies in my stomach flew in an easy formation. Sage and I quietly sailed through the week. Jackson had an air of indifference, but I knew he would do well in his exams. He always did.

Friday night after the last exam, Cooper's father invited over some of the seniors and their parents. He had a proposal, that a small group of the twins' friends could stay at their holiday house for the school term. It was more remote, a smaller, safer community. Ava's rape had rattled everyone. As a general practitioner, Dr Lewis was frightened by the injuries he was seeing, victims of violent crime, especially among young adults. The parents readily agreed with the idea. At the beach house, we could isolate, complete our online school lessons, and wait this out. There would be regular visits from one of the parents on weekends.

The Taylor family and the Lewis family were close friends. Mia Taylor and her younger sister, Alice, were confirmed to go. Technically Alice was not a senior but was only a grade below us at school. Cooper had clearly included me on the list, and by association Sage and Luca. Evan, Cooper's friend, who went to another school, was also coming. Although, I had only briefly met Evan a couple of times, I sensed a lively character, cheeky and charming. He had been getting into a lot of trouble, breaking into cars, and stealing and his parents hoped Cooper would be a good influence. They wanted to get him away from his other friends. Mia's boyfriend, Kenji, needed to stay with his family and help with his younger siblings so would not be coming. Imogen was not included.

We all agreed to be on our best behaviour.

Yeah right!

14

We gathered at the Lewis's home early on Sunday. Eight of us, subdued and anxious, feeling like we were escaping some tragedy. We drove slowly through town, as if in a funeral procession; Cooper's car, followed by Luca's, then Jackson on his motorbike. The effects of the spreading hostility were obvious. Looting had left broken windows and smashed doors. Shops were closed, some abandoned. An eerie silence cloaked the streets. Houses were locked up. Everything was shut tight. No children played, no dogs were being walked, no lawn mowers, no cyclists.

Once on the highway, the misery shroud lifted. Away from the buildings, it was cleaner and brighter. In Cooper's car, Evan chattered non-stop. His eyes glimmered as if they held a secret, and his wide mouth beamed with mischief. He had not known Ava, and although respectful, he was not as affected by what had happened as the rest of us. He kept us entertained with funny stories from his school and his droll spin on things was infectious.

Mia messaged me from the back of Luca's car, asking about the sleeping arrangements at the house. There were four bedrooms.

Are you going to share with Cooper?
No. We're only just back together. I'm not ready.
I get that.
Sage and Luca?
Definitely.
You could share with Jackson.
Hahaha. You can.

We arrived mid-morning. Before unpacking the cars, we held a house meeting to sort out rooms. Sage and Luca took one bedroom. Mia and Alice another.

"Do you want to share?" Cooper asked me.

His eyebrows were raised, hopeful, but I sensed a hesitation in him that matched my own.

"Umm. No. I don't think that's a good idea."

He nodded, a little reluctantly. "Okay, you take the other room and I'll share with Evan. Jackson can sleep on the couch."

Jackson shrugged and nodded his agreement. People went off to get settled.

The days eased into a routine. On weekdays it was online school. Virtual classrooms, homework, webinars, worksheets, tutoring by video conference and open book exams. Our practical work became theoretical case studies. Despite the strange conditions, our senior year was important, the basis of our future decisions. Although Alice was a year below the rest of us, she followed a similar routine. A spirit of collaboration and support pervaded the house. Household chores were divided by roster and rotated. Weekly house meetings provided a chance for ideas or grievances. Jackson ran them, with Mia. They were natural leaders and there were few complaints.

We created our own entertainment. The beach was at our doorstep and was usually deserted. Late April was a little cold for swimming, but Evan teased each of us mercilessly until we braved the icy waves with him. His favourite thing was night swimming and then creeping up underwater to scare us. Even when I expected it, he still took me by surprise. Our small backyard was big enough for a tight game of football. The boys set up a home gym in the garage. Sage and I used it as a yoga studio as well. With one television, we compromised. Board games and jigsaw puzzles came out of the cupboard. Privacy was available in your own room, but we mostly hung out altogether. Spending time with each other was the only social life we had.

With routine and isolation, came boredom. No sports were being played, no concerts, no cinemas, no picnics, and no parties. The pubs and restaurants were closed. Cafés were open for take-away food only.

Cooper and I took long walks on the beach, and there was a cosy glow between us, a renewed sense of trust and belonging together. The absence of Imogen made it easier.

Mia was particularly creative in ideas to stave off boredom. As the school musical was cancelled, she directed a house version of the Wizard of Oz. Jackson got on board and persuaded the rest of us. It was a distraction. Mia was Dorothy, and Thomasina, my cat, who had made the move with us, was an unwilling Toto. I was the Scarecrow, Jackson the Tinman, and Luca the Lion. Cooper made a great Wizard, Sage was the Wicked Witch, and Alice played Glinda, the Good Witch. Evan was the Munchkin Mayor, pretending not to care, while he was easily the most enthusiastic. My old clothes became a scarecrow costume. There was very clever ad-libbing and one-line quips, especially from Cooper and

Evan, who had such a quick wit and played off each other so naturally. A manic laughter bounced through the house.

Time rolled into May and brought colder southerly winds.

There was a continual barrage of social media posts about the terrifying hostility all around the world. Reports from home described neighbours coming to blows in the street. Home invasions. Raiding in shops and supermarkets. People purchasing guns for protection. Others arming themselves with knives and household tools. The police were overwhelmed, and their response was often just as violent as the crime they were called in to stop. It seemed no one was immune to the spreading aggression.

News headlines continued to tag the warrior gene. It made me miss my father. I wondered what he would have said about it all, if only we'd had that chance to talk.

I was conscious of being a conduit for the anger around us. Without warning, my stomach would drop, my chest would tighten with fear and my veins would simmer with fury. *How could I be happy when my father had been murdered and Ava raped?* Cooper took me for a run, physically burning off the rage. Sage calmed me with her down-to-earth view of things. Evan made me laugh. Thomasina was an excellent pet therapy companion. They helped me feel safe and loved. Overall, the beach house rested in a peaceful, harmonious space, in an irrational and dangerous world. Sage believed it was my influence that things ran so smoothly, but I was only reflecting the friendship I felt.

Out of all of us, Evan was the moodiest. He was funny and cheeky when in good humour and his pranks and stories kept us laughing. Prompting a round of practical jokes, he swapped sugar for salt, vodka for water, left plastic spiders in people's beds, and wrote messages on the toilet paper. He was also the most likely to complain about other people's cooking or to be frustrated by waiting to use the bathroom. A dark cloud would settle over him and to shed his irritability, he went off for a walk on his own. When he returned, I could feel the change, a happier, lighter tone. Evan brought back little gifts as a way of apology. Often it was for the whole house, a couple of fancy coffee mugs or a doormat. Sometimes it was a present for one person: a scarf for me, a football for Cooper, a pair of slippers for Mia, a toy for Thomasina. I had sensed an odd hidden pocket in Evan and when he brought back a brand-new kettle for the house, I realised that hidden pocket was a secret he was concealing. I suspected that he had been break-ing into other houses and stealing these gifts. I mentioned my concerns to Cooper, who also had suspicions.

Cooper waited until the others were down at the beach. "Evan, where did you get the money for that kettle?"

"I just had some money and wanted to get something nice for everyone."

We were standing in the kitchen and Evan dropped his elbows to casually lean across the bench.

"That's great mate, but not if you stole the money to buy it," Cooper said.

"I didn't steal money." Evan grinned as he emphasised the word *money*. "All these empty holiday houses are owned by rich people who wouldn't even notice their nice things are missing." He gestured at the neighbouring houses, many of which were standing empty for the winter. "Really, it's there for the taking."

"Evan, that's breaking and entering, stealing. You'll get caught."

"Sorry, not sorry. The police have a lot more on their hands than worrying about me. And the owners won't even notice until they come here for summer. If then. I'll be long gone." His tone was still light and dismissive, but his grin looked forced.

"That is not the point, Evan. It's not right," I said.

Evan stood up straight, tall and intimidating, staring down at me and I felt a swell of annoyance.

"It's none of your business, Miss Perfect."

"She's right, Evan. It's illegal and you shouldn't do it." Cooper's voice was critical.

"You would take her side."

Evan's anger rose and with it was a level of aggression similar to what I had felt with Troy, at school, and with Alexander, that night at the Lewis house. It was an uncontrolled fury bubbling beneath the surface just waiting for someone to launch at. I placed my hands flat on the kitchen bench, its smooth surface a comforting stability in the rising tension.

"Coop, be careful," I warned quietly.

I edged away from Evan, moving closer to Cooper, seeking the safety of his arms.

"Shut up." Evan turned on me again, his eyes wide open and a little bloodshot.

The rage found its outlet. He bent and grabbed my wrist between his hands as if to twist my skin, his fingers digging in tight. I gasped and my eyes turned watery as I struggled to pull my arm away. Cooper moved quickly and pried Evan's hands loose, pulling back his fingers, until he yelped in pain. As Evan leaned forward to cradle his fingers, Cooper dropped his shoulder to shove Evan aside. Cooper's shoulder slammed against Evan's nose, which drew a spurt of blood and a grunt. It was enough to quell Evan's rage. His hands lifted to his nose and his eyes were soft and confused. I rubbed at the red marks on my wrist that were already fading. My blood still burned with an anger I didn't want to feel.

"Oh shit. Nova, I am so sorry. I didn't mean to hurt you." I felt the sudden change in Evan and the flush on his face was now embarrassment.

"What the hell, mate?" Cooper glowered at him.

I moved to the lounge and sat on the couch, all my energy suddenly drained. Evan dropped beside me, a tissue dabbing at his nose, though it had already stopped bleeding. I could tell his energy was also low.

"Nova, I really am sorry. I didn't mean it." The anger was gone.

"Don't worry about it. I'm fine." I was still uneasy though, both with having absorbed Evan's anger and having it directed at me.

"Yeah. Well, you should be sorry. That was ridiculous." Cooper was not ready to forgive him just yet. "And no more stealing."

"Yeah, alright. I promise. Sorry mate."

The two of them were joking and laughing again by the time the others returned from the beach, Evan's good humour restored.

The knot in my stomach remained. It was a reminder that our safety in the house could turn in a moment, and the danger was not just from someone outside.

15

A small local supermarket supplied most of the groceries we needed, and the café offered pizza and burgers. Once a week we took turns to drive into Yarram, a bigger coastal town, about thirty minutes by car. It had more shops, more variety. Jackson took the motorbike, and I was keen to join him. It was loud and attracted attention, but with the isolation restrictions there was not much traffic, and it was freedom. The element of danger just added to the excitement.

The shopping was done, and we were heading home. I struggled to shoulder my heavy backpack which was full of groceries. Two guys appeared. One, tall and lanky, a navy hoodie hiding his face. The other, shorter, stockier, dark sunglasses, and more menacing. Even from a distance, hostility rolled off them and it pitched and burned in my chest.

"Hey Jock, isn't that my bike?" The tall guy strode towards us, holding a knife at his side. "I'm sure that's my bike."

Jackson mounted the seat and his apprehension shivered through me. "Hurry up." His voice was low and urgent as he started the engine.

"You're not going anywhere on Archer's bike," said Jock, the stocky guy.

Jackson kept his tone steady. "We don't want any trouble."

When Jock reached for the handlebars, Jackson jumped the bike forward and Jock leapt back. Combined with the weight of my backpack though, it tipped me off balance. I wobbled and fell to one side, as Archer reached forward with his knife. It pierced my arm, through my jacket sleeve. I felt a warmth, not pain, but shivers ran up and down my spine. With one hand, Jackson steadied me, pulling me closer against his back. The other hand steered the bike forward in another jolt. I wrapped my arms tightly around his waist. Archer stepped back with a growl of anger, while Jock pulled a knife of his own. He swiped at us, and it slashed across my side, but Jackson had us clear. It was a bit shaky, but we were moving off, down the road.

"He got me with the knife." I shouted above the engine noise, close to the side of Jackson's helmet.

There was a dull pain at my side and my jaw ached from clenching my teeth.

"Hang on. I want to get further away." Jackson concentrated on steadying the bike and picking up speed.

Fifteen minutes later, well clear of the town, Jackson pulled off the highway. Tall gum trees bordered both sides of the road. Dense green and brown foliage of the smaller scrub trees hid us from passing cars. Ominously quiet, it was surreal after the roar of the bike engine. Jackson swung back to face me, unlocking my hands from around his waist. He pulled down the sleeve of my jacket to inspect my arm.

Blood welled slowly in the puncture, just above my elbow. Jackson used his shirt to press against the wound. His expression was grim.

"I don't think it's very deep, but there's a bit of blood." His voice was eerie, as if in a tunnel or underwater.

I took several deep breaths. My heart thumped. I was cold. Nausea rose in my throat.

"Are you feeling okay?" he asked.

"Yeah, just dizzy and a bit sick," I said. "I'm not great with blood."

My stomach pitched and rolled. I made a conscious effort to unclench my fists, a hangover from the anger I had absorbed from our attackers.

Jackson watched me warily. "I'll see if I can clean it up a bit."

"Jack, I think they got me twice."

I lifted my arm and my shirt, exposing my side. Jackson flinched and swore. There was a long slash, from below my ribs at the front around to my back, still bleeding. The guy had managed to strike across my left side, where my jacket ended, above the waistline of my jeans. The deep crimson blood was quickly staining my white shirt, the colours a stark contrast. I yelped when Jackson touched the wound. It stung. His face was lined with anxiety, and I bit down on my tongue to keep quiet.

Jackson moved with a quiet confidence, creating tight makeshift bandages out of both our T-shirts. They soaked through quickly but slowed the bleeding. He passed me a Coke from our grocery supplies.

"Here. You need fluids and sugar." He studied my face through narrow worried eyes. "You are not going to faint, are you?"

"I don't think so, but let's get going," I said.

I could sense his wariness and concern; we didn't know if the men would come after us. I tried to cover my cringe as Jackson helped me back into my jacket and the backpack.

"Hold on tight and don't let go."

I nodded, hoping I was putting on a brave face, but he saw through it.

"This is my fault, coming in on this stupid bike." Jackson's voice was bitter with self-recrimination and his guilt felt heavy across my shoulders.

"Hey, it's not your fault. I'm fine. I love the bike. We were just unlucky." I tried for a smile.

He smiled back but it was more of a grimace. His eyes lacked their usual sparkle.

"Nova, you sure make it hard for me sometimes." It was a quiet mumble.

We got home safely, and everyone fussed over me. Cooper was furious with Jackson, who just took it, still blaming himself. Mia's mother did a phone-video examination and decided the cuts would heal okay with just butterfly tapes and bandages. My wounds were cleaned and dosed with antiseptic, while I almost bit through my tongue to keep from making a sound.

Later in bed, I had some flashbacks. When shaking tremors took over my body, I hugged my knees to my chest until I could regain control. My stomach churned, and tears rolled down my face. All too easily, I could recall the irrational rage of our attackers. Eventually, my body wore itself out. I went to get some water and found Jackson in the kitchen. He covered his unease with an affectionate smile, but I could sense the anger and fear he was trying to hide.

"Can't sleep?" he asked.

"No. You?"

Jackson shook his head. He nodded towards the couch, which had been made up as his bed and we sat down. Cooper appeared and I guessed he had come to check on me. He sat on my other side.

"Do you want to talk about it?" Cooper asked.

"Not really," Jackson and I said together, our eyes meeting in a shared acknowledgment.

Cooper reached for my hand and our fingers entwined. His love was a warm, weighted blanket, secure and comfortable. I let it soothe me. The three of us sat quietly in the semi-darkness.

"Nova is that you?" Jackson asked after a while.

"What?"

"I can feel … I don't know …" he hesitated, searching for the right word. "Happiness or contentment I guess."

I shrugged. "Maybe."

"I can feel it too," Cooper said.

An identical look of wonder was reflected in the twin faces.

I gave a quiet laugh. "It's what I feel from you two. I'm just sending it back."

Jackson moved in closer to me. Cooper noticed and I felt a stab of jealousy come from him, but I did not forward that on. It simmered and faded out when I tightened my grip on his hand.

"Come on, let's go to bed. I'll stay with you." Cooper pulled me up.

I sensed Jackson's clench of annoyance, betrayal. It slid to embarrassment when my reproving glance let him know I could tell.

"Nova, you are scary sometimes," Jackson muttered, with a wink.

In this volatile world, I knew my emotional sensitivity was growing. It was not just about sensing people's feelings, I was also able to send out my own, influencing how others felt. I was an echo chamber, absorbing and reflecting emotions, and I was getting stronger and better at controlling it. It was a little scary. *I was weird.*

<h1 style="text-align:center">16</h1>

With so many businesses closed, casual jobs were hard to come by, but our beach community was small, and we had become locals. Cooper and Evan got jobs at the small Woodside Beach supermarket, working for a few hours at night re-stocking shelves. Jackson secured some casual hours at the adjoining pizza café, as a kitchen hand, on Friday evenings and weekends. These businesses were a ten-minute walk from the house. Often, one of us went down to walk home with Jackson, helping him carry back the free pizza he scored from work.

In his second week, after the Friday evening shift, Jackson came home on his own.

"Where's Alice?" Mia asked.

"I don't know, I didn't see her."

"What do you mean? She went down to meet you." Worry crept into Mia's voice.

I felt the rise of panic in the room.

"She left here like twenty minutes ago, to go to the café to meet you. Where is she?" Mia was frightened.

We rang Alice's phone; it vibrated on the kitchen bench, where she had left it.

"Nova, can you sense anything?" Sage asked.

Alice would have walked to the shop, along the footpath, in the fading twilight, a safe, familiar route. It would have taken her about ten minutes. I stretched my senses, searching.

There was a guy we all saw regularly, though he kept his distance. He lived ten houses further along the beach. His eyes watched us, staring without acknowledgment and it set my hair on end. There was something about him, a darkness, anger, but deep and hidden.

Sweat drenched my skin. There was a throbbing behind my eyes. My fingers involuntarily curled into a fist, nails digging into my palms. I had a feeling, and it was not good.

"I think it's something to do with that creepy guy," I said at last.

Mia let out a hollow screech. They knew who I meant.

"Shit." Cooper's concern surged.

After Ava's rape, we did not want to take any chances. Mia left messages for her parents, who were both doing nightshifts. Her mother was a nurse, and her father was a policeman. The closest police station to us was in Yarram. Whilst they took down the details Mia provided, they sounded busy and distracted, hardly interested in a girl missing for twenty minutes, even if she was a policeman's daughter. Mia could not wait for her parents to call back and wanted us to check out the creepy guy's house. I had no proof, but Sage and Mia trusted my feeling. Evan was sceptical, although with Mia's obvious panic, he did not say much. Cooper and Jackson were both wary and undecided. I was not even sure I trusted myself. Eventually, we agreed to go and see if there was anything suspicious. Quietly and carefully.

The beach route was less conspicuous than the street. Darkness had fallen and the night was quiet. With a half moon, our dark clothes camouflaged us, but our faces shone as pale outlines. I pulled my hood lower over my forehead. There was an air of nervous tension between us.

On reaching the creepy guy's house, Mia hopped from one foot to the other, breathing in shallow, quick gasps. She was close to full blown panic. Luca persuaded her to stay out on the sand dunes in case her parents called back. Cooper and Evan crept down the left side of the house, while Jackson and Luca took the right. They would meet at the front. Sage and I had the back of the house, facing the beach.

A low-set wooden shack, it was older than ours, weather worn and dilapidated, paint peeling from the walls. Big windows and glass sliding doors were closed tight, reflecting the night, dark and foreboding. We listened and pressed our faces to the glass, peering through the gloom inside. At the slightest sign of trouble, we were poised to run. It was eerie. My breath came fast and shallow and my heart thumped.

Phones vibrated with a group message from Jackson.

Come. RH side, halfway. QUIET.

We met as directed and had a whispered conversation.

"There is a light here and I thought I heard something, but Luca didn't hear it so it could be my imagination." Jackson motioned to the window. "Nova, can you sense anything?"

The faint light in the room curled around heavy curtains. Everyone was quiet, waiting on me. Attempting to block out the emotions emanating from my friends, I concentrated on what I could detect from inside the house. There was a flutter of butterflies in my stomach, maybe fear and a sense of help-lessness. I was not sure if I was just imagining it. Then we all heard it. Someone talking quietly, the creepy guy. An icy shiver ran down my spine and wrapped around my heart, it was cold anger. I decided that was coming from him. The butterflies still swarmed, fright, anxiety. That came from someone else.

"Is it Alice? With him?" asked Cooper quietly.

"Yeah. Maybe. Sorry, I'm not sure." I had a strong feeling that it was, but who was I kidding, I could not be sure.

"We need to get in there," Evan whispered.

"No, we should wait for Mia's dad to convince the police to come," said Sage.

Jackson held a finger to his lips and then pointed to the dunes. "Be quiet. Let's see what Mia wants to do."

We crept back to meet with Mia. She hardly gave us a chance to explain, nodding her head frantically, like a bobble-head doll.

"Nova, you think it's Alice in there, don't you?" Mia's voice was pitched hysterically high.

I shrugged. "I think so, but I can't be sure. I'm sorry."

"We should just call the police again." Sage pulled out her phone.

"Evan mentioned he might be able to pick the door lock." I could see Jackson's brain working, forming a plan.

We all knew Evan had skills, though I was not sure if the others knew about his recent breaking and entering.

"We can't do that. I'm with Sage." Cooper was nervous. "Let's call the police again."

"And tell them what?" Luca jumped in. "That we were snooping around a house because we think he has our friend? Based on a feeling? No offence, Nova."

"None taken," I said. "I could be wrong, maybe she's not in there.

"Then who is he talking to?" asked Mia sharply. "It's Alice."

"Where is Evan?" Sage asked suddenly, looking around at all of us.

"Damn!" Cooper messaged him, but there was no reply.

"Come on. We'll check if Alice is there, and we'll get Evan." Jackson spoke firmly.

Sage, Mia, and I were not going to be left behind, but we agreed to stay outside the house. If Evan had indeed picked the lock and gone inside, Jackson, Cooper, and Luca were going in after him. They hoped, with three of them, to be able to overpower the guy if they needed to. Of course, we did not know if he was armed. A lot of people carried guns or knives these days.

My knees wobbled and my stomach twisted in knots. It was my fear but also what I was absorbing from the others. I sensed the adrenaline rising in Jackson and Luca, as they squared their shoulders and flexed their hands. Cooper pulled me close and kissed my forehead. His anxiety was a blast of cold water, but I also felt his determination and my heart warmed with his courage.

"Stay safe," Cooper whispered, with no expression, no smile.

"You too."

I shivered and pressed my knuckles to my mouth. Sage squeezed my other hand and a degree of calmness flowed through us both.

"Stick together?" she said quietly.

"Like glue." It was our thing, and the familiarity was reassuring.

The back sliding door was ajar. Evan had been successful in getting in. Jackson went through first, disappearing for a second and then reappearing. He beckoned to Luca and Cooper. They hardly made a sound. Sage and I held our breath and listened carefully. I could hear Mia swallowing and worried that she was going to faint.

Suddenly, we heard the commotion. Shouting from the house. My body was on fire, scorching hot, with anger, but not mine. There was the sound of breaking glass, and three people tumbled out through the open sliding door. Cooper and Luca had Alice between them, stumbling but upright.

"Move!" Luca yelled at us, as Jackson and Evan followed behind them, at a run.

Luca and Cooper helped Alice as we raced across the dunes. She was whimpering. The uneven sand hampered our progress. Jackson had blood pouring from his nose and smudging all over his face. Evan was nursing one of his arms and groaning. But we still ran. Sage gripped my hand to pull me along, and I dragged on Mia's hand. It seemed darker than before, and I kept looking behind us. There was nothing to see, just blackness. Emotions rushed at me, crowded me. My skin felt like it was being jabbed by needles and there was a stone in my stomach, but exhilaration pumped through my blood and kept me moving.

At the house, Alice sank to the couch, her shoulders hunched forward. Untidy, knotted hair hung over a pale face where her tears had tracked grimy lines. I twisted my own hands together as I felt her smouldering fear. Her eyes were deep, dark reflections of a nightmare. Mia patted her arm and would not leave her side.

Alice's breath came in short pants, as she explained what had happened. He had come up behind her in the street, with a large knife. She described his voice as deadly calm, while his eyes were angry and red.

"I've seen your friend, sneaking into people's houses, taking things. He doesn't think anyone sees him. Well, I see him. Now, I'm taking something ..." he had said.

As one, we all glared at Evan, who stared at his feet. He looked ready to pass out. His pain was an aching throb in my own arm. I wondered if it was broken.

Alice had been terrified. The guy had forced her to come back to his house and locked her in a bedroom.

Jackson took over the story. When he entered the house, Evan was waiting outside the bedroom door. They could hear the creepy guy talking to Alice and her voice answering him. It was just a jumble of words and lot of swearing.

"He didn't actually touch me, and he didn't yell," Alice added quietly. "He just paced up and down and ranted. He kept asking me what was happening to him, and I said I didn't know." She shuddered.

The four boys had burst into the bedroom, with Jackson and Evan diving to tackle the guy. Cooper and Luca grabbed Alice and fled. The creepy guy wasn't carrying a weapon, but he fought against the boys. He punched Jackson in the nose and pushed Evan into a tall mirror. The mirror collapsed under Evan, who flung out an arm to break his fall. At least, the glass had not cut through his clothes. The guy had bolted from the room. Jackson and Evan made their escape, not waiting around to see if he returned.

I couldn't help but feel we had been lucky.

Mia finally made contact with her father, and he was on his way with Cooper's father, a doctor. He also rang the Yarram Police. Cooper, Jackson, and Luca kept watch in case the creepy guy came after us. It was over an hour later, when the police car turned into our driveway and Mia's father had arrived. Jackson and Cooper gave the police officers a variation of the truth, with no mention of the break and enter. They claimed that Alice had called for help, leaving out the part about it being a weird feeling of mine. The creepy guy had gone by the time the police officers checked his house.

Dr Lewis took us all to Yarram Health Urgent Care Service. No-one wanted to be left behind. It was silent and deserted. People avoided coming out at night unless they had to. Alice was taken to a private room with her father and Mia. She had no physical injuries. While attending to Jackson and Evan, Dr Lewis made the rest of us wait on the plastic seats outside. A hospital smell wafted out through the doors, sterile and antiseptic. Jackson's nose was broken. Evan's arm was fractured.

It was well after midnight by the time we got home. Evan was left behind, needing a plaster cast for his arm. Jackson's nose was swollen but straight, a tape across his face. He had dark smudges under both his eyes, and he was a little high on painkillers. Alice was asleep, having been given a sedative, and her father carried her into bed.

Although exhausted, we all simmered with leftover adrenalin and nervous energy.

"Are you psychic?" Mr Taylor asked me, and I sensed a strange level of respect.

"No. It was just a feeling, a lucky guess," I said, shaking my head.

Cooper and I sat close, arms linked, and I let the drone of everyone's voices soothe me. In return, I sent out good vibrations to calm the turmoil. Gradually, the room quietened, and as the first light of dawn was breaking, we all went to bed.

I checked on Jackson. "Hey. Are you sure you're okay?"

"Hey, beautiful. I'm fine. We did a good thing tonight." His voice was nasally.

"We sure did. It was pretty scary though."

He shrugged, and his hand went to his nose. I felt the twinge of pain, too.

"What's life without a little danger?" He winked at me and leaned over to kiss me.

"Those drugs must be good." I scolded, pushing him away.

He used puppy dog eyes on me, but I shook my head. "You are amazing though." I figured he wouldn't remember in the morning anyway.

"You too." His voice was a faint whisper.

Mia's mother arrived a few hours later and brought Ava with her, as a surprise.

Mrs Taylor hugged me tightly, crying with relief. "How did you know, Nova?"

"I wasn't sure; it was just a feeling. That guy has always been creepy, and angry. Well, most people are angry these days. But I just thought it was worth checking out."

I did find it easy to connect with my close friends, feel what they were feeling. It was an instinct. I had searched for an imprint of Alice, and I had found it. It had never happened like that before, but then I hadn't needed to try like that before. I was not sure what I was, but I did not like people thinking I was psychic.

Evan was collected from Yarram. He was going home with Dr Lewis, to his parents.

He took me aside for an unusually sincere goodbye. "Nova, I need to thank you. You and Coop stopped me going over the edge. I'm sorry about that day ... when I got a little crazy. You're so easy to be around. You give off kind vibes.

You're a really nice person." Evan's voice trailed off with embarrassment.

The heat rose in my cheeks, but I managed an awkward smile. "You're pretty nice yourself."

I was rewarded with his cheeky grin.

Alice was being taken home as well, at least for a while, so her mother could look after her. Her parents had a big discussion about taking us all back and I sensed their uncertainty. The violence at home was worse than ever. It was dangerous going out even during the day. Gangs from Melbourne made regular raids. There was an 8 PM to 6 AM curfew and the police patrolled the streets to enforce it. Even with what had happened with Alice, the parents still believed we were safer at the beach house. We got instructions about stricter safety measures, and they were going to make more regular visits to check on us.

Jackson also made the decision to go back home. It took me completely by surprise.

"Jack, why?" I asked when we had a moment alone.

"I just need to get away from here for a while."

It was all he would say, but his resolve was firm. All I could sense was confusion and frustration, but I was not sure what lay deeper.

Jackson, Dr Lewis, Evan, Alice, and the Taylors left after lunch.

It was suddenly very quiet around the beach house.

17

Ava's arrival provided a much-needed distraction. She brought gossip from home and filled a spot in the house. Yet, it was clear she was different, a quieter version of her former self. She stayed inside and sudden noises made her jump. Sharing a room with me, she spent a lot of time in bed. Nightmares still flared most nights, sometimes mingling with my own, until we both woke. I sensed strong feelings of shame and anger, as well as twinges of anxiety and fear. She had broken up with Prisha. The rapists had not been apprehended and they were probably long gone. She was seeing a rape counsellor, via online sessions, which helped. We surrounded her with gentle support and compassion.

The whole house battled the despondency that settled over us. The changes and uncertainty in our world took its toll. We stressed over school assessments and struggled with homesickness. Mia's worry about her sister was a heavy load. Luca and Sage seemed to be quieter than usual. Cooper took over as house leader with the manner of a football captain. Trying to boost morale, he went on and on about teamwork. It did not help and all the while I could tell he was miserable himself. Since Alice's rescue, he had been jumpy and anxious, and he clearly missed Evan and Jackson. We were all on edge.

May was slipping into June and the days turned chilly. The beach was often deserted, great for walks, but too cold for swimming. It was no longer patrolled by the lifesavers, just the seagulls. When the westerly winds swept up the waves to a decent swell, only a couple of persistent surfers braved the icy seas.

There were tangible changes in our community, and I felt the anger all about me. Houses were fenced with barbed wire; windows were boarded up. People peered out from behind their curtains, staying inside, but it did not stop the sound of angry shouting and domestic disputes that spilled onto the streets. The supermarkets and pharmacies were still open but barricaded, to restrict the number of customers entering. All of them had security guards. Customers fought over the last packet of pasta, shouting, and pushing until staff intervened. Except for one incident, where Cooper and Luca broke up a fight between teenagers at the end of our street, we kept our distance from people. It was dangerous to get involved. The changes that initially we had considered a little weird, were now depressing and horrifying.

Yet, we knew that our beach community was safer, more sheltered than the bigger towns. The major cities were the frontlines of a war zone.

The violence had left its mark on us. Physically and emotionally. While my cuts had healed from the knife attack, leaving only a thin shiny scar, I still had bad dreams. The murder of my father was never far from my mind. Mia fretted about her sister, blaming herself for letting Alice go out alone that evening. And Ava, she had been permanently changed.

The fear and anger around us vibrated and echoed through my very core.

Three weeks after Alice's ordeal, Mrs Taylor made her regular visit to see us, and Jackson and Alice came with her, to stay. It had seemed an eternity since they had left.

The mood in the house lifted at once.

Mia was overjoyed to have her sister back. As Mr and Mrs Taylor were so often at work and Alice was home alone, they agreed she was better with us.

While I was not sure why Jackson had changed his mind, I was glad he had. He could be moody and brooding but I now saw a strength and energy to Jackson that was inspiring. His teasing and sense of mischief brought fun and laughter.

On his first night home, Jackson and I sat up waiting for Cooper to finish work at the supermarket. Thomasina sat between us on the couch, getting pats from both of us, in turn.

"Did you miss me?" Jackson asked with a cheeky grin.

"Are you talking to me or the cat?" I laughed as he shrugged. "I don't think Thomasina even noticed. The rest of us did a tiny bit. The house was much cleaner without your mess."

"Huh! So, you hardly noticed I was gone?" Although he was still smiling, it seemed a little more forced now and I sensed some hurt.

"We all missed you. It was awful without you. Everyone was jumpy and depressed. Coop really missed having more guys around." I spoke truthfully but was careful not to make it too personal between us.

"Yeah, well, it drives me nuts being here." He didn't look up from Thomasina. "But not being here drives me nuts too."

My head clouded with confusion. I was absorbing Jackson's feelings.

"What do you mean?"

"I'm just a guy, who's fallen for a girl, who thinks she's in love with my brother." Jackson's voice was light, but I sensed his sincerity.

So much for not making things too personal. I concentrated on tickling Thomasina under her chin, who was basking in all the attention.

"That's not fair." I kept my voice even, not letting him draw me in.

"It's not fair for me, either." He looked at me now, and I felt drawn to meet his gaze.

His eyebrows angled up, his eyes were wide, but the corners of his mouth were drawn downwards. My chest tightened with his internal conflict.

"Jack, what do you want me to do? I love Coop, and I love you too, just differently." I wriggled on the couch, my legs jiggling up and down, and received a glare from Thomasina.

"Yeah." I felt the resignation in Jackson's sigh. "I just wish you'd loved me first."

I did love them both. They were two of my closest friends. I was saved from saying anything further when Cooper arrived home, with perfect timing.

I'm not sure if it was the aftermath of the conversation with Jackson but I started noticing changes in my relationship with Cooper. He was drawing away, not from me, just more into himself. I knew he loved me; I could feel it. So, I made a point of saying the words to him, so he would be sure of my feelings. We did not argue but I didn't feel like we were really connecting either.

Sage noticed. She was always looking out for me.

"Are you and Coop okay?" she asked. "You don't seem to spend as much time together as you used to."

"I don't know," I replied honestly. "Sometimes I think it's been a bit much for him. We just got back together and moved in together. And it all happened so quickly."

"Yeah, it gets hard, all living together." Her tone was reflective. "Luca drives me crazy sometimes, and I need my space, but I need him more."

"I think Coop misses footy and school and his mates," I said.

"We all miss things. That's not your fault. He's got you."

"Yeah, I know. But … I don't play footy. I'm not as fun as his mates. Maybe I'm not enough." My voice cracked a little, despite my best efforts to sound nonchalant.

"You're more than enough. He's lucky to have you." Sage was quick to rise to my defence.

I shrugged. "Thanks."

"Hey! You and me, stick together?" Sage said.

"Like glue!" I gave her a weak grin.

The following week, Cooper, Jackson, and I took a walk on the beach. The twins were quizzing each other on biology exam questions. I tagged along and dropped in an answer occasionally. The winter sun was warm, but the cold sea nipped at our bare feet, a reminder that it was June. About a kilometre down the beach, we saw a group of young teenage boys huddled in the sand dunes. They watched us advancing, four of them, about fourteen years old. Caps and sunglasses hid their faces. Two of the boys were squatting, while the other two stood close together as if to block our view of the dune behind them. Their voices carried, the words indistinguishable, but they held a cruel mocking tone. As we got closer, we could see an elderly man laying back on the dune, at their feet. Even from several metres away, I could sense his fear. Shivers ran up and down my spine. There was anger and a sinister excitement, like steam, that rose off the boys.

"Coop, Jack, there's something wrong over there."

They both nodded at me and without needing to say anything, we changed direction so our steps would take us closer to the group. The boys saw us approaching and crowded together over the old man.

"What are you kids doing?" Jackson was casual and friendly.

We stopped a short distance away.

"Nothing."

"Piss off."

When I leaned to the side, I could see the elderly man's hands and feet were criss-crossed with bloody scratches. A blonde boy had his hands resting on the old man's shoulders, and at first glance it seemed harmless, but his knuckles were white as if he was exerting significant pressure, holding the man down. Another boy, wearing a striped, blue shirt, held his hand behind the man's back and I glimpsed the flash of a blade.

"I think they are torturing that man," I said quietly. "He's bleeding and the boy in the stripy shirt has a knife."

"What are you doing to this poor guy?" Cooper's voice was loud and challenging.

The boys stood their ground, glaring at us. They were not afraid, and the hostility rolled off them in burning waves. It seared my skin and burned in my throat. The old man looked up at us helplessly, but kept his mouth shut. My heart thumped with his fear.

"I told you to piss off." The blonde boy spat at us.

Aggression surged towards me as a sharp spear.

"These kids are really angry," I observed pointlessly.

"Coop, are you up for this?" Jackson spoke in a low voice.

"Yeah, I guess." Cooper said. "I'll go for the tall one and you take the one on the left. Then we'll tackle those two." Cooper inclined his head towards the blonde boy and the one in the striped shirt kneeling by the elderly man.

Jackson's acknowledgment was a tiny nod. "Watch out for the knife."

Cooper turned to me. "Nova, stay out of the way and see if you can get to the old man."

I nodded. "Be careful."

Jackson's eyes were bright with the anticipation of a fight. Cooper's face was grim but resigned. He flexed his hands. The twins were fit and strong, taller, and bigger than any of the younger boys. I could feel Cooper's fear, like ice between my shoulders, but his adrenalin coursed through my body as well. There was no fear from Jackson, but his wariness gave off a cautious strength.

Cooper and Jackson launched themselves at the boys without warning. The young boys scrambled. It was a noisy brawl, messy choreography. Fists smashed into faces. Shoulders slammed into chests. Feet kicked out at legs. There was swearing, grunting, and panting.

My stomach was tight but not with fear, and a tingle ran through my body. I reached the old man and helped him to his feet. White haired, slim, and frail, his clothes were well-worn but comfortable. His face was lined like an atlas and his mouth drooped in weariness. He was still silent.

"Come with me. I'll help you," I reassured him.

Blood dripped from his wrists, a stark red on the fine white sand. His feet were bare, and the delicate skin was marked with harsh cuts, also seeping blood. On reaching the water's edge, I stopped and looked back at the fight. Three of the boys had backed away, yelling insults, while Jackson held the fourth in an arm lock.

"Get out of here before we call the cops," Cooper threatened them.

Jackson pushed the last boy away as they all took off at a run. He and Cooper joined me at the shoreline. With a gentle expertise, they took over cleaning the old man's hands and feet, who yelped with the cold sting of salt water.

"Are you two hurt?" I ran my eye over each of them, looking for injuries.

Scratches and red marks covered Cooper's face and arms and would probably turn into bruises. Jackson was the same and held an arm across his ribs.

"Nah." Cooper was dismissive. "They were pretty useless really. I don't think we'll see them again." His confidence had returned, and he was feeling smug.

"Once we kicked the knife away, they didn't seem so tough." Jackson held up a small utility knife.

Although his face split with his usual cheeky grin, he still held an arm protectively in front.

"You didn't break a rib?" I asked him.

"Nah, that tall kid kicked me though and it still hurts," he admitted ruefully.

I turned my attention back to the old man and focused on being calm, hoping it would spread to the others. Lindsay introduced himself. He lived further down the beach with his wife. He was having a walk when the boys started harassing him. His energy and vigour were returning. The elderly man's cuts were not deep, most of them were just scratches that had stopped bleeding. We walked him home, propped up between Jackson and Cooper, to meet his wife, Betty. The twins dressed his wounds properly with disinfectant and bandages, while I made tea. I doubted that the old man would venture out much again. It was an extremely dangerous world for the frail and elderly.

That night Cooper and I talked. We sat out on the patio, side by side on the wooden bench seat. Even though it was a cold night, it was private outside, away from the others. The sky was clear, and the stars sparkled within an infinite space. Thomasina was rubbing up against our legs. Cooper leaned back, looking up, but his feet jiggled nervously.

"I hate days like this." His uneasiness was all over his face. "Something is always happening to someone. And if it's not one of us, it's complete strangers. Why do you always want to get involved? I worry one time it will all go wrong."

"Do you think we should have kept walking today?"

He shook his head sadly, his brow furrowed. "No. I guess not. It just never stops."

"People need to support each other, to try to stop this violence," I said firmly. "Don't you want to be a paramedic? That's on the front-line helping people."

"That's different," he said defensively. "I'll be older, and I'll have had proper training."

I could tell he was annoyed with me, but I kept going regardless. "Coop, I want to help people. I don't want to wait until I'm older. I wish I could make a real difference, now, and stop this anger in the world."

He looked at his hands and fidgeted. I stayed quiet, waiting for him.

"It's too intense. Maybe you can do it, but I can't. We never have fun anymore. When was the last time we just had fun? I want a normal life. School, parties, friends, getting drunk, playing footy. This is too serious. You are …"

He spoke quickly, like it was a relief to get it all out, but then stopped without completing his last sentence, and shrugged. I lifted my knees up and wrapped my arms around them, hugging myself for warmth, and took a deep breath. His eyes were fixed on the stars. I did not want an argument and I could tell he was struggling with working out his feelings and thoughts. My skin was a pincushion being pricked with anxiety and apprehension.

"I'm what? Too intense, too serious? Sorry, I don't mean to be. I just want a normal life too," I said gently. "But right now, the world is a mess. If I can do something to help make it better for someone, I will."

"Are you expecting me to marry you?" His question came out of nowhere.

I watched while Cooper pushed the hair out of his eyes, which was a gesture I loved, but he still avoided looking at me. *What was this conversation really about?* My head spun with his confusion and my own. I couldn't tell what he wanted from me.

"Coop, I haven't said anything about marriage. Ever. Right now, you're my boyfriend and we are trying to stay safe and finish school. I thought that was what you wanted too. I know it's a weird world, but I can't help that. I want to have fun too. We do have fun … don't we?" I heard the hesitancy in my own voice.

He finally looked at me and nodded. With a smile, he hugged me, but I could tell he was holding something back.

The next day Cooper announced he was leaving. Going home. He had already packed. I was not really surprised. It explained what I had been sensing, his withdrawal.

"I love you, but I can't do this anymore." He was apologetic.

"Do what?"

"Be here. It's like there is one thing after another that we have to deal with. I want to go home and be a normal person again."

"Coop, I'm not sure there is a normal anymore, even back at home."

"Maybe not, but it's something I need to do."

"Are we breaking up?" I asked.

My throat felt tight, and my heart contracted. I felt my anger start to swell.

He shrugged. "I think it's for the best."

"So, that's a yes." My voice was cold.

He shrugged again. "Sorry, Nova. I can't be what you need."

I felt the dig of annoyance but kept my voice even. "Coop, I don't need you to be anything. I want you to be you."

"Well, this is not me, not here."

I searched his feelings. They twisted in my body. He was afraid and overwhelmed. And somehow it was my fault. He wanted the stability and security of home, his parents.

"Okay, go then. Good luck with everything. I hope it's better for you at home." This time I let the anger I was feeling resonate in my voice.

"I'm sorry," Cooper said again.

"Me too." I blinked several times in succession, to hold off the tears.

That was that. I walked away.

"Look after her." I heard him tell Jackson.

"I will, but I'm not doing it for you." I could feel Jackson's irritation at his brother.

Cooper went back home. He messaged that he had arrived safely. I didn't respond.

His abandonment was another betrayal.

My heart was heavy. My body was weary.

My world was falling apart again.

18

Those of us remaining at the beach house shuffled around. Ava and I moved into Cooper's room, together. Jackson got his bedroom back. We revised the rosters for cooking and cleaning. Jackson took Cooper's shift at the small local grocery store, stacking shelves a few nights a week, with Luca. We didn't go out much, just for a run or walk, always in pairs or a small group. We were extremely cautious. Safety first.

I missed Cooper. My bones felt heavy, and my mind was a wrung-out sponge. Clearly, I was too intense, too serious, too demanding for him. That was the impression I was left with. Sage insisted he did not really know what he wanted, and he would regret his decision. She also said that I was better off without him. Although I tried to be rational, mostly I just slumped in a deep hole. As always when my emotions plummeted, my head took me back to the grief of my father's death and dumped that on me too. Never had a day passed without me thinking of him, but now that loss returned, a painful ache all over again. My heart was raw and bleeding.

The house fell into a depression. Probably it was my fault, my depression.

The weather turned bleak and grey.

With two weeks till mid-year break, we worried about school workloads and assessments. We worried about the reports of violence from home and the safety of our friends and family. We worried about ourselves and our own safety.

One afternoon, I was helping Alice clean up the kitchen after lunch. She had a piece of broken glass, running the water over it. Caressing it, she pressed her fingers to the edges until a spot of blood appeared on her thumb. Thinned by the running water it swirled down the drain, out of sight. My movement caused her to flinch, and she covered the glass with her fist, hiding it.

"Hey, fancy a walk?" I asked.

Alice looked doubtful and I felt her fear. Like Ava, she was uncomfortable leaving the beach house now. I didn't blame them, given what had happened.

"Let's just walk down to the water's edge. We won't go out of sight of the house."

I mentally promised to keep her safe. She must have sensed something because she reluctantly nodded.

"Feel like talking? You don't have to."

I had found that walking often made a difficult conversation easier. You didn't have to make eye contact. I let my compassion be a bridge between us, emotionally extending my hand, but letting a comfortable silence fall. Eventually she spoke.

"Nova, I'm scared nearly all the time. Being with all of you helps, but then it comes back."

"Well, I'm not surprised. You had an awful experience."

We had reached the water and let it surge around our bare feet. It was so cold, we both shivered and jumped back, laughing. The sun sent our shadows stretching out in front. We watched the waves swell, break and crash.

"Alice, I saw the piece of glass," I said gently.

"I'm not cutting. It just helps to hold it. I sometimes feel like I want to … cut, make the fear bleed out. The pain would be better than the fear."

"What does your counsellor say?"

"That it's a temporary release. It doesn't solve anything."

"She sounds right." I was gentle but firm.

"Yeah, I know." She sighed.

"Do you want to go back to your parents, back home?"

"No! I want to be here. You help, Nova. Mia helps. You all help. Even Ava."

I nodded. Healing would take time.

"Don't tell Mia about the glass." She watched me carefully, needing to trust me.

"Well, I think you should, Alice. She'll be okay about it."

"I will, when I'm ready." Her voice rang true, and I believed that she would.

"Alright, I won't tell her. You can talk to me anytime, you know."

"I know, thanks Nova."

The fear in Alice lightened a little, but she was still broken. I wanted to mend her but didn't know how, so I wrapped her in a blanket of care.

Ava's mood had deteriorated, too. She was having nightmares again and would wake me screaming and struggling, tangled up in the sheets and blankets, wet with sweat. Some days, she had no interest in anything. She was not eating much and had lost a lot of weight. Mia and Sage encouraged her to exercise with them, and we gave her the same food portions we took for ourselves. Sage tried to engage her in jigsaw puzzles and lent her books. They discussed school assessments with her, but she was apathetic. I was not much help.

"Nova, I hate myself." Ava confided one night as we sat on the couch.

Jackson was in the kitchen behind us, and I could tell he was listening.

"It's my fault I was raped. I shouldn't have run home. On my own. Or I should have run faster. I should have fought harder."

The guilt was not in her heart but in her brain. It squeezed and clawed at me too.

"Oh, Ava, that's heavy. It was not your fault. You did nothing wrong. There were two of them. You had no chance. You did fight. I saw your bruises and cuts. Any harder and they might have killed you."

"But now I'm … damaged. No one will ever want to be with me." She sucked in a breath and held it as if scared to breathe out.

"That's not true. You are a beautiful person. You have a kind heart; you're fierce and brave. Anyone would be lucky to have you."

"No, I'm not. I'm sad and scared all the time. I thought I was getting better, but I'm not. I'm a burden for all of you."

I struggled for the right words to say. Her pain was an open wound. I tried to let my love and acceptance close around her.

"Ava, it's okay to fall apart, even when you thought you had it under control. You are not weak. You are not a burden. Give yourself a break. Be kind to yourself. You are healing; it's just going to take time. You are strong and amazing. And as for a relationship, it will happen when it's right."

I hoped I was saying the right things. I was better with feelings than I was with words. Jackson nudged me as he sat down beside us.

"Sorry to interrupt, but I need to say something. Ava, I know you're not into guys, but if you were, I'd be interested in you. You're courageous and funny. I'm honoured to be your friend." His sincerity got through to Ava. "What happened wasn't your fault. Sometimes I'm ashamed to be a guy."

Ava was crying now, but I felt a shift as if she was more at peace with herself.

"We all love you," I said. "I'm here for you, if you want to talk, or not talk."

Jackson nodded emphatically.

"Thank you, guys, for saying that. And for making me feel normal." Ava said at last. "I love you guys, too."

Later, it was just Jackson and I on the couch. It was a night for deep and meaningful conversations.

"Nova, can we talk?" It was his serious tone.

I nodded.

"Your mood affects us all. That is why this place works and there are no disagreements. But, right now, you are moping over Cooper, and it is bringing us all down. It's affected Ava and Alice. All of us are sulking. You have to get over it."

I felt the annoyance and resentment rise within me, the heat in my chest and a bitter taste in my mouth. "That's not fair. You are full of shit! You can all be happy if you want, that's not on me. I can't help how I feel."

His eyes narrowed with a frown. "I'm not putting it all on you. I'm just saying your emotions rub off on all of us, whether you mean them to or not."

"If I'm so powerful, why didn't I make Coop stay? Why did he leave?"

I knew Jackson could feel my irritation, but I glared at him to make sure he got it.

"Because you don't use your powers like that."

"I don't have powers. And you can't tell me how to feel, Jack."

"I can if it's affecting all of us. You are the one full of shit! You know you can influence people's feelings, Nova. Usually it's for good, but right now it's miserable."

"Can we NOT talk about this?" I brought my knees up to my chest and wrapped my arms around them.

"We are definitely going to talk about it," he said firmly.

Jackson shivered and I knew he had just felt my angst, a sharp stabbing jolt. I wanted to hurt him. I twisted the knife further. He closed his eyes, grimaced, but took a breath and opened his eyes to glare at me. I felt his strength pushing at me.

"Wilson, it's lucky you're so beautiful because you can be a real bitch. You're doing it now. I can feel your pain if you are wondering. I get it. I don't want to feel it."

I stopped, knowing I had more control than he probably realised. He stretched out his legs, long and straight, and sat up a little taller, as if a load had been lifted. I had a begrudging respect for him, for standing up to me. But it was still hard to hear.

"Nova, I just want you to be happy," Jackson said gently.

His eyes had softened, though were still wary, in case I caused him more pain.

"I know." I relented a little bit.

"Well?"

"Well, what, Lewis? Okay. I'll try." I was terse and ungracious, but he nodded.

"Thanks, WILSON." Jackson emphasised my last name, raising his eyebrows while the corners of his mouth quivered as if resisting a smile.

He brushed his hair off his face, and I tried not to think of Cooper.

"I wish there was a potion I could take to make me stop loving him, stop hurting," I said.

"Do you really want that?"

I shrugged. "Yes."

"I wish you'd take that too."

I raised my eyebrows. He shrugged this time.

"There are other people around that you could love instead." Jackson's voice was low, almost inaudible.

I pretended I had not heard. "You're a shit, but you're a good friend."

"The dreaded friend zone."

"What do you mean?"

I felt the shot of courage he gave himself as he shifted on the couch to move a little closer. "What if I don't want to be in the friend zone?"

"What do you want now?"

"You."

"Jack, stop it."

"You asked."

I shook my head. "Coop has just left."

"Yeah. He's gone. It's his loss. He doesn't get you like I do. He wants a fantasy. White picket fence. That is not you. I want reality. I want you, now, in all of this … the good and the bad."

"And the ugly?" I couldn't help myself.

"There is no ugly from where I am sitting."

I pointed a finger at my mouth and pretended to vomit.

"Romance is wasted on you, Wilson." He shook his head, smiling.

I knew Jackson had a point. He and I were often on the same wavelength. But I did love Cooper. My mind swirled in circles and my heart refused to unlock. I held my hand over Jackson's mouth to stop him saying any more, but he playfully bit my fingers.

"Jackson Lewis, you are impossible."

"You're feeling better though. I can tell."

I laughed, despite myself. "If I try not to be so miserable, will you stop flirting with me?"

"It'd be easier to stop breathing." He squeezed my hand and threw me his most mischievous smile. "You are like a song, stuck in my head."

I laughed, feeling lighter, happier. Jackson had a way of cheering me up, even if it was a little brutal and confronting.

I slept better that night, and Ava did too.

19

With so many shops and services closed now, none of us had been to a hairdresser for months. Mia decided we all needed home-haircuts. Her enthusiasm was infectious and after Jackson's talk, I knew I had to try harder.

Jackson's straight hair had grown long, tickling his shoulders. Mia cut off a few centimetres all over. I was admiring his face, a strong jaw, his slightly crooked nose, and defined cheek bones, until I got to his cocoa brown eyes. They glittered with amusement at my attention. The heat rose in my cheeks. Luca got the same treatment, a light trim. Mia was next. Her dreadlocks were growing out and she wanted to cut her hair short. She cut it herself, spiky short over her whole head, using a mirror. It was uneven and patchy at the back and Sage tried to neaten it up without much success.

"Okay then, I'll shave my head," Mia declared. "Will someone do it for me?"

"I'll do it. It's just like shaving my face, I guess," Jackson said.

"You hardly even shave!" I teased, pointing at his rough stubble.

He laughed, light at first, then it developed into a deep belly laugh. A sound that had not been heard in the house for over a week. It spread to Mia, then me, until all of us were giggling and gasping.

Mia looked wild with her shaved head. She took the scissors back and did Sage, then Alice, a neat trim off their long hair. Ava's hair curled and just sprang back when cut. They all looked good. Mia pointed to me.

"Now you."

"Okay, go short." It was a sudden whim.

Mia cut my straggling, long hair into a neat pixie cut that framed my face. I was admiring myself in the mirror when Jackson and Luca came back in from their run. Sweating and puffing, they were in good spirits. The haircuts had already made a difference.

"We're all done," I said. "How good is Mia?"

Luca smiled at all of us and planted a kiss on Sage's forehead. Jackson wolf-whistled at Sage, Alice, and Ava, and then his jaw dropped when his eyes landed on me.

"I got my hair cut short." I mumbled, embarrassed by his stare.

"I liked your long hair, but I've got to say, this short hair is HOT!" He winked at me.

Reaching out, he ruffled my hair and stroked my cheek, his fingers dropping to cup my face before he took his hand away. It was a very intimate gesture, and his eyes were locked on mine.

"Ahem!" Mia cleared her throat.

I looked away, feeling my cheeks flood with the familiar warmth, which then spread all over my body.

The haircuts were the turning point. No more moping around. The house felt lighter, brighter. We finished the last two weeks of school, helping each other with final assessments. Exams had been changed to assignments, so it was a more manageable stress. I tried to promote feelings of confidence and well-being throughout the house.

Special occasions were not much fun anymore, with isolation, curfews, and the ever-increasing danger, but we wanted to celebrate the end of term. Just at home, but fancy dress. Mia and I went to the local grocery store to get party snacks and drinks. Ava and Alice put up some decorations. Sage made a playlist. Luca and Jackson volunteered to do food.

We modelled our costumes down the hallway. Alice was Alice in Wonderland, with a blue dress and white apron. All in green, Mia made a wonderful elf with pointy cardboard ears. Sage wore her sexy red strappy dress, heavy black eye makeup, and devil horns. Luca dressed in a checked shirt, jeans, and a cowboy hat someone had found in the cupboard. I wore my black leggings, black T-shirt, a headband with cat ears, and Mia drew whiskers on my face. Ava wore some hospital scrubs left by Dr Lewis. In his skinny black jeans, black shirt, and black eye makeup, Jackson was a vampire, with lipstick blood running down his chin.

The house was in party mode. Jelly shots, loud music, good friends. Jackson danced while cooking the spaghetti. Sage and I belted out song lyrics. Mia weaved between us pulling people up to dance. We grinned and laughed like idiots, happy to be together, in our own little safety bubble.

By midnight, we were tired and content. Music played quietly. Mia dozed in an armchair. Alice and Ava sat on the floor, scrolling through movies. Luca and Sage snuggled on the couch talking quietly. Standing at the kitchen bench overlooking the lounge, I basked in the ease within the room. Jackson shuffled up beside me and bared his teeth.

"I vant to suck your blood," he leered, in a terrible vampire impression.

"Eww!" I laughed and pushed him away. "You still have blood dripping down your chin from your last victim, or is that spaghetti sauce?"

He laughed with me, casually draping his arm around my shoulders.

"It's been a good night. You seem happier."

"It's been a great night. We all needed this."

He shared in my delight as we observed the others.

"I noticed you had some pretty fancy dance moves earlier when you were cooking," I teased him, digging my elbow into his ribs.

He reached for my hand, holding it above my head, to spin me around in a pirouette. "Will you dance with this bloodthirsty vampire?"

I giggled. "Only if you promise not to drain my blood."

His body bumped against mine, urging me into dance steps. He led me, with an easy grace, in a loose waltz around the kitchen. When we stopped, he placed a hand on the bench on either side of me, so I was pinned between his arms.

"I promise not to drink your blood, if you'll honour me with a kiss." His face was split with a cheeky grin.

"You don't give up, do you?"

"Nope. Not when it's something I really want."

Penetrating dark eyes twinkled at me. His grin was a dare.

"One kiss, sir." I relented and stood on my toes to plant a quick peck on his mouth.

"That's not a kiss!"

He leaned in and his lips pressed hard against mine, his passion and hunger literally sweeping me off my feet, while I clung to him. I lost all sense of time and place as I kissed him back, recklessly. He was as breathless as me when he set me down and stepped away. I glanced around at the others, my heart racing, but no one was looking.

"I can't help it, Nova."

He watched me closely, challenging me. I was caught in a whirlpool, being pulled in different directions. It was clear that Jackson wanted to move our friendship into a deeper level, but I didn't know if I was ready. It was too soon.

"Must be a vampire thing." My shoes kicked lightly against the tiles as I kept my gaze lowered, and my voice light.

"Sure." I sensed his annoyance. "Let's call it a vampire thing then."

I could hear him take long slow breaths, like he was calming himself and deciding what to say next. I continued to concentrate on the floor. At last, he swung his arm around my shoulders and bumped his hip against mine, without saying anything. Our friendship status was restored. Yet, I was aware of his simmering emotions, just beneath the surface.

"Let's go watch this." I indicated the horror movie Ava and Alice had settled on.

We moved into the lounge and sat apart. Thomasina jumped up into my lap and I focused on her. I could feel Jackson watching me from time to time, but I deliberately avoided making eye contact.

Although we did not talk about it, the kiss was there the next day, in the space between us when we got breakfast. It was reflected in Jackson's face when I stole a sideways glance at him. The mirror reflected it on my own face. It was an undertone to the casual words we said to each other. There was the delightful memory of our mouths meeting, our hearts racing, our breathlessness. And the longing to repeat it.

Cooper was still in my thoughts most days. I wondered if he had found it less intense at home. I heard from friends that he was drinking a lot.

One night he messaged me.

I caught up with Imogen today. Wanted to tell you before someone else does.

It's not really my business anymore is it? We aren't together.

I know but I still care about you.

I'm not sure what you expect me to say.

Imogen messaged me too, just mentioning Cooper had dropped by.

Sage hugged me. "They deserve each other. Don't you dare let it get to you."

Jackson heard about it, too. He came into my room and dropped down on the bed, where I was studying. He lay on his back and looked up at me.

"Coop said he told you he's hooking up with Imogen again," he said. "Are you okay?"

"Well, he didn't actually say it in those words to me, but yeah, I guess."

"So, you're alright?" His eyes were scanning my face.

I shrugged, a pretence at nonchalance "We're not together anymore."

"Yeah, I know, but you still love him. And … it's Imogen."

"Bloody Imogen!" I sighed. "What a friend she's turned out to be."

"Yeah, probably cross her off your Christmas card list, I reckon."

I gave a half-smile, but my heart was not in it. I couldn't say anything because I was still trying to assess what I was feeling. Maybe annoyed, still hurt, certainly tired of it all.

"Well?" he probed.

"I'll be fine."

He raised his eyebrows at my sharp tone. "You know, if you want to move on, you can practise on me."

Although Jackson was being playful, I could hear the serious subtext.

His cheekiness had managed to lift my mood though, and I fought against a smile. "Maybe I should."

His eyes widened, and his jaw dropped. For once he was lost for words.

"Or better still, maybe I need a break from all Lewis men!" The sarcasm hung heavy on my words.

I closed my laptop with a snap, stood up and turned to walk out of the bedroom.

"Oww!" he cried out loudly, forcing me to look back.

Jackson clutched at his heart and pulled out an imaginary dagger, but he was laughing.

I knew we kept wavering between being just friends and being something more, and I was not sure what to do about it.

Despite the safety bubble that pervaded the beach house, the violence was never far away. It plagued our thoughts and provoked our fears. All our house meetings included discussions on better ways to keep safe.

The media platforms were saturated with horrifying reports:

Violent crime death toll in Victoria worst in Australia.

Rioters out of control. Seventeen dead.

No-one is safe.

There was also the predominance of organised gang crime, on a scale never seen in Australia before.

Family of victim plead for gang violence to end.

After a bloody weekend, police call for ceasefire to gang warfare.

Teenagers abusing curfew laws taken as gang recruits.

The conspiracy theories were still rampant. The warrior gene. Government experiments. Chemical warfare. Mobile phone towers, preservatives in our food, vaccines. A government engineered strategy for population control.

There were conflicting stories but no evidence. No solutions and no cure for the aggression.

20

We still made a regular trip into Yarram for groceries that were not supplied by the local store. Like other larger towns, a huge food bank had been set up there, with armed security. Luca and Jackson had made the last trip. This time, Sage and I were going too, with a list from the other girls for clothes, cosmetics, and various personal items.

Luca's car took us through the scrubby coastal bushland into stretches of more open woodland with tall eucalyptus trees that looked like sentinels standing guard. The air was cold, and the sky was washed with grey. An earthy, clean fragrance wafted through the car.

The large food bank was a supermarket and department store in one. There were a few dozen customers, and we avoided getting too close to strangers. Always on alert, I probed for a sense of the people close by. It was calm and business-like, everyone intent on ticking off their lists. The four of us stayed close. We made decisions and choices quickly, continually on the move, always checking to our sides and over our shoulders. Despite the tension, I rolled my shoulders and grinned at no one in particular. It felt good to get out.

With no self-service options, we chose the checkout with the fewest people and kept a good distance behind the man in front. He was big, both tall and solid, with long, greasy hair and sunglasses. His baggy jeans and bulky khaki jacket could have easily concealed weapons. On his turn, there was an immediate change in the emotional climate. I tugged on Jackson's sleeve and nodded towards the checkout girl. It was unnecessary, he had already noticed. The man was harassing her, and she was terrified. I started to move towards them, but Jackson put his arm around me and held me still in a grip tight enough to bruise my forearms.

"No, Nova," he said under his breath.

"But …"

"No." Jackson cut me off, in a tone that allowed no argument.

I stopped resisting and we watched the interaction unfold. The guy argued about prices, claiming the scan was wrong. I could feel the instant the girl succumbed to her fear. She adjusted the total for him. His aggression left a dirty smear in the air.

Our turn. We had two trolleys and Jackson and I went first. He loaded the groceries onto the counter. The girl was pale and sweating. Her eyes were wide and startled, a deer caught in headlights. There was no cheery greeting.

"Are you okay?" I asked her.

She didn't answer. Holding one hand to her chest like she had pains, the other was clenched at her side in a tight fist. Her breathing was loud and getting faster.

"Jack, she's having a panic attack." I kept my voice low.

"Damn!" he said. "What do we do?"

I reached across the counter and gently touched her arm, letting my hand rest there.

"Eve." I spoke gently, acknowledging the name on her badge. "You're safe now; just breathe."

She blinked, looked at me, and gave a tiny nod.

"He's gone. You did the right thing." I kept my voice warm and soft, a light summer breeze. "Breathe with me, in to the count of 5, hold for 3, and breathe out for 7. Will you try with me?" A trick I had learned from online meditation.

Another tiny nod.

"Breathe in 1, 2, 3, 4, 5. Hold for 1, 2, 3. Out for 1, 2, 3, 4, 5, 6, 7. Good. You're doing great. Let's go again."

I repeated twice, breathing with her, and I heard Jackson joining in. Focused on being calm and content, I let the peace settle softly like dew.

"How are you doing?"

Her breathing had settled, and her anxiety seemed to be under control. She gave me a watery smile, in response.

"Do you need to sit down?" Jackson asked her quietly.

Eve glanced around furtively, taking in the queues, and shook her head. I felt her tension starting to build again.

"It's okay. Let's breathe slowly while we get these groceries scanned."

I helped her scan and Jackson bagged the items. We kept breathing with her, counting quietly.

"I'm going to stay here, while you do the next customer," I told her, after we had paid. "They're my friends."

I let Sage go ahead of me with Jackson and stayed at the register with Eve and Luca. I kept talking to her quietly and counting breaths. By the time she had put through the rest of our groceries I could tell she had things under control again.

"Thank you, so much." She squeezed my hand like a hug.

"No problem. Thank you for doing such a great job and being so brave." I gave her a friendly smile and squeezed her hand in return. "Stay safe."

She nodded at me and smiled. "You too."

We left her to attend to the next customer and I hoped she would get through the day without any other panic attacks.

Following Luca and the shopping trolley, I was stopped from exiting the store when a man materialised in front of me. About thirty, he was dressed casually in jeans and a simple white T-shirt that hugged his muscled body. His eyes were an honest blue and sparkled with a sense of humour. Fair hair, gently tousled and a face weathered just the right amount suggested a love of the outdoors. I tried to close my gaping mouth and raised my eyebrows at him in a nonverbal question. I could tell he meant no harm. In fact, I was picking up good vibes.

"You handled that really well." His voice was soft and musical.

"Oh. Wow." It was all I could manage, as I was still trying not to gape at him.

"You're an empath, aren't you?" His head tipped to one side like a curious bird.

Suddenly jostled as Jackson and Luca appeared close at my sides, I felt Jackson's arm wrap protectively around my shoulders. Sage was at my back. My bodyguards had arrived. The spell was broken.

Jackson's distrust radiated with Luca's wariness, while Sage was captivated. It seemed the guys were not as open to this man's charms as Sage and me.

"I'm so sorry." His smile now included all of us. "I need to introduce myself. I'm Sawyer Young."

"I'm Nova." Finally, sensible words came out of my mouth. "This is Jackson, Luca and Sage."

I nodded at the others. "He's okay guys."

There was no doubt in my mind. Sawyer was a good person, and he was like me. We were communicating by sharing emotions.

"I'd really like to talk with you." Full round lips curved in a friendly grin, with brilliant white, straight teeth. "But maybe we should continue outside before someone takes off with your groceries." Sawyer gestured to where Luca had abandoned the trolley to come to my aid.

We moved outside, glancing around furtively. A group of five people could attract unwanted attention. Luca and Sage took the trolley to the car.

"I know you have no reason to trust me yet," continued Sawyer. "But would you be willing to talk? You can follow me home."

Sawyer addressed all this to me. Jackson stiffened at my side, so I took his hand and squeezed it, to reassure him. I nodded in confirmation at Sawyer.

We followed Sawyer's car to his house, several streets out of town. I explained that I had an emotional connection with Sawyer, and I knew he was trustworthy. Jackson urged us all to remain on alert.

"Just because he's flirting with you, doesn't mean he's okay."

"Jack, it's not like that; I can sense his honesty. It's real I promise."

"He is awfully good looking," murmured Sage, getting a glare from Luca.

The house was a normal residential home but inside we passed two guys in army fatigues playing video games, and a young woman, also in uniform, working on her laptop. Sawyer nodded at them on the way through to the kitchen. As they came behind us, Jackson and Luca bristled, tense and alert.

"Please, everyone grab a seat," Sawyer said, indicating the chairs.

It was a sleek modern dining table and chairs set, wooden seats and tabletop with black steel legs and backs. The kitchen was sparkling clean, though the dishes were still in the sink after their last meal.

Sawyer made introductions. "This is Jet and Finn, and Rayna back there. They are Army, the elite Special Air Service regiment, SAS."

Jet and Finn nodded and smiled. Rayna yelled out a hello.

I could sense Sawyer creating an emotional climate of cooperation and friendship. He sent his dimpled grin my way, knowing that I could feel him. As he started to talk, Jackson and Luca relaxed as if coming under his spell.

"We're with the Federal Government. The Department of Violence Eradication or DOVE for short."

This got a smile from everyone.

"It's a new department. We work in partnership with the state governments, to re-establish security and order. We are one of the teams in Victoria and we travel from town to town, helping the police, doing what we can. Our priorities are food and medicine. Making sure the hospitals are safe and operating. Setting up food banks like the one here and increasing their security if necessary. Then we start to work on eradicating the violence, and in particular, any gang violence. There are about ten of us in Yarram now and they have us billeted in various houses around the town. There are other teams in the north, out west and all around the state. Then of course in all the other states and territories."

"Sounds cool," I said, impressed that something was being done. "Is it working?"

"We are trying but I'm afraid it's going to be a lengthy process." Sawyer made a face.

"What do you actually do?" Luca had a sudden sense of hope.

I felt it in Sage and Jackson too. They wanted to be reassured, to know everything would be okay, even if it did take a while.

"I'm just a mediator. I help keep the negotiations peaceful and try to calm things when there's hostility. To be honest it really just means I sit in on a lot of meetings." Sawyer threw us that dimpled grin.

"He's too modest." Jet spoke up for the first time and chuckled. "Sawyer is usually right in the thick of things."

Jet was lounging against the kitchen bench, looking every bit a soldier, with a tall, muscular frame. He was dark skinned, with thick eyebrows hovering above deep brown eyes. I imagined he could be very intimidating but now his face was split with a friendly, encouraging grin.

"So that brings me back to why I wanted to talk with you." Sawyer leaned forward and fixed his eyes directly on me. "You're an empath, aren't you?"

Luca turned to me in confusion, but Jackson and Sage nodded at Sawyer.

"Well, if you mean I can sense other people's emotions, then sure."

"No, it's more than that." Sawyer shook his head. "You can influence their emotions too, can't you?"

Again, Jackson and Sage were nodding solemnly. Finn and Jet were looking at me with interest and Rayna had appeared at the door. She had obviously been listening. I squirmed under everyone's scrutiny.

"Maybe, sometimes, a bit."

"She definitely can," Sage said proudly. "She's amazing."

I was shaking my head, but everyone ignored me.

"We could really use your help," Sawyer said.

"Doing what?" I could sense that Jackson's curiosity had been stimulated, but he was still wary and a little defensive on my behalf.

"We need empaths like Nova to try and modify people's anger. To calm this violence." Sawyer spoke as if it was the easiest thing in the world to do.

"Nova, I'd really like to work with you, help you develop your skills, and you could help me in mediations and negotiations. We are heading into Melbourne soon and it is far worse there. But I believe we will slowly get this violence under control, and not through more violence, but through calming people's anger, getting a better understanding of what is going on and using peaceful solutions." He had a smooth but genuine persuasiveness.

Sawyer turned back to the others. "How old are you guys? Have you finished school?"

"Eighteen, except Nova who is still seventeen. We're still in school, well, home schooling, Year 12," Sage told him.

I felt Sawyer assessing the emotional ties between us, and he knew he would not get me without them.

"I'm not sure school will be continuing much longer. This could be work-experience for all of you, through to the end of the year. We work in hospitals and welfare centres, security, and even scientific research. It depends on what you are interested in." Sawyer paused and turned back to me. "Nova, you're only seventeen. You will need your parents' permission. Do they know you are an empath?"

"My parents are dead." My words sounded so blunt, so final.

"I'm sorry." Sawyer sent me immediate compassion.

I felt the room swell with sympathy. It helped. I nodded.

"Anyway, the offer is there for the four of you. If you are interested, we can work out the details. You would be supervised and paid a small wage. You'll get accommodation and food. It's not without danger, but these guys look out for us." Sawyer gestured to Finn, Jet, and Rayna, who nodded confidently.

I could feel Sawyer drawing them in. The chance to change the world, a step back to being safe and normal. Jackson's eyes shone and Sage was smiling at Sawyer with admiration.

"There's more than just us four. We're safe; we look after each other. I don't know about going to Melbourne." I was the only one with doubts now.

"It can be dangerous, but it's exciting and rewarding. You will make a difference."

It was a good sales pitch, but Sawyer spoke with such sincerity, that we knew he believed it, so we believed him.

"We really should get back to the house before the others start to worry about us." I wanted to talk this through away from Sawyer's influence.

"Look, can I give you my number? Have a think about it and we can talk further." Sawyer exchanged numbers with Jackson.

We stood to go. Sawyer focused his attention on me once again.

"Kindness, compassion, peace." He listed them off. "Just keep spreading these. You will change people."

"Maybe." I barked out a doubtful laugh. "I really don't think I will make much of a difference."

"Oh, you'd be surprised. You helped that girl today," Sawyer said. "Think about it, Nova, please. With your empathic abilities, maybe you have a responsibility to help save the world, or at least this part of Australia."

He was issuing a challenge.

Jackson had us all laughing on the drive home, away from Sawyer's allure, as he quipped in an imitation of Sawyer's voice, "Nova, with your power, comes great responsibility."

It did set me thinking though. I did want to help. I did want to make the world a better place.

21

As soon as we drew near Woodside Beach, I knew something was wrong. Fear hung in the air.

Thomasina, my cat, had been killed. Shot with an arrow. Alice had found her and bundled her in a blanket. She was cold, so cold. Her eyes were closed as if sleeping, but her mouth was open, mid-breath. The arrow's tip stood upright, her fur stained with blood around the puncture, where it was buried in her side. A trail of blood had soaked into the grass, scarlet red on the green lawn. I pulled at the arrow, but it would not come loose.

"Let me," said Jackson quietly.

He pushed it through until it came out the other side, leaving a hole staring back at me like one dark eye. The blood stained her fur, thicker and darker than that on the grass. Sage wrapped the blanket tighter around the cat, covering the wound.

Jackson and Luca dug a hole in the back garden to bury Thomasina, and we stood with bowed heads. I couldn't cry, couldn't talk, I just stood there. The sadness moved through me, soaking into every part of my body until I was weighed down by its weariness. There had been too much loss.

It was impossible to know if Thomasina's murder was an attack on us personally, or just someone passing through, but it was a stark reminder that violence could intrude without warning. That night, Luca and Jackson stayed awake, on guard.

The meeting with Sawyer was momentarily forgotten. Our brief feelings of hope were dashed.

Then the following day, we heard from Sawyer.

Please call me. Wondering if Nova can get up to Yarram today. Need help with a situation.

A phone call gave us more details. Two armed teenagers were threatening staff at the Yarram Health Service, and it had become a hostage situation. Sawyer was hoping I could relate to them better than the police, being of a similar age.

"Okay I'll be there as soon as I can." I ended the call. "Jack, will you take me?" I still did not have my licence.

"Of course, but are you sure you feel like it?" Jackson asked.

"Yeah, it will take my mind off things." I shrugged.

Sawyer had piqued my interest. I wanted to help. I was tired of all the misery.

"We'll take Luca's car," Jackson said.

"What about the bike?"

"You really want to take the bike?" I sensed his reluctance.

Jackson had refused to take out the motorbike since we had been attacked, in Yarram, and I had been stabbed. I saw the flush of concern in his face as his eyes dropped to my arm and then my side.

I nodded. "I really do. I don't know, it helps clear my head, blows everything away."

I felt his reservations fade and his adrenaline rise. He was keen to take the bike out, too.

"Okay, but don't do anything stupid, like get stabbed." His face dropped in horror as he realised what he had said, after what had happened with Thomasina.

"I promise." I gave a weak smile.

Jackson started the bike and pulled on my arms, so I was sitting up close against his back. "Stay close and hold on tight." I could sense his smug satisfaction.

Yarram Health Service had an urgent care department which served as a small hospital. Three police cars blocked the carpark and a small group of uniformed officers stood huddled together. The noise of the bike drew their attention and Sawyer beckoned us over. Jet and Finn stood to the side, nursing rifles. Despite the police presence, I was reminded of when we had been here the night of Alice's abduction. My heart fluttered with the memory.

"Nova, will you come in with me? I want to see if they will talk to you. None of us have had much luck." Sawyer was brisk and matter of fact, a professional.

The police were looking at Jackson and me with curiosity, two silly teenagers.

"There are three young men; one is injured. They are armed. There are seven other people inside, being held as hostages. I want to get this sorted out without anyone being hurt." Sawyer glared at a young police officer whose hand hovered over his gun holster.

"What do you need me to do?" I asked.

"Follow my lead."

"I'm coming too." Jackson stepped forward.

"You can't. Don't worry, I'll keep your girlfriend safe." Sawyer had sensed his anxiety.

"I'm not his girlfriend," I said.

"She's not my girlfriend," said Jackson at the same time.

We glanced at each other, then away again.

"My mistake. I thought ..." Sawyer stopped and looked at both of us.

He raised his eyebrows. Jackson's face split into a self-satisfied smirk, while I shook my head. The heat rose in my cheeks. I gestured toward the Health Service building, hoping to redirect the conversation. Sawyer smiled and nodded.

We went into the lion's den.

At the Urgent Care Department doors, Sawyer put me in front of him, so they could see me. "We just want to talk," he said clearly.

He had his hands held up in surrender, so I did the same. I could feel his calming influence already. Without a word spoken he was letting them know they could trust him, that we meant no harm. Behind us, the police and Special Forces guns were trained on the entrance. A tall, blonde guy let us in. While his appearance suggested he was about seventeen, his dark eyes hinted at a maturity born of hardship, beyond his years. I was hit by surges of pain, fear, and resentment as we walked through the doors. For a second, I could not breathe, and sharp needles stung behind my eyes. Sawyer's push of serenity sent calm waves rippling across the room, a soothing breeze across a lake.

With none of the usual hustle and bustle of an emergency department, it was spookily silent. The walls glared white, only marked where trolleys and beds had bumped against them. A faint aroma of citrus disinfectant was in the air. Hostages sat on the floor, except for two patients laying across the seats.

The blonde teenager had a pistol pointed at Sawyer, while his companion had his trained on a doctor. The third boy lay on a trolley, pale and still, his eyes shut. Blood stained the front of his shirt, wet and shiny. They all looked about my age, angry faces, but also afraid. I sensed that they were overwhelmed, they were in over their heads.

"Nathan needs a doctor, and no one is leaving until he's stitched up."

The blonde, spokesman of the trio, was demanding. His eyes glinted with suspicion, flicking between Sawyer and me. I could tell he was wondering what my role was. Sawyer nudged me.

I took a deep breath and gave a half smile, hoping they could not sense my fear. "I'm Nova. This is Sawyer. We want to help."

The teenager's fists clenched and unclenched. Sweat lined his forehead and top lip. That he was also clutching a gun made his anxiety more frightening.

"What happened to Nathan?" I focused on remaining calm and hoping that would spread to the boys.

"He's been stabbed, and this doctor won't even look at him." He swung the gun around to point at the doctor, who now had both guns pointed at him.

"I'm not doing anything while someone points a gun at me." The doctor's stubbornness was a rod against my back.

Sawyer moved towards the doctor, and they spoke quietly. He exuded co-operation and calmness. I felt it swell through the room.

"If we get the doctor to sort out Nathan, can you put the gun away?" I asked.

The teenager glanced at Nathan who was silent and unmoving. He nodded. That was all he really wanted. At

Sawyer's insistence, the doctor and two nurses wheeled Nathan into one of the consultation rooms. The blonde teenager went with them but passed his gun over to his friend.

"Nova, can you manage things out here?" Sawyer indicated the waiting area, while he followed the doctor.

I knew he felt my uncertainty, but I nodded reluctantly when he smiled in confidence. "You've got this."

"I'm sure Nathan will be alright," I said to the remaining teenager.

He was holding both the guns awkwardly down at his sides. He opened his mouth to say something to me, then changed his mind, and closed it again. I could feel his indecision and a restless anger that lay beneath the surface.

"You can talk to me," I said. "What's your name?"

"Tom."

"So, Tom …" I smiled encouragingly.

"We didn't mean for this to happen," he said eventually.

"Shall we sit down?" I gestured to the waiting room seats.

Tom nodded and gave me a half-smile of relief. Stretching out his long, skinny legs, I felt the release of tension. Tousled, thick black hair fell to his shoulders and his eyes were a mesmerising granite grey. Relaxing some more, he placed the guns on the chair next to him and slumped back against his own uncomfortable chair. He did not look dangerous now, just vulnerable. The remaining four hostages watched us warily.

"I haven't seen you around before," Tom said.

"No, I'm not from around here."

"Are you with the police?"

"No." I chuckled quietly. "I'm just here with Sawyer. He's the negotiator."

"Oh. We're probably going to get into a lot of trouble for this. I was hoping you could put in a good word for me."

"I'll try but I think you are overestimating my importance."

His face was well defined, but it was his returning smile that hooked me in. It was playful and cheeky. I was not sure what would happen to them, but I hoped it would not be too bad.

My heart beat steadily, and I let its rhythm soothe and balance me. I focused on being reassuring and kind, hoping that would keep the situation under control. I smiled reassuringly at the hostages. When Sawyer returned with the blonde teenager, Tom and I were discussing school.

"Nathan has been stitched up and is going to be fine," Sawyer told Tom.

I heaved a sigh of relief. Sawyer reached for the guns, and the teenagers exchanged a glance. There was a surge of anxiety, but Sawyer quelled it.

"It's okay, guys. You need to face the music, but let's keep it cool and level-headed." Sawyer directed for me to lead them all out. "We'll let these good people get on with their work of saving lives."

As soon as we stepped outside, I saw the rifles lift, trained on the boys. Sawyer held up his hands and when Finn and Jet lowered their weapons the police followed suit. The two boys were led into a waiting police car. Jackson was beside me in an instant, his eyes travelling up and down, assessing me. I lifted my chin and smiled smugly. He gave my hair an affectionate tousle and poked his tongue at me.

"Will they get into a lot of trouble?" I asked Sawyer.

"The fact that they were armed will go against them, but I'll see what I can do. The courts don't really want to be dealing with minors."

"I think the doctor could have handled it better," I said.

Sawyer shook his head. "You can't blame him. He doesn't deserve to have a gun pointed at him."

I nodded reluctantly. He had a point, but I still sided with the boys.

There was something else niggling at me. "You could have gone in before I got here, but you waited for me, didn't you?"

Sawyer grinned, as if caught out. "Yeah, I did wait. I wanted you to see the sorts of things we do, and how you could help if you come with us. And you were a big help. Thanks."

I shuffled my feet and shrugged.

"So, have you given any more thought to coming to Melbourne with us? I could really use another empath."

"I'm not even really sure what you mean by that, an empath."

"Well, an empath, is someone with the psychic ability of empathy, like you and me. We feel the emotions and sometimes the physical pain of the people around us as intensely as if it is our own emotion, our own pain. And it's all emotions, both positive and negative. So, if someone close by is excited, we feel excited. If they are angry, we feel angry. The feelings may have nothing to do with what's actually happening in your life, so it can seem completely random at times."

I nodded as he explained, relating it to my own experiences. Jackson nodded along with me.

"Emotion researchers have claimed that empaths have the ability not just to sense other people's emotions, but also to imagine what someone else might be thinking. They call it cognitive empathy, and it allows us to accurately identify and understand another person's perspective."

"But I don't read minds," I interrupted.

Sawyer laughed and shook his head. "No, it just means you are more readily able to understand the other person's viewpoint. Because of this cognitive empathy, you often know the right thing to say, or the best way to deal with people. That's what I use in negotiation."

"Okay. You make it sound really cool."

"It is cool. People with empathic ability, like us, can use emotional energy to help or influence the people around us. We can spread positive vibes to keep things calm and cooperative. I use this ability in my work, and I've seen you do it, today, and that day at the supermarket."

"But I'm nowhere near as skilled as you are. I could feel you doing it in there."

"Actually, Nova, I think you're stronger than me, but I've just had more practice." Sawyer touched my arm, and I could feel his belief in me. "Now, you need to decide how you can best use your abilities, especially in this current climate of violence."

Jackson was silent throughout Sawyer's explanations, and he was still deep in thought as we climbed aboard the motorbike to head back. Several kilometres down the highway, he pulled off the road into the shelter of the coastal scrub bushes and stopped the bike. Our knees were touching as he swung around on the seat. He took off his helmet and then mine, while I watched him, waiting.

"Nova, I was so scared you were going to be hurt back there," he said. "I need you."

He lifted me until I was on his lap and my legs were wrapped around him. His head bent towards me, and his lips brushed against mine, a tease which left me cold for a second until he claimed my mouth. A flame raced through my body. Left over adrenalin ignited with desire. Jackson's passion soared and mine rose to meet it.

"Tell me to stop and I will." His voice was husky as he checked in.

I shook my head. I needed him too. Our second kiss was softer but no less passionate. His hands hooked around my hips holding me in place. My arms were locked around his neck, but I pulled one hand back to run down the length of his nose. It was still slightly bent from being broken when we had rescued Alice. He scrunched up his face at my touch and smiled affectionately. We rested against each other, forehead to forehead, until our breathing slowed, and heartbeats had returned to their normal pace.

"We better go, before I try and kiss you again." He lifted his head and sighed reluctantly.

22

We returned to the news of a devastating tragedy.

Sage's parents had been killed. Her sister had rung her, and they wanted Sage home. It was an attack, a robbery, in a supermarket carpark. The thief had shot them both. Dead. A random, senseless act of violence.

Sage and Luca were leaving immediately for her sister's place. The shock and the chore of packing had stopped her from breaking down. Until we came through the door.

Sage fell into my arms, sobbing. A blackness descended. There was an impenetrable curtain of grief. No one was safe in this world.

"Oh, Sage." If ever I needed my empathic abilities, it was now.

I tried to calm the upheaval and the desperate sadness I sensed within her, while my own raw loss lurched through my heart, my whole body.

"I know there is nothing I can do or say that will help, so I'm just going to hug you and hold you." My arms were tight around her. "And I want to remind you that I love you. And

I'm not going to say sorry because that doesn't help. I loved them too."

Tears flowed, Sage setting off a chain reaction among all of us. I knew she needed my comfort, and I gave her what I could, even though my own resources were running low. There was a weight in my body, pulling me down. Everything felt heavy and dark.

More violence, more death, another loss. It felt like this would never stop.

I held Sage, feeling helpless.

"It's like this is a dream. A nightmare," she said at last. "I have all these memories playing over in my head. I mean, I spoke with them yesterday and I'm still annoyed with them. Mum can't work out how to video message and Dad always asks embarrassing questions about Luca. Does that sound terrible? I want to wake up and … this can't be real." Her words came in broken sentences between her sobs. "I didn't get to tell them I love them."

"They knew."

"Yeah." Her anguish was calming, a little. "How the hell did you cope with this, when your dad …?"

"I didn't. Well, not at first. You helped me." I smiled through my own tears.

Our friendship was strong, and it surrounded me, a steel frame holding me up. I used that feeling to wrap support and strength around Sage, sending it through the tips of my fingers, my palms, my arms.

"Do you want me to come with you?" I asked, although I knew all her sisters would be there and they only wanted immediate family.

"No. I think just Luca and I will be the safest." She squeezed my hand. "I know you know how I feel."

I nodded. "Like shit?"

She gave a croaky laugh. "Yep, you got that right."

Her eyes were a watery blue, a deep ocean. When her glasses fogged up, she took them off to wipe them, finding comfort in the routine task. We sat in silence until the crescendo of sorrow between us settled into a quieter rhythm. I knew that it was only a temporary reprieve from the grief.

"Nova, you have to do something. With Sawyer. You must stop this violence. Make the world better. Promise me."

I nodded, but my stomach pitched and rolled at the impossible task she was setting me. It was a big ask.

Eventually Luca came for Sage, and they left for her sister's.

The house went through the daily motions of preparing meals, eating, cleaning, making conversation but it was all mechanical, like we were passengers in our own bodies. Sorrow hung over us, an old heavy bedspread, familiar but rough and scratchy. Fear rolled just beneath, a tangle of bedclothes, a mess waiting to strangle us. Anger and frustration bubbled in Jackson. Ava regressed again, and I felt the sudden lurch of terror and dread when she had flashbacks or nightmares. Mia and Alice deliberated returning home. Grief ran its course. It was exhausting.

Sawyer's words ran though my head about my ability to calm and influence people's emotions and help them. I tried to cast off my own weariness. It wasn't easy. Sage's parents were family to me. And I missed her, and worried about what she would be going though. However, she had set me a task, to make the world better. I could start here. I focused on the small things. A warm winter's day, the sun breaking through the clouds, a walk on the beach. Mia's soft laugh, Ava's involuntary smile, Alice's warm hugs. Jackson's secret wink at me when he caught me observing them. Gradually, I felt the climate lighten around us.

<h1 style="text-align:center">23</h1>

With the death of Sage's parents, I felt like my life was a derailed train, hurtling on its journey, but out of control. I wondered if I would ever get back on track.

I missed Sage and found myself drawn to Jackson's strength. We often sat up after the others had gone to bed talking about Sawyer and what he had offered. Those dark quiet hours were intimate, talking through the night. I shared more of my thoughts and feelings with Jackson than I had with anyone ever before, even Sage. It was cosy and special, but I was also playing with fire. There was no denying the attraction between us, and it was burning at a low smoulder.

I woke with a start, sprawled on the couch, my face resting on Jackson's chest, a wet patch on his shirt.

"How long was I asleep?"

"Long enough to dribble all over my chest."

"Sorry." I giggled quietly. "Sorry," I said again.

He chuckled. "It's okay. I fell asleep too."

I sat up and stretched. It was cold. We were sharing a blanket and body heat, apparently. He pulled me back against him, and put his arm around me, as he often did in a friendly way. But he was also playing with the hair that curled around my face and that felt more personal.

"This is … you are …" he stopped, the last word hanging between us.

"I'm what?"

His eyes studied me, serious and intent. He opened his mouth but shut it again without saying anything. It was clear he was still thinking.

"Say something. I'm what?" My nerves fluttered.

"Annoying, beautiful, calm …"

"Calm?" I choked off a laugh.

"It starts with C."

"Oh. So, what is this, an alphabet thing?"

He didn't answer and just continued. "Dangerous, enigmatic, fearless …"

"Enigmatic?" I interrupted him.

Jackson's usual cheeky grin appeared. He stretched out his legs, which were long and hanging off the end of the couch.

"Gorgeous, hot …" he continued, until I interrupted again.

"You are idiotic, juvenile."

"I am much better at this than you." Jackson interrupted me this time. "Kind, lovable."

"Moody." I jumped back in.

"Nice."

"Nice?"

Jackson shrugged, his grin widening. "Outstanding, perfect."

"You are quarrelsome," I said.

"Radiant, sexy." He winked at me.

I shook my head, laughing at him. "Stop."

"But I haven't finished. Thoughtful, unique, virtuous, wonderful, extraordinary, yummy and zany." He finished with a small bow.

"Extraordinary is cheating."

"Now, who's the quarrelsome one?"

When I turned to glare at him, he kissed me, carefully. Our previous kisses had been passionate and heated, but tonight he was tender and soft. His skin was warm and smooth, smelling faintly of soap. Deep brown eyes shone with suppressed emotion, but looked at me fondly, without demand. He reached for my hand and moved it up to touch his face. I stroked his cheek and pushed his hair out of his eyes.

"Do you want this to happen?" He spoke softly, asking my permission.

"Yeah." It seemed inevitable.

"What about Coop?"

"We're not together."

"Yeah, but what do you want?' Jackson persisted, gently but firmly.

I thought for a moment, then answered him a lot more broadly than he had implied.

"What do I want? I want to be loved and to love in return. I want passion and I want adventure. I want to make a difference in the world."

"Is that all?" Jackson chuckled. "Okay, then let's go do that. Together. Love, be loved, have passion, adventure and make a difference."

"We have to take this slowly." I twisted my fingers nervously. "I feel like my life is a disaster waiting to happen."

I wondered if I would scare him away, like I had with Cooper.

Jackson just nodded. "As long as I can share in that disaster."

We kissed again and a reassurance crept over me. Jackson gave himself so openly, I could sense every part of his being. There was nothing hidden, nothing buried. My heart galloped and his rode along with it.

I woke in the morning on the couch, warm and comfortable, with Jackson nuzzled up against me.

"I get what Ava says. I sleep better when I'm lying next to you." He cuddled in closer.

He made me feel more secure too. Although the grieving was never far away, these small moments of happiness and contentment lifted my energy. They helped put the train back on its tracks. And in return, I knew I was lifting the energy of the whole house. It was just as Sawyer had said.

When Sage returned a few weeks later, we took a long walk. Her grief was still fresh, but I could feel a gradual return to her naturally buoyant, practical self.

We discussed Jackson. "I think you should let a relationship develop. It is happening anyway," Sage said.

"What about Coop? I don't want to hurt him."

"What about him? He left you. He hurt you. If he was good for you, you would still be together. I like Jackson. He's stronger than Coop, and you need that."

"I care about them both."

"Nova, you care about everyone." Sage shook her head at me in friendly frustration.

It was only a short reprieve in our grieving.

There was a shooting at the food bank, in our hometown.

More violence, more death, more horror.

Five people were dead, including one police officer. The police officer was Mia's and Alice's father, and Ava's mother was also one of the five.

It was time to go home.

My train had not just derailed, it had crashed.

24

With loud, heart wrenching sobs, Alice and Mia were inconsolable. Ava sat as still as a statue, silent, yet equally distressed. After all, there was nothing anyone could say or do that would help.

Jackson, Luca, Sage, and I moved about quietly, packing up the house and everyone's belongings, and loading the car. Sage's discreet tears ran down her face. My body moved as it was supposed to, but my mind was blank, and my heart was frozen. I was becoming numb to so much loss. The violence, death, grief, all over again.

Luca drove with Sage, Mia, Alice, and Ava in the car. Jackson and I went on the motorbike. It had been months since I had been home, and the differences were devastating. Streets that had once been filled with families and children were now deserted. Discarded plastic bottles and rubbish littered the gutters. We passed a car still smoking and others completely burnt out. Houses were closed and dark windows were boarded up or smashed. The roar of the bike engine was obtrusive in the quiet.

Sage stayed at my house. It was musty and cold after being closed up and there was a noticeable emptiness, the distinct lack of my father. At least we had each other.

"Stick together?" I asked, knowing her answer.

"Like glue."

Our friendship supplied the warmth we both needed.

It was already a week past the start of term when we received notification that school was suspended indefinitely. So much for completing Year 12. It was unclear what was happening about exams and our final two terms. The teachers sent through messages encouraging us to keep learning and keep busy, but there was no guidance or support. No one knew when this aggression and isolation would end. There was just uncertainty.

We left Mia, Alice, and Ava to mourn with their families. Sage and I knew from experience what they must be going through, the heaviness of losing a parent.

I had not seen Jackson for a few days and assumed he would be busy catching up with his family. He turned up on Sunday night with news from Sawyer.

"Hey, Wilson."

"Hey, Lewis."

I hugged him clumsily, feeling stiff and self-conscious. Being back home had stirred up memories of Cooper and me, and what things had been like before.

"The DOVE team is heading to Melbourne. They'll pass through and collect you if you want to join them. Sawyer said there was room for me too, if I want to do work-experience at the hospital." Jackson sounded ambivalent.

Since the incident in Yarram, I had decided to go with Sawyer. I wanted to learn from him. Sage had challenged me to make the world a better place and this was an opportunity to do something good. She had talked with Luca, and they wanted to come with me, to help in a hospital or welfare centre. There was nothing here for us anymore, no school, no parents. We had tried the safe thing, isolating ourselves at the beach, but it hadn't worked. Violence had still found us. It was time for a change. Things were at their worst but hopefully with DOVE we could make a difference.

"Jack, I'm going with them. I need to. Sawyer can teach me so much. But I understand if you want to stay here with your family. You don't have to come."

"Don't you want me to come?" His voice was harsh with hurt.

"It's your decision. It's nothing to do with me."

He narrowed his eyes at me, and I could feel his frustration rising.

"I do want to come," he said. "I want to do my part."

"Only if you're sure. Don't do it because of us."

"Is there an *us*?" His tone was annoyed.

"It's complicated."

"That's a cop out, Nova. I thought we were just starting to work on an *us*."

"We were." I kept my voice even, not wanting to upset him.

My own emotions were a blurry mess. The grief from recent and previous losses still weighed so heavily in my body, I didn't know if I could allow myself to be happy with anyone. The future was hazy. I dropped my gaze to the floor, feeling uncomfortable under his scrutiny.

"And now? Have you changed your mind? Is it Coop?"

His need was unmistakable, but I could not give him the reassurance he craved. I was not sure what my heart wanted, and my head was not offering any clarity at all.

"Jack, I haven't even seen him." I met his eyes again and sent a silent plea for understanding.

"Okay." He nodded reluctantly. "But I am coming with you to Melbourne."

The following afternoon, Sage, Luca, and I sat out on the back deck. The bare trees stood proud and still, offering little refuge for the chattering birds. It was cold, but sunny, and we lifted our faces to the rays like sunflowers. Jackson arrived, without advance notice, bringing Cooper too. There was an uneasy tension between the three of us, while Sage and Luca made polite conversation. I wondered if Jackson was forcing me into making a choice.

Cooper followed me into the kitchen when I went for drinks. "I've missed you."

"I've missed you too, Coop," I said lightly.

"Jack says you're going with these DOVE guys."

"Yeah."

"Isn't that dangerous?" He sounded dubious.

"I think we can help, and I'm sure they'll keep us safe." That was the plan, anyway.

"Are you and Jack a thing now?" he asked.

It was a quick change of subject. My head spun.

"What did Jack say?" I shuffled my feet, wishing I could escape.

"He told me to ask you."

Thanks for that. Jackson was probably waiting to hear my answer as much as Cooper.

"Right. Yeah. I guess we were heading that way." I concentrated on gathering the drinks I had come for, so I did not have to look at him.

"But nothing official?"

"Not really."

Cooper was pleased, I could feel it. It just added to my confusion about how I felt. I did not mention Imogen. I did not really want to know.

"Are you doing okay?" My turn to change the subject.

"Yeah, I'll probably just help Dad in the surgery now that school is off. He is still open."

"That's good experience if you want to be a paramedic."

"I miss us, Nova." He was not going to let it go easily.

I felt dizzy and I needed to end this conversation. "I better take these drinks out."

I was left feeling flat and hollow. Cooper and I seemed to be drawn together but we did not fit properly. Not in this world anyway. Love was cloudy and painful.

We had not planned any big farewells. Ava and Mia were still grieving with their families. To my surprise however, they came to say goodbye, with Cooper too. Mia's face reflected her grief, pale and drawn. Her eyes mirrored the hurt I had seen in Sage's and my own after the loss of a parent, when you realise all the things that would never be said and the experiences that would never be shared. I wondered if she had seen Kenji and worried that her time away at Woodside beach had affected their relationship. We gripped each other's hands tightly.

"We'll stay in contact when the phones are working," I said.

"Of course."

Ava's face was blank. I felt the resistance. She was not allowing herself to grieve. I would have to talk with Mia about keeping an eye on her. We hugged and I poured love and understanding into my touch. I felt her receiving it, and there was a glimmer of gratitude in her eyes. Hopefully, that was a start.

"Take care."

Cooper hugged me, gripping me like he could not let go, would not let go. This time I was leaving. Eventually we broke apart and I shuffled my feet awkwardly. I did not know what to say. He was silent too, but his eyes spoke volumes. They shone with love and sadness. I sensed Jackson watching us and wondering.

It was time to go, time for a different direction.

25

The trip into Melbourne took longer than usual. We had to leave the highway and take the back roads in some areas. Roadblocks and barricades loomed large and foreboding around towns that had isolated themselves, for protection. I was driving the DOVE jeep to get some practice in. I still wanted to get my licence if VicRoads was even open anymore. Thankfully, there was minimal traffic, and no need to do any reverse parking. Jackson sat with me in the front and pretended to be relaxed, but I felt his underlying anxiety at my inexperience. Sage and Luca were in the back, regularly giving me annoying driving tips. We followed Sawyer and his team in their jeep.

We found ourselves in a war zone as we entered the outlying suburbs. Smoke rose from burnt out buildings. Sporting fields were carved into mud and dust where schools and public spaces had been used as combat arenas. Striped police crime scene tape decorated buildings like Christmas tinsel. Police cars roamed the streets and their drones hovered in the skies, yet looters continued to trash stores in broad daylight.

It seemed they were fighting a losing battle to enforce the curfews and control over the ever-increasing violence.

Sawyer had explained that there was a fierce rivalry between highly organised criminal gangs. Melbourne was divided in half. A crime lord called Frank Murphy ran the northern suburbs, with a ruthless brutality. We were headed to the south-eastern suburbs, comparatively an island of relative order in the anarchy. It was ruled by another gangster, called Abraham, and his followers.

There was a checkpoint for entry, a border crossing. People that had nothing to offer, too old, too poor, or those not prepared to follow Abraham's rule were refused. There was an extensive line of cars and a trailing queue of people. Tempers flared. Fights broke out. Order was restored when a gunshot was fired in warning. It was chaos, madness, and mayhem.

Following Sawyer's jeep, I passed under the road signs that now read *Abraham City*, and stopped at the border gate. Although it was still daylight, huge floodlights glared overhead. A security fence laced with barbed wire blocked the road. Carrying automatic weapons, which had been outlawed in Australia for years, the scowls of the guards froze my blood. They were civilian soldiers, militia, gang members keeping order with violence and intimidation. Anxiety and fear poured through me, turning my stomach, and burning my chest. My throat tightened as I sensed a heavy undercurrent of cruelty. The air reeked of sweat and urine.

"We're with them. Department of Violence Eradication." I pointed at Sawyer's jeep that had just passed through.

"ID's?" The guard ignored me.

We handed over the passes we had been given. He gave them back and nodded to the gatekeeper. As the barrier started to roll back, the car behind slammed into ours, and kept accelerating. My chest smacked into the steering wheel, and Jackson's head only just stopped short of the dashboard. Luca and Sage, in the back, fell forward straining against their seatbelts.

"Holy Shit!" Jackson's eyes were wild. "Nova, keep your foot flat on the brake." He pulled up the handbrake as well.

People swarmed down the sides of our jeep, hoping to gain entry through the open gate. Guards shouted and raised their rifles. Warning shots were loud above our heads. People ducked but keep pushing through. The barrier was rolling back towards us, closing the gap. My foot was planted on the brake, but with the car behind locked onto our rear bumper, we continued to inch forward. The wheels spun and screeched.

After interminable seconds, the gate latched shut again, with our jeep resting hard against the wire, but still on the outside. Guards converged on the car behind and hauled away the driver. They were efficient and brutal.

"All of you, out of the car." A guard had his gun pointed at my head.

I instinctively put my hands in the air, tasting my fear.

"But we didn't do anything." My protest was ignored by a grunt and a further wave of the rifle.

"Just get out." Jackson spoke quietly, keeping his eyes on the guard at my door.

"I can't." Sage gestured at the press of people blocking her door.

"Come out this side." Luca was sitting behind me and there were less people on our side.

Jackson also climbed across to come through my door. We were marched into the adjoining building, hands above our heads. It was an old brick hall, cement floor and grey walls, dirty and drab, and it made me think of a prison.

The guard grunted at two others. "Check them for weapons."

While one pressed his gun against my chest, another moved his hands over my body.

"Hey!" Jackson was indignant. "Leave her alone."

The guard used his rifle like a club, striking Jackson in the stomach, who doubled over in pain.

"It's okay." My legs wobbled and my heart was racing, but I closed my eyes and took slow deep breaths.

I sent my thoughts to a warm summer day at the beach, concentrating on flooding the room with a calm wave. A couple of the guards lowered their rifles.

I kept my voice soft and even. "We aren't carrying anything."

Jackson swore under his breath, and I raised my eyebrows at him.

"I have a knife." He was still winded, and his voice was a wheeze.

I rolled my eyes at him.

"Except for a knife … or two." I amended when Luca cleared his throat meaningfully.

I glared at them and noticed Sage looking at the floor, avoiding eye contact. She had known about the knives.

"We're with the Department of Violence Eradication." I held out my ID again. "We're not with those people trying to push through the gate."

The room was getting calmer, the guards more receptive.

"You look a little young." One of the guards hung on to his last shreds of doubt.

At that moment, Sawyer breezed in, bringing an air of authority that no one wanted to argue with. "Thank you for keeping my team safe."

That was that. Within minutes we were through to the other side, while a guard went to retrieve our jeep. Sawyer could move mountains; I was sure of it.

"He completely changes the atmosphere in a room." Jackson was in awe.

"So does Nova." Sage was my cheerleader.

"True," agreed Jackson, grinning at me. "And her witchy powers are sexier."

"Oh, please." I poked him in the ribs, and he groaned, still tender from being struck by the rifle. "So, I'm a witch now, am I?"

"Well, if the shoe fits." Jackson dodged out of my way so I couldn't poke him again.

We all laughed.

Our jeep was a little battered, front and rear, but there was no major damage. Luca took over the driving. Leaving the checkpoint and highway behind, the suburban streets were a narrow, winding rabbit warren. Homemade barricades made driving difficult. Fences and walls were vandalised. Graffiti provided colour but was mostly angry and vulgar. Litter blew across the road. Houses crowded together in clumps, cold and unwelcoming. Traffic lights blinked for non-existent traffic, and the rare pedestrians scurried off like rats. Like an apocalyptic scene from a horror movie, there was a feeling that something was inherently wrong. And yet, it was better inside the border than outside.

The four of us were billeted in an apartment above a Vietnamese restaurant, with Sawyer and his team in neighbouring rooms. An old building, it stretched down the whole block, tenanted by shops and cafés, all closed. We entered through the back door, to the dining area, where chairs were stacked on tables and covered in a layer of dust. In contrast, upstairs was bright and inviting. Wide windows overlooked the main street, empty now but reminiscent of a bustling workday. Someone had been in to clean and while a smell of disinfectant drifted through the apartment, there was still a dominant aroma of lemongrass and coriander. The door opened to a lounge, with a nook for the dining table. Leading off this room was a kitchen with modern, shiny appliances. It had hardly been used. The previous tenants had probably been fed by the restaurant below. A short hallway led to the bathroom, behind the kitchen, and two bedrooms on the other side, each small but cosy. Sage and Luca took one, while I took the other. Jackson offered to sleep on the couch.

Jackson and I exchanged awkward glances and polite conversation, skirting around each other's personal space. Neither of us wanted to bring up Cooper, but his presence hovered between us. My heart lurched from Cooper to Jackson and my head still spun. I wanted someone to tell me what to do. I cared about them both.

"You need to work it out." Sage's counsel was not helpful.

"I'm so grateful to have you as my best friend. You are so wise and full of *sage* advice." Sage poked her tongue out at my sarcastic tone.

The following morning, Sawyer showed us around. We visited Box Hill hospital where Sage and Jackson would do their work-experience, and the community organisation where Luca was going to be helping with the teen programs.

Sawyer planned to spend some time each day teaching me to better understand and use my empathic ability, and then I would join the others at the hospital. He also had to go and present himself to Abraham, the self-nominated president of this region of Melbourne. He wanted me to come along.

Abraham's headquarters were an inner-city high school. The chunky red brick buildings were reminiscent of my own school, but the familiarity ended there. This school was littered with debris. Mounds of half burnt furniture had been left around the playground. The walls were covered in scribbles and drawings, sharing colourful opinions about the recent school administration, none of which was favourable. I wondered if my own school was in the same state of disarray.

Abraham did not need a surname. His authority was absolute. A permanent guard of his followers watched us curiously, silently. Sawyer was flanked by his own protection, Finn, and Jet, while I stood behind, trying not to attract any attention. My heart was ready to explode from my chest. Everyone was armed except me. There was a base line of anger and hostility in the room, but it was not the same as the raw aggression I felt out in public. These men used their brutality as a means of control. However, the control was stretched taut, a balloon blown up to its limit. One pin prick and it could all explode.

"Thanks for seeing us, Abe." Sawyer's voice did not waver, any fear was well hidden.

Abraham received us in the principal's office. The walls were grey, and the room had one window, which faced the main road. On the large desk, a stack of papers sat under a pyramid paperweight that I suspected was left by its previous occupant. It would make a handy weapon. Just being there made me feel anxious. I had never enjoyed being sent to the principal's office. It was rarely for anything good.

"Who is this young lady you have brought me?" Abraham watched me like a cat with a mouse.

"This is Nova, my assistant."

"I look forward to getting to know you, Nova."

I nodded at him, unable to say a word. Something dangerous lurked within Abraham. It almost had a smell, dank and rotten. Maybe I was being melodramatic, but it took everything I had to control the shivers running down my spine.

I will not be afraid, I said to myself and repeated it, forcing myself to believe it, forcing myself to stay calm.

The conversation turned to the supply and safe distribution of food, medicines, and essential items through Abraham City. Deliveries were being hijacked by Frank Murphy's gang and Sawyer had offered to negotiate between the men. He worked hard to create a cooperative atmosphere and I could sense the strain. Sawyer argued for creating more food banks, ensuring hospitals were safe and well-equipped, and providing security for delivery routes. I focused on keeping my breathing regular and relaxed. To dampen my anxiety, I let the drone of voices become a background of white noise. It seemed to work.

26

The next month settled into a routine. Sawyer and I spent an hour together most mornings where he taught me to better understand and control my empathic skills. I would then assist him with his duties, or I would join the others. Sage and Jackson had work-experience at Box Hill hospital and Luca at a youth agency. We were back in the apartment by mid-afternoon. As I improved in my control of my emotional environment, and thanks to Sawyer living next door, we lived in a small bubble of happiness. As soon as I left the apartment however, the jabs of anger I sensed from people in the streets were like dogs biting at my heels.

Sawyer often had me attend when he met with Abraham. These meetings were an ongoing debate about what Abraham could and could not do. When the violence had been at its worst, Abraham had claimed control of this part of the city, using his gangs to deliver their own form of street justice, providing protection for a price, and terrorising those who opposed him. Sawyer was trying to re-establish the traditional government structure, from the legal procedures and policing, to the transport of goods through the city, and the health and welfare systems. It was a slow and volatile process and Sawyer claimed he needed my help in keeping the negotiations calm. Although my efforts seemed like small nibbles at a huge cake, Sawyer said I did make a difference.

Abraham's olive skin was heavily inked, and his dark hair closely cropped. Beneath his thick eyebrows, cold eyes probed with a direct stare. With a nose that had obviously been broken, perhaps a few times, he looked exactly as expected, like a person raised on aggression. He had a warped moral code and a complete disregard for other people.

Careful to keep me safe, Sawyer rarely had me talk. While they faced each other across the desk, I sat in a chair to one side. I avoided locking eyes with Abraham and concentrated on building a conducive emotional climate. It was not easy. Abraham's temper would explode without warning. If I got distracted, frustration and animosity would surge through the room, and voices would rise in anger. Every day, I felt more in control, and I got better at sensing Sawyer's cues. A bow of his head and a twinge of anxiety meant he needed me to concentrate harder as Abraham's irritation was rising.

In the first few meetings, Abraham mostly ignored me. It was not until our fifth meeting that I felt his curiosity piqued, and his gaze kept flicking towards me. I was careful to keep my face neutral. Sawyer's fingers drummed nervously on his armrest.

"You can call me Abe." He spoke directly to me.

"Thank you." I could not help the nervous waver in my voice.

"You're a little young for a negotiator."

"I'm just doing work-experience with Sawyer."

"I see. And what do you do exactly? You don't take any notes."

"Umm, I'm just learning about negotiation."

I felt Sawyer's anxiety rising, but we could not leave until Abraham gave his permission. At some secret signal, Finn and Jet went on alert. They rose from their seats at the back of the room, and took a small step closer to me, as if ready to guide me out. It seemed everyone was on edge, except Abraham, who treated it like a game. I was the toy.

"Sawyer, I think that's all for today. I want a few minutes alone with Nova." Abraham was used to being obeyed.

Sawyer rose from his seat. "Abe, that's not possible. She's under my protection."

Sawyer was still influencing the room, to keep it calm and cooperative, but I felt his silent shudder of dread, and Abraham's flash of annoyance. Sawyer and I both pushed harder to keep things peaceful.

"Sawyer, don't be ridiculous. I'm not going to hurt her. I just want a minute."

Abraham had more men than we did, more heavily armed. He could do whatever he wanted.

"Nova, I'll be right outside the door," Sawyer said clearly.

I nodded with a confidence I did not feel. Finn and Jet followed Sawyer.

With a flick of his hand, Abraham dismissed his own men, and we were alone. He clearly did not feel the need for his protection detail with me.

"Nova, I won't hurt you. I just want a bit of information. I've heard rumours and although they sound ridiculous, I'm not sure. Can you read minds?" His voice was as smooth and hard as steel.

My horrified expression brought a sneering smile to his face. "I've heard that's why he has you with him."

"Of course not. That is ridiculous." Although I tried for bravado it came out as a nervous stutter.

I repeated my mantra in my head. *I will not be afraid.*

"Sawyer is a particularly good negotiator. But after the two of you leave, I often feel uneasy, like I've been managed." Abraham watched me, without blinking.

"Sawyer would never do that."

Abraham's face tightened, his eyes narrowed, and his chin jutted outward. He had no fear, no compassion.

"Perhaps. I'm still not sure about either of you," he said.

After a few seconds of silence, he dismissed me with a wave of his hand. I held my breath and forced my jelly legs to walk to the door.

"Nova," Abraham called, as my hand reached for the door handle. "What am I thinking now?"

My stomach lurched with a wave of hatred. My hand involuntarily went to my abdomen, but I forced myself to stand up straight.

"I have no idea."

I opened the door and left the room with his cruel laughter ringing loudly. Although, I could not read minds, I honestly believed that if Abraham thought we were deceiving him, he would not hesitate to hurt us, possibly kill us. I also caught a glimpse of Sawyer's anger and fear before he buried it with his usual calm demeanour.

Jackson, when he heard about what had happened, was openly furious. Sage too.

"You said she'd be safe," Jackson confronted Sawyer.

"I am trying to keep you all safe." Sawyer's voice was composed as he sent comfort to Jackson.

"Try harder," said Sage.

"Jack, Sage, I'm fine," I said.

Sawyer nodded at me and left us.

Jackson slammed his fist on the table, and a scorching heat tore through me. I sent out gentle waves of reassurance, but he looked at me with irritation.

"I can feel what you are doing, Nova. Stop it. I'm pissed off, and I have a right to be. I care about you."

"I know. Thank you. I'm okay though."

"You're too zen about this whole thing," Jackson said and frowned at me. "This guy is a serious criminal."

"I'll be careful."

"I hate that I can't protect you."

"You don't need to."

He sighed and shook his head at me, still upset, as was Sage.

I was worried too, but I couldn't let it show. One wrong step with Abraham could result in dire consequences.

The next day, I caught another glimpse of Sawyer's concern. "He's a narcissist and won't hesitate to use people if it will benefit him. Let's keep you out of the picture until he forgets about you. And don't ever mention being an empath to anyone."

I spent the next few weeks doing work-experience with the others. Sage was in a special part of the children's ward at the hospital, for orphans and victims of violence or domestic abuse. There were young boys and girls, with varying degrees of injury, harm, or neglect, being kept at the hospital because there was nowhere else they could go. Many had been orphaned when violence had killed their parents. A lot were found wandering the streets and brought in by police. Child Protective Services were trying to place them in safe homes, but it was harder than ever to find people willing to take in a child, especially one who had suffered trauma.

Unlike the rest of the hospital, the children's ward had colour and personality. Although every surface was spotlessly clean, the air had a sweet scent, masking the disinfectant. Toys and books crowded the tables, and the walls were splashed with bright, loud art. The nurses were friendly and welcoming, moving with an unhurried composure from room to room on their rounds. The low murmur of a television came from the communal area.

A large majority of the children confined to beds were recovering from injuries, but their energy was an inspiration. Those that could move about, ran to greet Sage when we arrived, pleading for games. A good deal of noise and rowdiness invariably accompanied this play. Bright eyes, enquiring minds, tiny bodies waiting to dance and jump. They chattered and giggled, and while Sage answered a question from one, ten more questions queued from the others. Her mind was alive with ideas for craft activities and storytelling. They all loved her. We read to them, played games, and showered them with cuddles. I rarely needed to prop up the ward's emotional levels and instead they revived my flagging energy.

Luca worked in a neighbouring youth agency for young teenage boys, a drop-in centre. These children had less chance of being fostered out and their wounds stayed long after the physical injuries healed. With no school anymore, they wandered the streets in gangs. The social workers were trying to keep them out of the clutches of Abraham's followers, where they would be groomed as soldiers. Many presented after initiation rituals, where they had been beaten within an inch of death. It was a cruel culling process. Abraham's followers beat the kids to make them stronger, so they would not break when it really mattered. Those who were not good enough ended up at the hospital. Most of the boys were skinny and malnourished. They modelled the swagger of older teens but lacked the physical coordination. Confusion, guilt, and fear rolled off them.

Organising exercise programs for the boys at a nearby gym, Luca talked with them while they worked out and he gradually won their trust. Helping him, I learned about Luca's own background, as he shared with these broken teenagers. Luca's mother was an alcoholic and his survival had meant looking after himself. Never knowing whether she would be there after school, unable to rely on her to make dinner or school lunches, she was violent long before this recent pandemic. Luca had learned to keep out of her way, recognising the signs. As with these boys, it was normal for him to be on the receiving end of a backhand slap across the head, or worse, and it was a relief if she had already passed out. Never any money, no security, and no sense of safety. He did not know his father, nor any other family. Luca grew up amidst chaos and fear. It gave him a solid connection to these young teens.

Jackson worked at the hospital wherever he was needed. He got to observe in theatre, shadow doctors and nurses in their rounds, assist in measuring blood pressure and blood sugar levels. Having had some similar experience in his father's surgery, he felt quite at home. As blood made me queasy, I only spent a little time with him and mostly felt I was in the way.

The DOVE team came with its own Army Special Forces protective detail, and while Finn and Jet were with Sawyer, Rayna was at the hospital. The few times I went looking for Jackson, I found her close by. Rayna had an understated kind of beauty. She did not wear makeup, but her skin was flawless. Tall and slender, she was fit and strong, usually dressed in simple army fatigues. Her eyes were surprisingly soft and when she smiled you could not help but smile with her. I could feel the attraction that flowed between her and Jackson. Their heads bowed towards each other as they shared a joke. Rayna laughed and touched Jackson's arm. An unwelcome cold twist of irritability and possessiveness plagued me until it became a stone in my throat.

I waited for Sage and Luca to go to bed. In the kitchen, Jackson and I worked side by side doing the dishes.

"Rayna's nice." I kept my voice light.

"Yeah, she's really cool. She trained as a medic and knows all about treating injuries. She's so hands on."

"Yeah, well, she had her hands on you." I couldn't help myself.

"She what?" Jackson's eyes opened wide in surprise.

"She's been flirting with you." My heart fluttered.

"Has she? Really? An older woman too." He grinned wickedly, linking his hands behind his head, which pushed out his chest and flexed his biceps.

It was like watching an animal preparing for a mating ritual.

"So, do you like her … like that?" My voice was a weak stutter.

Jackson raised his eyebrows. "Nova Wilson, are you jealous?"

"What? No! Don't be ridiculous." I focused on putting the plates away.

"You are." His voice was a laughing tease.

"No, I'm not."

"Really? So, if she does like me and I like her, you won't care."

"Well, she's old enough to be … a much older sister, at least."

"So?" He watched me, eyes narrowing. "Wilson, you are totally jealous."

His voice was high and teasing as he repeated 'totally jealous' and flicked soap suds at me.

"Lewis, … how old are you?" I aimed to hide my embarrassment with mockery.

"Old enough." Jackson laughed easily. "Nova, if you want this," he pointed his thumb at his chest, "you better make a move soon, because I won't wait forever."

"I don't … I'm not … you're an arrogant …" I could not complete a sentence.

Jackson laughed again, his dark brown eyes twinkling with mirth.

"Yes, you do. You are. And I might be arrogant but I'm also very sexy." He blew me a kiss.

I opened and shut my mouth, still unable to make a coherent sentence.

"Now, I'm going to see Rayna." Jackson pulled the plug on the sink.

"You're not?" My voice was uncertain.

His grin almost climbed off his face as he waltzed towards the door. Rayna was in the flat next to ours.

"Jack, wait," I called out.

He turned instantly, lounging in the doorway, and waited. I watched him push his hair back from his face. It was a loveable gesture.

"Do you really like her?"

"Nova, I love that you're jealous. Your green eyes are glowing." Jackson was taking too much pleasure in my discomfort.

"They are not."

He ignored my protests. "It's time you admit how you feel about me, Wilson."

"And how's that, Lewis?"

In one stride he was beside me, pulling me in close, lifting me up to meet his demanding mouth. He kissed me, long and hard, until I saw brilliant stars behind my eyelids, and had to pull away, or faint. I drank in his smell and delighted in the warmth of his body. Finally, I opened my eyes to find his boring into mine, challenging me to acknowledge what he already knew. That I wanted this as much as he did.

"Do you want me to kiss you again?" He needed me to admit it.

"Yes." My voice was husky.

He kissed me again, more gently but his mouth was still insistent. Normal time paused, for us to breathe in each other. Nothing else existed outside our space.

"Nova, it's you I want, not Rayna." He spoke into the side of my neck, nuzzling against me. "Ever since that first time you climbed onto my bike and wrapped your arms around me, it's only been you."

In his eyes was the sincerity I felt in his heart.

"So, we blame the bike?" I hid an internal smile.

"Well, it was a hell of a ride."

This time my mouth found his and was just as demanding. My hands were buried in his hair, while his arms held my body up against his. Our mouths merged; our tongues entwined. It was my turn to leave him breathless. I could feel the matching passion stirring in his body and the love in his heart joining with mine. We had kissed before but this time it was a commitment and we both knew it.

"Are you sure?" His voice held no arrogance, no demand.

"Stop talking," I whispered, and he snickered.

We resumed kissing and moved into the bedroom to lie together, dishes forgotten. We talked and laughed and later as we lay in a comfortable tangle, I waited for his breathing to deepen into sleep before I whispered quietly.

"I love you, Jack."

I was mistaken though; he was not asleep.

"I love you, too, Nova. Always." His voice rang out clear and true.

We clasped hands and let our hearts drum to the same beat, soothing the way into a peaceful sleep.

I woke the next morning, safe and content, Jackson's body spooning mine. I stretched and moved slightly away so as not to wake him. Jackson felt my movements though and scooped me back against his body. He was as warm as an electric blanket.

"I love feeling you stretch against me," he said drowsily. "You're like a cat."

I made a purring noise while he proceeded to wrap his body around mine. Sometime later, we emerged from the bedroom to find Sage and Luca making breakfast. Sage took one look at my face and jabbed Luca in the ribs.

"I won," she said.

Luca looked at us and grinned. "Well, well."

"What?" I asked innocently.

Jackson just looked smug and shrugged his shoulders.

"Just a bet we had," said Sage, vaguely.

Nothing more was said, but I knew Sage would want all the details later when we were alone. Jackson snatched a piece of toast off my plate and leant down to plant a big wet, noisy kiss on my lips. It left no room for doubt, that we were a couple. Our laughter filled the room. I was brimming with love. The four of us continued our breakfast with companionable chatter, preparing ourselves for the day ahead.

I floated around in a haze of happiness and love.

Sawyer noticed my mood. "About time," he said.

Jackson found that hilarious. "He's like a seer."

"He can't see the future. He just senses how people are feeling."

"Well, he called it before you would admit it."

"He was just guessing."

"Yeah, keep telling yourself that."

The usual end to these conversations was us kissing, while Sage and Luca made vomiting noises. They were content too, though. The whole team was happy, and I realised it was my emotions spilling out.

27

It was the end of August, and we had been in Abraham City for six weeks. Winter still held us in her clutches, the southerly winds bringing goosebumps when they brushed across bare skin.

Abraham held a tight grip on the city reins while the government was still in disarray. With various retirements and a couple of deaths, there were several political seats needing to be filled when we eventually had an election. Abraham wanted one of these; he wanted legitimate political power. I was sure he fancied himself as the next Prime Minister. Sawyer used this ambition, negotiating for more lawful ways of re-establishing order. They worked on keeping the police and hospitals functioning and re-opening the shops. These processes were hindered by the coercion currently being used to control neighbourhoods. Any disagreements, or anything Abraham had not authorised, was dealt with quickly and lethally by gang members. It seemed that half the police force also reported to Abraham. In his favour, he did not stand for domestic violence, nor petty crime, but he circumvented the court system, to deliver his own justice, and businesses paid him a protection tax. Then there were Abraham's illegal money-making activities, drug and gun trafficking, and prostitution, which he carried on regardless of Sawyer's disapproval.

Sawyer was extremely busy and not just with Abraham. There were DOVE teams working in other parts of Melbourne, and he often travelled to help them out, sometimes staying away for days. The northern suburbs, under Frank's rule, were the most dangerous, and negotiations were difficult, trying to keep services open and transport flowing around Melbourne.

Although, overall, I had been staying away from Abraham and spending my time at the hospital, I had developed a shadow. There always seemed to be one of Abraham's guards not far from me, and while they never came close, I felt them watching me.

Early one evening, the four of us were enjoying the warm refuge of our apartment. We talked softly and listened to the muted clatter of the restaurant owners below. They were re-opening in a week and the aroma wafting up the stairs grew more tantalising by the day. Darkness fell with a comfortable serenity, until the quiet was shattered by loud booming noises. Fireworks, screams, and glass smashing. Although it was dangerous to venture out, especially at night, Jackson was instantly alert and curious.

"Shall we go and see what's happening?" He was looking at Luca, who nodded.

"No, you can't, it's almost curfew." Sage grabbed Luca's arm, and turned to me for support.

"It is dangerous," I said half-heartedly.

I could feel the adrenalin rising in my body, and my skin tingled.

"What if someone is in trouble?" Jackson insisted.

There would be little point arguing with Jackson anyway, once he had made up his mind. His impulsivity and fearlessness were infectious.

"We'll be careful," Luca said, patting Sage's hand.

"I'm coming too," I said.

"Damn." Sage stood up as well, accepting her fate.

In the blanket of night, the streetlights created bright halos at regular intervals. We crept along the dark edges to avoid being too conspicuous, following the booming noises. When we came on a group of three adolescents, we huddled under the shadow of a shop awning and watched them. Only just old enough to have lost the traces of childhood, they were laughing and shoving each other, stumbling, and weaving around the footpath. Boxes of fireworks lay open at their feet. One waved what looked like a stick of dynamite and flicked a lighter in his other hand. Another, in a bright red shirt, pulled out the remaining glass shards from the smashed shop front window. A girl sat on the gutter edge cheering on her friends. Having cleared the window frame, Red Shirt snatched the lit firecracker off his friend and threw a perfect underhand pitch. It sailed through the opening, the fuse vivid in the semi-darkness. There was a bigger, brighter flash of light inside and then a muffled explosion rocked the night. Further glass shattered onto the pavement. The girl shrieked, another harsh noise in the otherwise hushed street. The boys staggered about in laughter. Neighbouring dogs set off a volley of loud barking, adding to the cacophony, but the shops and houses stayed dark and quiet. I suspected that even if people were home, they were remaining silent.

"Throw another one!" Red Shirt was urging his friend who was choosing another firecracker.

My stomach shrank as I felt their teenage angst. Their resentment about their lives and the world. Their anger was as volatile as the fireworks. It was a hot branding iron against my skin.

"Shall we call the police?" Sage asked dubiously, keeping her voice low.

We all shook our heads. It would just get back to Abraham, and we did not want to see what justice he would dish out. With Sawyer in the northern suburbs somewhere, we had to handle this ourselves. I knew Luca wanted to keep them out of trouble. They were just kids.

"What if I try to talk with them?" I suggested.

The others nodded, and I felt their support wrapping around me like an extra coat. I stepped out into the light, sending out calm, friendly overtures.

"Hey guys, what's happening?" I asked.

I hesitated mid stride when Red Shirt waved a gun towards me. "Get lost."

Someone swore. Jackson leapt past me, tackling Red Shirt around his knees. They both went down as the gun flew into the gutter and exploded with a loud boom. I felt a pull on my arm and looked to find a spot of blood soaking through my jumper. I realised the bullet had grazed me, but there was no pain. Jackson had Red Shirt on the ground and Luca was locked together with the other boy in a wrestling skirmish. I stood still, momentarily dazed.

"Nova, are you okay?" Sage's voice brought me back, as she examined my arm.

"I'm fine." I brushed her off.

Jackson had his foot on Red Shirt's back, who was face down. The other boy was on his hands and knees with Luca standing over him. Sage retrieved the gun, holding it gingerly.

The girl had been still and silent while her friends were struggling with Luca and Jackson. When she rose to her feet, her movements were stilted and mechanical. I felt a surge of hatred, then the tip of a knife at my throat. With her body pressed close to my back, her arm came across my chest. Her anger surrounded me, a red mist. It had escalated quickly.

"Don't move or I'll slit her throat." Her voice was strangely flat and distant.

She kept her gaze focused on Jackson, but her eyes were cold and empty. Everyone froze, even her friends. Time was suspended. The only sound was the loud breathing from recent exertion.

"If you hurt her," Jackson had his hands raised in surrender, but slowly took a step towards us, "I will kill you." His voice was cold.

I knew he was trying to work out how to take a dive at her, without hurting me.

"Jack, don't."

I felt his anger. It was as dark as hers and it was pulling me in. I fought it. Slowing my own breathing, I focused on being calm and relaxed. I thought of the friendship and happy memories I shared with Sage and felt the mood around me shift.

"No one is going to get hurt." I kept my voice even and soft.

The knife dropped a few centimetres, and the girl moved to stand by my side. Unnaturally pale, her skin was like wax. Her eyes were blank, her face lifeless. But behind this mask, there was hot anger. I mentally reached out to Jackson, who was still fuming, and flooded him with my love. His eyes had not left my face. As he felt me pushing at him, emotionally, he gave a deliberate, slow wink. I returned his wink and let myself relax a bit more. As a result, my love for him seeped into everyone. I felt the girl sway as it affected her. Her fury was cooling, and she was confused.

"Jackson, Luca can you let the boys up?" I asked, calmly.

Luca held out a hand to Red Shirt. Sage surreptitiously passed the gun to Jackson, who tucked it into his jacket pocket. The boys moved to stand beside the girl. She lowered the knife and backed away. I surrounded everyone with a serene peace.

The spell was broken when one of Abraham's men strode out of the dark. I was sure it was one of my shadows.

"It seems you're having some trouble." His attention was focused solely on me.

"No, not at all, just chatting," I said.

My stomach tightened as I felt everyone's fear building once more.

"And yet … you're bleeding." His voice was gruff and challenging as he pointed to my arm.

I wondered what he had seen before he had made himself known. His sly smile was smug with arrogance.

"Just caught my arm on a piece of glass."

I nodded at the ground. The shards from the windows were scattered beneath our feet. He raised his eyebrows in disbelief.

"It's almost curfew. You shouldn't be on the streets." He growled at the adolescents.

They needed no further warning and slid silently away, into the night.

"We're just going, too." Jackson reached for my hand.

"Be seeing you then." Abraham's man strode away, turning to look over his shoulder once, before he became a dim outline.

"Holy shit!" Jackson said.

We all let out the breath we had been holding. Weariness slammed into me, my own, but from the others as well.

"Nova, were you sending us love?" Sage asked, awe in her voice.

"That was for me," Jackson said dryly and squeezed my hand.

His eyes smouldered but softened as he realised, I was almost at my limit.

"Let's go." Sage recognised the signs in me too.

We walked home quickly. I concentrated on putting one foot in front of the other. Jackson and Luca scanned for further danger, eyes darting side to side, front and behind.

The blood on my arm had dried and clotted over the bullet graze. Jackson dabbed it with antiseptic tenderly, while I gritted my teeth and pretended it didn't hurt. I was getting a fine collection of scars. Sage sat close and let her energy and love refill my cup, until our familiar environment was renewed with a sense of wellbeing and safety.

"That girl was creepy," said Luca.

"She was like a zombie," said Jackson.

"A zombie?" I giggled, a little hysterically.

"Yeah, her eyes looked dead, and she moved like this …" Jackson was defensive as he moved his arms up and down.

"You make a good zombie!" Sage snickered.

Jackson's laughter started as a rumble and developed into uncontrollable snorting and gasping, as much from the relief of being safe again, as our comments. It was so contagious, we all joined him, rolling about on our seats and the floor, letting go of the last bit of tension.

Although I was struggling to keep my eyes open, Jackson and I stayed up talking.

"That guy was watching us before he came forward." He confirmed my own thoughts.

"He's one of Abe's. He had a triangle A tattoo on his neck. I've seen it on some of the other followers. They're watching me."

Jackson nodded in agreement.

"Nova, be careful, you're flying too close to the sun."

"I'm what?"

"You know, Icarus."

"Yeah, I know what you mean. But I'm not doing that."

"You're taking chances, with your life. Cutting it too fine sometimes."

"I'm not. Honestly. And anyway, I don't have wings."

"Yes, you do. Even if you can't see them. I can. Angel wings."

"Oh, come on. You are either overly sweet or delusional. And I'm thinking it's the latter."

The two of us swayed with laughter. We gulped at air, snorted, and set each other off all over again. In a world of violence and uncertainty, the best times are these simple moments. Love, laughter, silliness.

"If I'm Icarus, who are you?" I was finally able to ask.

"Eros, the god of love."

"Oh please, don't make me laugh again." I clutched at my stomach. "What about Hades, god of hell?"

Jackson poked out his tongue at me.

"How about Hercules? You are strong and heroic," I said, with a straight face.

"Now you are delusional."

I grinned widely. "You're really coming out with it tonight. Icarus. What have you been reading?" I teased him. "You know, intelligence is very sexy."

"So, you think I'm intelligent?"

"Oh yeah." I laughed and poked him in the chest. "And sexy!"

"Are you happy being with me?" He caught my finger and held it, suddenly serious.

"Of course." My voice was firm, yet my head had clouded with his uncertainty.

"I'm pretty sure Coop thinks the only reason we're together is because he isn't here."

"Well, he's wrong. Although, you've never officially asked me to be your girlfriend."

"I'm waiting for you to get over Coop."

"Pfft." I let out a sigh of annoyance.

He shrugged. "It's true, Nova. You're not over him."

"Whatever." I said and pushed at him, but he scooped me into his arms.

Our kiss was slow and comforting, but passionate at the same time.

"Kiss me like that again," Jackson said quietly.

"Like what?"

"You kissed me like you're in love with me."

I laughed. I kissed him again. I flooded him with love, reminding him of how it felt earlier. His doubt eased and his natural confidence returned, but now my doubt lingered. I pushed it down, deep. Jackson was here, now. Hour by hour, day by day I was falling more in love with him. It was different from Cooper. Jackson challenged me, he protected me, but he also made me stronger.

"Please don't share that feeling with anyone else again. It's mine." He was playful again.

We laughed and loved together, all doubts forgotten. A perfect moment in time.

28

The next morning, Abraham's man knocked at our door. Our presence was requested, all four of us. Sawyer and the team had not yet returned from his most recent trip to the northern suburbs. We had no choice but to go.

Abraham waited for us at a café in Camberwell. A tiny dark space, it huddled despondently among the newer, flashier places, but it was open while a lot of them were closed and vacant. Black metal chairs and tables crowded together on the terracotta tiled floor. Small vases of red plastic flowers supplied the only spot of colour. All the patrons were clearly Abraham's followers; I could see the neck tattoos, a small triangle A symbol. Everyone was armed. Looking tired and nervous, the barista took our order. I sensed a glimmer of sympathy, and worried that it was a sign of what we should expect. The door was locked behind us. Sage's fear was freezing cold ice between my shoulder blades. Luca and Jackson stood straight, but shuffling feet and clenched fists betrayed their anxiety. None of them had ever met Abraham before. I knew I had to be strong.

"Hello, Nova, lovely to see you again." Abraham was ridiculously cheerful. "Will you introduce me to your friends?"

I made the introductions politely. He shook hands with Luca and Jackson and motioned for us to sit with him.

"Mick says you had some trouble last night." Abraham spoke only to me.

I shrugged, staying silent, praying the others would do the same.

"He said you handled it. He thinks you controlled the children, with your mind. The girl had a knife to your throat, and you messed with her mind until she backed down."

"I can't control people with my mind." I kept my tone light, as if it was a joke.

"But you can read minds." It was not a question.

I felt Jackson about to say something and put my hand on his arm. He stayed silent. I knew we were on dangerous ground, so I concentrated on peaceful thoughts.

"What am I thinking now?" Abraham asked.

"I don't know. I can't read minds."

"What am I feeling?"

"I really don't know." But I did know, it was a simmering irritation.

Abraham nodded at one of his men, standing behind our chairs. I felt the hard, circular shaft of a gun barrel between my shoulder blades. There was the taste of bile in my mouth, and I fought to control the chills racing down my spine. Jackson half rose in his chair, but one of Abraham's men pushed him back down.

"You will remain seated," said Abraham.

He nodded at his man and Jackson's hands were cuffed behind with a plastic zip tie. Jackson glared at Abraham, his anger obvious, but stayed quiet.

"Anyone else need to be disciplined?" Abraham spoke as if offering us a drink.

Luca and Sage stayed quiet, and I felt the pricks of their fear needling my skin.

Abraham was baiting me. I clenched my teeth and hung on to the remnants of my strength. *I will not be afraid.* As always, when with Abraham, I repeated this over and over in my head until I believed it. Mostly.

"Nova, I think you can manipulate people's feelings. Tell me what I'm feeling now. If you get it wrong, I shoot you."

I could sense his insincerity, so I shrugged. Jackson struggled against his restraints. Making a tiny shake of my head, I hoped he would stay quiet.

"I can't tell you what I don't know."

Abraham's frustration was a storm cloud in my brain. I was on dangerous ground.

"What about now. What am I feeling?" His tone had turned impatient.

At a nod, the gun turned on Jackson, pressing into his back. Jackson sat up straighter and turned to wink at me. His courage gave me courage. With a mocking smile, he turned back to Abraham. Suddenly, a hand reached across and struck Jackson across the face. I flinched. Jackson's smile fell, and his dark brown eyes were watery, but he still sat up tall and straight. There was a red handprint across his cheek.

Abraham raised his eyebrows, and I had a sense that he respected Jackson's show of bravery. I stayed quiet, waiting.

"Nova, you are a pain in my arse." Abraham was like a rubber band, stretching, and I was not sure when the breaking point would be. "Maybe this will help you talk."

At his nod, the gun was turned on Sage. It was pressed to her temple. Sage whimpered, her eyes wide with terror. Abraham watched me, impatient, ruthless, waiting.

Waves of dread threatened to engulf me. I knew I could be strong, but not on a day like this, when I was still recovering from last night and my friends were now at risk. I was only human, and I got lost in those waves and conceded.

"You're annoyed. You feel contempt for our weakness. You're cold and hollow. You need to be in control, and you are desperate to hang on to that control." I spoke mechanically.

"That's enough." His voice was loud, firm.

Abraham had got more than he bargained for. At another nod, the gun dropped away from Sage's head. I worked on getting my own control back. Focusing on a gentle centre in a storm of fury. I set aside the panic. Closing my eyes, I let my limbs fall loose and tilted my head back. A mental picture formed in my mind, the air clear, the weather fine, birds in the sky. I relaxed. The tension eased. Sage sighed. Jackson let out the breath he had been holding. Abraham smiled, but it was more like a sneer. He had felt it too.

"You can read people's feelings and you can influence them, too. That is a useful skill. Your potential is wasted with Sawyer. I wonder if he has tested your genetic makeup." It was almost as if Abraham was talking to himself.

I did not say anything. The exhaustion was a stone in my stomach, or more like a giant boulder. As I slumped in the chair, the relaxation in the room turned into a crushing fatigue. Abraham sighed this time and rubbed his temple, feeling its weight. Like my friends, he was getting more perceptive to the subtle changes I could make.

"Nova, a bit of advice. Your compassion for your friends makes you weak."

I did not reply, but I heard Jackson let out his breath in a hiss. Abraham ignored him.

"Thank you for visiting with me, my young friends. I hope we can spend time together again, soon."

Abraham nodded to a follower, who cut the handcuffs from Jackson's wrists. After rubbing his arms, Jackson reached for my hand, supporting me, sending me his courage. He scowled at Abraham.

"I will admit that you have very loyal friends, Nova. I like them." Abraham chuckled.

It was an unnerving sound. We were dismissed and the coffee had not even come.

Sawyer and the others were back by the time we returned to the apartment. Sawyer was furious with Abraham, but there was nothing he could do.

"The trouble is I'm not sure he'll leave you alone now."

"Maybe we should get out of here." Sage's normal buoyancy had been knocked off balance by the whole episode.

"You might be able to, but I doubt he'll let Nova go. I don't know that you'd be any better off anywhere else," said Sawyer. "Sometimes the safest place is right under the nose of the enemy."

"Guys, I'm so sorry. You're in this because of me," I groaned.

"Nova, we'd probably be dead already, if not for you. I mean look at this world." Luca spoke from the heart but lightened his comment with a chuckle.

"It's all a bit much, isn't it? We're teenagers, we should just be doing stupid fun things," I said.

"I promise we'll do lots of stupid fun things, as soon as all this is over." Jackson spoke seriously.

"Yeah, lots and lots of stupid fun things." Sage's optimism had returned.

"How stupid?"

"Very! And very fun!"

We all laughed. I loved these guys.

"Sawyer, what did he mean about you testing my genetic makeup?" I caught Sawyer before he left.

"Well, they are doing research at Melbourne University on violent offenders and what causes the aggression. That includes people's genetic makeup. Abraham has put up the money and is taking a keen interest," Sawyer explained. "I don't really trust his motivations, but we do have to work out how to stop the violence. The prisons are overflowing. The police have all but given up. People are isolated but the violence continues behind closed doors. You've seen how busy the hospitals are."

"So how are they doing the research?"

"They test violent offenders and then a control group of people who haven't shown any aggressive tendencies. Genetics, blood, brain waves, looking for patterns."

"Have they found anything?"

"Well, they know how to stimulate the anger but not how to stop it. They are looking at the warrior gene, various enzymes and hormones, parts of the brain. Nothing they didn't already know and nothing that has shown how it can be controlled."

"Why did Abe wonder if you had tested me?"

"I guess because there might be something in your genetics that can help us understand how to reverse the anger in people. Like the opposite of a warrior gene. I was a little reluctant to have people know about you, or even me, but I suppose it would be good to include you in their sample base.

Me too." Sawyer turned thoughtful. "What if I take you out and we have a look?"

"Sure, it sounds interesting."

"What's up?" Jackson asked me later. "You're doing that thing you do when you're trying to avoid saying something."

"What thing?"

"You bite your bottom lip. To stop yourself from speaking."

He was right, I was biting my bottom lip. "I do not." I pouted to prevent myself doing it again.

He shrugged and just waited.

"Do you ever think that coming to Melbourne wasn't our best idea? I mean is all this too intense for you sometimes?" I asked eventually.

After our run in with Abraham, it was my turn for doubts.

"What do you mean? Abe? Melbourne? Or being with you?"

"All of it, I guess. The danger. But my emotional overload as well."

"You call it danger, all I hear is adventure, excitement." His tone was flippant.

"But am I too intense?" I needed serious reassurance.

"The more intense you are the better." Jackson kissed my head and wrapped his arms around me. His hips thrust against mine suggestively. "I'm right where I want to be."

"That's not what I mean."

"Look, we tried the safe thing. We stayed isolated at the beach house, and it was still dangerous. And people we loved still died. At least here, we are all making a difference. Yeah, it is dangerous and intense, but so is everywhere. Here, you are learning from Sawyer, I'm helping at the hospital. We don't have to do our VCE exams and we're getting paid."

"That's very glass half full of you."

"I'm a glass half full kind of guy."

I smiled, enjoying his warmth, his strength. My stomach was still churning though, and he could tell.

"This is about Coop, isn't it?" His voice was gentle. "Nova, I'm not him."

"I know." I shrugged.

"He's a jerk. We might be twins, but we are very different." Jackson held me at arm's length and looked into my eyes. I could see his sincerity. "I like flying so close to the sun. With you."

"You say that now, but it's exhausting being around me. I exhaust me."

"Nova, being around you is inspiring, it's magical."

"And the danger we're in? Isn't that exhausting?"

"Darlin'," he drawled, "danger is my middle name!"

He winked at me, playful and deliberate. I gave him a good-natured punch, but I could feel the truth in him.

"Nova, you are extraordinary."

"What if I just want to be ordinary?" It came out in a sigh.

"Too late," said Jackson.

He ran his finger down my nose, over my lips, and below my chin, to lift my mouth to his. His love was a calming wind, gently carrying me along with it.

The next day Sage had a deep and meaningful with me.

"Nova, you know it's okay if you care more about Jack than you did about Cooper. You don't owe Coop anything and he wasn't always the best of boyfriends."

I knew she was referring to Imogen. She had never really forgiven him.

"Has Jack said something to you?"

"He just asked me if I thought you cared as much for him as you did for Coop."

"What did you say?"

"I said, I thought you did, but he'd have to ask you." She shrugged.

"Sage, I don't know. You can't just stop loving someone."

"Nova, you love everyone, and that's great. But you can move on, love someone else, like Jack, and let Coop be in the past. A friend, but not someone you're in love with."

"You make it sound easy. It's not." My head was getting cloudier by the minute.

"Jack is very much in love with you, and he's really grown on me. Are you hanging on to a love with Coop that's in the past? He's not here; he couldn't hack it."

"Maybe." I shrugged. "So, am I hanging on to Coop?"

"Jack thinks you are." She gave me a sympathetic smile.

"Now, I'm more confused than ever." I shook my head, trying to clear it.

Sage laughed. "Stop trying to think your way through it, just feel your way. Maybe we just live in the moment and stop over analysing."

I nodded vigorously. "Agreed."

"Stick together?"

"Like glue." That was never in any doubt.

29

We all wanted to go to the Melbourne University research laboratory. It meant going through a checkpoint, passing out of Abraham City. When we pulled up and passed over our IDs, I was singled out. They would not let me through, Abraham's orders. Sawyer's fury was hot and a little scary. I rarely felt a negative emotion from him. He made a phone call and although we could not hear him, it was clear he was having words with Abraham.

"This won't happen again." Sawyer assured me, returning to his seat and his normally well-controlled emotional state. "He can't keep you here. He is playing games. We have given him a lot of leeway to avoid blood-shed, but this is taking things too far."

We went through the checkpoint with no further hassles.

The research laboratory was all white and glass. White-coated scientists moved in an ordered chaos, typing into computers, and peering into microscopes. Machines handled hundreds of test tubes, turning them, sorting them, labelling them. The scientists examined, assessed, and documented, with a soft hum of machinery in the background. It felt like we were breathing artificial air as there was a total absence of smell. Some people sat in chairs, waiting to be tested. Jackson was fascinated. Sage, Luca, and I were overwhelmed. I was pleased that I did not see any animals in cages.

We were met by Sidney, one of the white-coated scientists. She smiled at us in the aloof, distant way that adults do with annoying children. Her serious face was devoid of any make-up and glasses perched on her nose. In contrast to her mask of professionalism, I could see a wrist tattoo of the Aboriginal flag peeking out from the sleeve of her coat and when combined with the tiny gold earring cuffs wrapped around her left ear and the green streak running through her loose dark curly hair, I knew she had some personality.

With a precise manner, she led us on a tour, moving purposefully from room to room. One area was for the samples sent from the test subjects in prison. These were the most aggressive perpetrators of violent crime. Blood work, genetic testing and various neurotransmitter test samples were sent to this laboratory for reviewing. Other test subjects came in off the street, recommended through the hospitals and medical centres. They were less violent but had still been exhibiting uncharacteristic episodes of aggression.

"Do you know what happens in our bodies to produce anger?" Sidney sounded like a teacher. "The prefrontal cortex is the thinking part of our brain, for logic and judgement. The emotional part of the brain is the limbic system. When we are experiencing and expressing anger, we are not using the cortex, but the limbic system. Make sense?"

We nodded. It felt like being in a classroom again, and it was kind of nice.

"Emotions begin inside the amygdala. That is the part of the brain responsible for identifying threats and sending out an alarm if we need to take steps to protect ourselves. It is responsible for our fight-or-flight reactions. If the amygdala considers a threat to be significant, it gets us reacting before the cortex, our thinking and judgement, can influence our actions. This means we act before we properly think through the consequences. When the amygdala overrides the cortex and goes straight to the emotional limbic system, it's called amygdala hijacking. This is not an excuse for aggression, because we can and do control our anger. Well, usually."

Sidney smiled at our attentive faces.

"When the amygdala is hijacked, neurotransmitter chemicals are released. These cause a burst of energy which lasts for a short time, normally, but much longer in our aggressive subjects, and it allows us to take protective action. Our muscles tense up, our heart rate accelerates, our blood pressure rises, and our rate of breathing increases. Our attention is focused on the threat. Other brain neurotransmitters and hormones are released too, including adrenaline. We are ready to fight."

Sidney paused, while punching a code into a security keypad to take us into another lab. There were strange pink samples in glass jars. I did not even want to know what they were. Nausea pitched across my stomach.

"So, if someone is coming at you, you get ready to defend yourself." Jackson was our science nerd.

"Exactly. But what we are seeing in the test subjects is emotions raging out of control. Normally the prefrontal cortex keeps our emotions in proportion, switches them off after the threat is gone." Sidney tapped her forehead.

We reached an empty consultation room with beds and machines. Sidney motioned for us to sit on the beds and continued her lesson.

"Anger has a wind-down phase. We start to relax when the threat disappears, even if that takes hours. It can take 20 minutes for a person who has experienced an angry state of arousal to calm, and move from functioning in the emotional area, to the thinking area of the brain. Our subjects are finding it more difficult to calm down, and it is taking much, much longer. Their anger arousal often lasts days, and because the aroused state lowers our anger threshold, it is easier to get angry and violent again. So, we are seeing people get excessively angry in response to minor irritations that normally would not bother them. Their ability to concentrate, think logically and remember things is also adversely affected."

Sidney paused, reaching into cupboards for sample jars, before continuing.

"Serotonin plays a key role in regulating anger and aggression. Low cerebrospinal fluid concentrations of serotonin are a marker and predictor of aggressive behaviour. Our aggressive test subjects are consistently low in serotonin and extremely high in cortisol. Too much cortisol will decrease serotonin, which makes you feel anger and pain more easily, as well as increasing aggressive behaviour. Elevated cortisol also causes a loss of neurons in the prefrontal cortex which prevents you from using your best judgement or making good decisions."

Jackson was nodding intently. I could almost see the cogs moving in his brain. We all wanted an explanation for what was causing this violence.

"So, what about the whole genetic thing. Is there really a warrior gene? Is that what is hijacking the amygdala and inhibiting the serotonin?" asked Jackson.

Sidney gave a half smile. "What have you heard?"

We looked to Jackson to speak for us all. He shrugged.

"They have been testing violent offenders and gang members in the US, and they all have the warrior gene. It means you are predisposed to violence." Jackson's face was earnest. "But that doesn't explain, even if people have this gene, why have they turned so violent, all of a sudden."

"Yeah, exactly. The warrior gene is like the gay gene or the alcoholism gene." Sidney's forehead creased in a frown. "It makes for good media stories but not scientific proof. The warrior gene occurs in about 30 percent of the population. Since the early 1990s, several studies have reported a link between violent aggression and a gene on the X chromosome that encodes for an enzyme called monoamine oxidase A or MAOA. This enzyme does regulate the function of dopamine, serotonin, and noradrenaline, which can cause anger."

Jackson nodded along with her.

"But the research is very unreliable. They have examined specific population groups and compared gender and there is no significant statistical difference between carriers and non-carriers reacting aggressively to stimuli. People get angry with and without the warrior gene."

Jackson looked about to protest, but Sidney held up her hand.

"Yes, there does seem to be a predominance of carriers amongst the samples we are testing here, and these offenders are usually carrying the warrior gene. But we do not have reliable past studies to indicate whether that has always been the case in violent offenders. And, as you said, we still do not know why the violence has escalated recently. In the past, people carrying the warrior gene were not automatically aggressive and violent, any more than people not carrying the gene. We also do not have enough evidence of the smaller incidents, the average person who has just had an angry outburst, which was a reaction more aggressive than normal for them. We don't know if they are carrying the warrior gene."

"What about synthetic biology or something artificial that has set off the warrior gene?" Jackson asked.

Sidney huffed and I caught a twinge of frustration. "Don't start on the conspiracy theories. We can artificially produce the enzyme that regulates dopamine, serotonin, and noradrenaline, but to produce the widespread violence we have seen, it would have had to have been given to people all around the world and I cannot see how that could have happened. It was not mobile phones or vaccines."

She shook her head when Jackson looked like he was about to ask another question.

"Come on, let's get you kids prepped for some tests."

She ran us through a complete physical as well as neurotransmitter and genetic testing. We were jabbed and poked, examined and measured, told to breath in, breath out, relax and tense. Samples were taken of our blood, hair, urine, and skin. It was intrusive, and I tried to breathe deeply, slowly, and not bring up my breakfast. Although, I had not said anything about being an empath, I was wondering if Sidney might find out that I possessed a special gene, as Abraham had hinted.

"Nova, was your father Harley Wilson?" Sidney asked quietly, as she was taking my blood.

"Yeah. Did you know him?" My mouth was suddenly dry.

"Not personally, but he was very well respected in the genetic engineering field. I wish he were here to help with all this."

"Yeah, me too." I choked a little on the words and Sidney's eyes softened.

"I'm so sorry about what happened."

"Yeah, thanks," I said. "Do you know what he was researching before he died?"

"I believe it was almost like the opposite of the warrior gene. He was looking for the specific gene that carries empathy."

This time, I really did choke and ended up in a coughing fit. I felt Jackson and Sage watching me, wondering what was happening. I would tell them later.

When Sidney led us out through the security doors, I was more aware of the armed guards and CCTV monitors. It was a high security laboratory.

The science was interesting but also made for a heavy day. I wondered if the answer to the anger was in the warrior gene. It was frustrating that we were no closer to an explanation, nor a solution. None of this explained what was different about me either. My father must have been researching me, but he had never even told me anything about me being an empath. I wondered if he had been an empath too, or my mother.

My head was swimming with questions that could not be answered, and my heart was heavy with the loss of my father all over again.

30

The visit to the research laboratory had just raised more questions. It felt like we took one step forward and two steps back. Violence and aggression had become so much a part of our lives. Day after day, I was tired, emotionally drained, and physically exhausted. I envied people that did not connect with the pain they saw every day; it was easier for them, safer.

Sawyer stepped up the practice we had been doing, to help me with controlling my own emotions and influencing others. We were experimenting with being able to individualise my impact, using my skills to direct my influence at specific people.

"People will push hate, anger, and fear at you, and it slows you down, confuses you. It is like having too many programs open on your computer. Empty your mind, so you are back in control, back up to full capacity. Use mindfulness or mental calmness. That will keep you in control. When you feel afraid or distracted, use mindfulness. Then reach out to who you want. Choose who you will influence."

I knew Sawyer had Abraham in mind when he spoke about me influencing a specific person. It was as much for my own safety as it was to help him in his negotiations.

"I'm flat out trying to keep myself calm, let alone Abe."

"He is a particularly resistant person, and as he now has a sense of what you can do, he is even more resistant. You are strong but you can improve. Practise on your friends. They know you too, so will be more resistant to your influence."

"But what difference is all this really making in the whole scheme of things?"

"No one can change the world with a single stroke, Nova, but each action we take helps. Every time you treat someone with kindness and take away their anger or pain you make a difference in the world; you brighten up the darkness."

Sawyer also wanted me to broaden my range, beyond the people in my proximity.

"Nova, I've been checking the statistics. You have left an emotional footprint, in your hometown and at the beach community. There is still less aggression and violence in those communities, compared to similar ones close by, even after you have left there."

"Really?" I was proud of that. "But I didn't do that intentionally."

"I know, but it shows your strength. You have been gifted."

"Huh! Sometimes I'm not sure if it's a gift or a burden."

"It's both, I guess. But think of it as more of a gift, and less of a burden."

I wanted to heal, to lighten the dark. I decided to rope in Jackson as a test dummy.

"Hey, Lewis. Can you do me a favour? Can I practise my empathic skills on you?"

He grabbed me by the waist, pulling me in against his chest. "Wilson, you had me at 'hey'." A small teasing smile flittered across his face.

"Okay. I am going to try and send you a feeling and then change that feeling. Ready?"

"I was born ready." Jackson's dark brown eyes twinkled at me.

I let my passion burn, a hot intensity. Something stirred in him; it took over his thinking. Everything was banished into the far recesses of his mind, except me. The only thing that mattered was touching me, kissing my mouth. We crashed together, soaring into a timeless existence. I broke away from the kiss, shook my head to clear it and switched my emotions to contentment. A warm blanket, a good book. But I did not count on Jackson's own feelings.

"Damn, Nova. You cannot just turn that off. I want it back."

He moved his body against mine and I felt his frustration. It was a pain in my side. When I stepped away, he pulled me closer. I calmed, he resisted. I slowed my breathing. Serenity, blue sky, fluffy clouds. He resisted.

"Jack, relax. You are making this too hard."

"You shouldn't have started like that. I'm not letting it go."

He ran his hands up my arms and the electricity sparked. I felt his need to kiss me. It was all-encompassing. Note to self, cannot start with passion when practicing on Jackson; he was too strong. I smiled a secret smile and let his emotions flow. We surrendered to each other, kissing with a fervent urgent need. I would practise some other time.

Sawyer had been busy, and some positive changes had been made throughout all of Melbourne. Police officers that were not on Abraham's payroll, nor Frank Murphy's, were now scattered throughout the force. The army had also been brought in to help provide protection to the various government services that had been re-opened. The courts were functioning, with protection supplied for judges and barristers. State emergency services were responding to calls, with additional security support. Social welfare services were given security officers of their own. Trains, buses, and trams were running again and regularly patrolled. The Chief Health Officer was liaising with hospitals and health services to ensure a safer, more efficient response to violence-related injuries.

In Abraham City, Abraham still held a lot of power and was reluctant to let go, but there had been a gradual shift of control to the right people. I had returned to the negotiation sessions and practised my emotional control with Abraham and his followers. Sawyer was working to open the border between Abraham City and Murphy's area, but Abraham wanted to keep his little territory. He hated Frank Murphy.

"I can control who comes in and out." Abraham's voice was cold and unyielding. "We don't want just anyone in Abraham City. We have far less violence and crime than him."

"Abe, it's all Melbourne. It can't stay divided like this." Sawyer argued with him carefully. "We need access to the goods and service outside these eastern suburbs. Besides there is still crime and violence here; it's just being instigated by you." The last part was said quietly, under his breath.

Abraham heard it and glared at Sawyer.

"Abe, let's call it a day," Sawyer said calmly, re-establishing the peace.

Abraham sighed with annoyance, but there was no anger, thanks to the efforts Sawyer and I made. "Nova, it's a pleasure as always." He made a point of ignoring Sawyer.

With a flick of his hand, we were dismissed.

The following morning red roses were delivered for me, from Abraham. My favourite, but not when they came from him. I gave them to Sage to take into the hospital. He sent another bunch the following morning, with a note.

"I'm disappointed that you gave away the roses. I hope you won't do it again, Abe." I read aloud. "How did he know?"

I ran my eyes around the walls and ceiling, as if expecting to see cameras.

"He's creepy." Sage shivered.

Jackson was furious. He took the roses from me, tossed them into the bin, and held up his middle finger to no one. The obscene hand gesture was a clear challenge and I looked around nervously.

The following day, I got home from work and dropped into a chair, shattered. Jackson sat across from me, with a solemn face and a handgun grasped tightly in his lap. He squinted his eyes as he let the magazine clip out. Bullets fell into his hand, but he quickly put them back in. He turned the gun in his hand as if it was a precious object. I knew that Jet and Finn had been teaching the boys some self-defence, but I had not realised that it had progressed to handling guns.

"You're holding a gun and loading real bullets. Do you even know how to use that thing? What the hell?" My voice was raised, and irritation bubbled in my throat.

"Nova, deal with it. I am carrying a gun. I know how to use it. I don't need your permission." Jackson's mouth was a thin line.

"What? So, you actually plan to shoot it? You could kill someone."

"I don't plan to do anything. I hope I never have to use it. But if there was a life-or-death situation, if your life or mine was threatened, then yes, I probably would use it, for protection." Jackson's voice had also risen, and I felt his stubbornness pushing at me.

"You work at the hospital. You want to be a doctor, to save lives, and you are talking about killing someone." I was still agitated, and my tone was harsh and challenging.

"I'm not, you are. You are blowing this way out of proportion. I'm carrying a gun, for our protection. End of story." Jackson was solid in his obstinacy, but his voice was calm.

I glared at him. He smiled sweetly in return, showing much better control of his emotions than me.

"We can't just rely on your superpowers. What if your magic doesn't work?" His grin was cheeky now, and I knew he was trying to distract me, lighten the mood.

"Why do you do that?" I frowned, even more annoyed at being dismissed so quickly.

"Do what?" he asked calmly.

"Avoid the issue with humour." I let my frustration flow into him.

He flinched. "Okay, Dr Phil."

"Like that."

"Look, Nova, it's my job to protect you. And I don't have any special gifts. I might need a gun to do it." His voice was serious.

I shook my head. "It's not your job. I can look after myself."

Jackson narrowed his eyes, and I felt his stubborn pride. "What if I want to look after you? I let you look after me, with your powers."

"Stop it, I don't have powers."

Frustration and annoyance rolled through my body and pulsed between us.

"I'm going to carry a gun. And I will do my best to protect you, no matter what. Especially from Abe." Jackson stood firm.

I suddenly realised this was all because of the roses. Jackson felt helpless against the power that Abraham wielded.

"I want us both to look after each other," I said, in a more reasonable tone. "But a gun, Jack. Don't I get a say in that?"

"No, you don't."

Although I stayed silent, I continued to let my disapproval jab at his stubborn wall. He pulled his shoulders back and sat up a little straighter.

"Nova, are we going to be okay about this? You and me?" I could feel his unease.

"Jack, I hate guns. A gun killed my father."

His sympathy was like a gentle hug, but it did not shift his conviction. "I know, and I'm sorry. But this is different." He looked at me expectantly, as obstinate as ever.

"You are completely impossible." I sighed in resignation.

His eyes smouldered while he waited.

"Yes, we are okay." I finally gave in, and his relief left a sweet taste in my mouth.

But it was not fair. Sure, we had matured in giant strides since the beginning of the year, but we were barely young adults and certainly not soldiers.

Jackson was studying his computer screen, intent and oblivious, when I entered the room, a few days later.

"Hey, Lewis," I said.

He slammed the laptop shut. The flash of guilt on his face was quickly replaced by an innocent smile. It didn't matter, as I could sense his discomfort. He was trying to hide something from me.

"Hey, Wilson."

"What are you doing?"

"Nothing."

"What were you looking at?"

"Nothing." A deep red colour rose in his cheeks.

"Well, it was clearly something."

"I'd rather not say."

"Now, I really want to know." I thought for a moment then asked reluctantly. "Were you looking up porn?" It was all I could think of to explain his guilt.

"No!" He was hurt.

"What then?"

"Nothing."

"Jack, show me."

The screen showed the components of an improvised explosive device. It was a how-to for making a homemade bomb.

"What the hell? I almost wish it were porn."

"Really?" He raised his eyebrows and chuckled.

"No," I said firmly. "But you can't make a bomb."

"I'm just exploring ideas. We might need a diversion to get out of town one day."

I knew it was about him feeling powerless against Abraham, again. The gun was one thing, but homemade bombs was another level.

"You can't blow something up. You might hurt someone."

"Nova, it's either that or porn."

"That's not funny."

"It's kind of funny." His face beamed with a cheeky grin. I shook my head.

"Come here, beautiful." Jackson hooked his fingers through the belt loops at the back of my jeans, pulled me in against his body, and rested his chin on my head. "I will do whatever it takes to protect you." There was a clash of steel behind his words.

"We would be as bad as him."

"Nova, you are being naive. It's not that simple." I felt his stubbornness but met it with mine.

"Jack, we don't hurt people. We are here to help."

He shrugged but stayed silent.

"Jack this one is non-negotiable for me. No bombs." I pushed harder against that stubborn wall.

He looked into my eyes, and I made sure he felt my sincerity.

"Okay," he said at last.

"Promise."

"Okay. I promise." He was not happy about it, but he meant it.

No more bomb research. The world was frightening enough.

We were never far from danger, despite the protection of Sawyer and the DOVE Special Forces detail. It had become part of life.

Sage, Luca, Jackson, and I stumbled on them by accident, two men looting the hardware shop. Tools made useful weapons. They did not just have hammers and picks though, they had guns. We were wanting some paint, to freshen up the apartment. A simple trip to the local store became a fight for survival. They released a warning shot above our heads when we appeared at the shop door. The blast was loud and the wood above the doorway splintered with the impact of the bullet. We ducked and backed out of the shop, taking cover behind some industrial bins. I felt their anger. It was blind, without reason.

"The next one won't miss," a voice spat from the other side of the shop.

We needed to get to safety. The paint would have to wait.

"Over there, see that lane." Luca pointed across the road. "Hopefully, they won't follow."

I nodded, Sage too. Our fear was a sour scent and clogged my nose and throat. My heart was racing.

"I'll distract them, you run," Jackson was rummaging in his backpack.

His eyes were hard and determined, his gun was gripped tightly in his hand. He carried it everywhere now, tucked into his pants or his jacket. With a quick look over the rim of the bin, he fired off a shot. I hoped he wasn't aiming at anyone. Sage and I took off. We made it to the lane and stopped, to wait on Luca and Jackson. I heard what sounded like two small explosions.

"Hang on, Jack's coming." Luca appeared behind us, his gun in his hand.

Then Jackson arrived, as if on cue, his backpack dangling from one shoulder. His courage was a solid rock beneath my feet.

"What was that noise? Was it an explosion?" I asked.

"Cool, hey?"

"Jack, you promised, no bombs."

"Nova, it was Mentos in a Coke bottle. You shake it up till it explodes out the top." He gave me a cocky grin.

"Oh." I gave him a weak smile.

"Come on, they might still follow us." Luca's voice was urgent.

At the other end of the lane, Luca waved at us to fall in behind him. He slipped around the corner. We waited, expecting him to reappear. Jackson stuck his head out to see, and then held his hands up in surrender.

"Got ya!" A man in black stepped out holding an automatic rifle.

They were the two men from the hardware store, and they were angry that we had disturbed them. Jackson and Luca were disarmed, quickly and efficiently. Jackson's mouth tightened into a flat line. Luca was watching the men through narrowed eyes.

"Nova?" I knew Jackson was asking if I could do anything.

A cold anger burned through my body like dry ice. They saw us as a threat, but more than that, they liked the violence, the power. I pushed at the anger with peace and tranquillity. I let happy memories pass through my mind and kept my breathing calm.

Bleak grey eyes, framed in the detached face of a killer, watched me warily. His experienced hands were steady on his rifle. Cords of muscle knotted across his neck and chest, straining the buttons of his black shirt. His friend's face was stern, yet indifferent as he swung his rifle to his shoulder, whistling tunelessly. Lean and lanky, this one did not have the look of a fighter, but his nonchalance made him seem the more dangerous of the two.

Sage shrank behind Luca, and I could smell her fear. Sweat trickled down the back of my neck. I directed all my efforts on the two men in front of me, focusing on calming the anger and the commotion I felt, smoothing it to make soft music. Deep slow breaths and quiet meditation. I created a mental picture of us walking away, no one being harmed.

I felt it take effect, with a softening of the anger. "Please, just let us go," I said.

The guy in black lowered his rifle. "They're not really worth the effort."

"Go on then, get out of here." The other man had already started to turn away.

We did not need to be told again. The relief from my friends flooded my body.

"Hey!" The guy in black called to us. "That was a cool trick with the bottle."

Jackson raised his hand in salute, but we kept walking, and broke into a run at the next corner.

Back at the apartment, I collapsed, drained, and relieved.

"Nova, I don't know how you do it," said Luca. "But thank you. That was freaking scary." He hugged me, trembling in appreciation and relief.

It still felt like one step forward, but two steps back.

31

The days of the week had ceased to have meaning. With no school, no specific holiday breaks, one flowed into the next. It was hard remembering what day it was, even what month it was. September came with a promise of spring. Warmer days to entice the flowers, bring new life. I hoped it was a pledge of hope, of a brighter future.

When I was not with Sawyer, I shared my time between the hospital with the children, and the university research laboratory, helping Sidney. She gave me mostly administrative jobs to do but at least it was something. Our test results had come back. I did not have the warrior gene and nor did Jackson, Sage, or Luca. I wondered about Finn, Jet and Rayna. They had chosen a career that can be characterised by control and discipline, but also violence and aggression. I had become especially close with Finn, who escorted me everywhere now, my own protection detail. Like Jackson, Sawyer worried about the roses and the attention I got from Abraham.

September not only brought warmer spring days, but also my birthday. I was finally turning eighteen, the last of my friends to reach this milestone. Legally I could now drink alcohol, vote, and I would receive the trust fund my father had left for me, to manage myself. With the world in its current state, a celebration was not possible, but Sage had insisted on making a cake. We had invited Sawyer, Finn, Jet and Rayna for supper.

Although internet and phone outages were now commonplace, I was lucky for my birthday to receive a truckload of messages. I devoured the news from home and shared it with Sage.

"Mia's mother has not gone back to work. She is at home with Mia and Alice. Mia has a part-time job in the supermarket, and Alice is doing a lot better. She's a big support to their mum. Ava says she is feeling okay, but Mia says she's like a robot. She functions but only just. Imogen has a serious boyfriend, and it's not Cooper." I paused to smile at that. "Cooper is helping his dad in the surgery. He sends his love." I paused again and a wave of soft, lulling affection flooded my heart. "But there is still a lot of violence, and no one goes out unless they have to."

While I was reviewing my messages there was a knock at the door. It was Finn. When in his army fatigues, Finn was clearly a solider. As part of Australia's Special Forces elite, he had been tasked with the most difficult missions in Afghanistan, and I sensed a hidden pocket of darkness that suggested he had taken lives in the line of duty. With the current onslaught of violence domestically, he could have been bored with this protection detail. Nevertheless, his cheery smile and sense of humour was always present. He was tall, muscular, and moved gracefully, with reflexes as quick as lightning. Today he was in civvies and the excitement spun off him.

"Hi guys! I know we are supposed to be coming by for cake later, but I'm just wondering if you are up for something different? Feel like going out?" Finn asked.

We all looked at him, our curiosity peaked. We didn't go out much.

"It's UFC, tonight."

I felt a surge of delight from Jackson and Luca, and it bubbled in Finn like a boy with a new toy.

"What's UFC?" I asked.

"Ultimate Fighting Championship."

"A movie?" I had not been to a movie in nine months.

"No." I sensed Jackson's hesitation. "A fight competition."

"Real fighting?" Sage asked.

"Yeah." Jackson was sheepish.

Their adrenaline had reached an all-time high.

"Come on, Nova, Sage. We never know when it's going to be on, until the last minute. They send out a text." Finn's voice was imploring. "And it's tonight. We're just going to watch."

He shook his heads at the boys, whose faces fell. I looked between them. Sage shrugged her shoulders at me. She was in the dark too.

"What is going on?" I asked.

"There's a UFC competition just outside Abraham City. Luca and Jack are going to fight with us. But not tonight. Tonight, is just reconnaissance. We are trying to see what is going on behind the scenes. We think Abe runs it and is recruiting from the fighters. We're not sure how voluntary that is."

I looked at Sage, who nodded in resignation.

"It's a night out. We can still have the cake when we get back." Finn was not giving up. "It'll be safe. We'll all be there. Well, except Swayer, because we do not want Abe to get suspicious. I reckon you might even find it exciting, Nova. I'm sure there is a fighter in you."

Luca and Jackson were already fully committed, and their excitement swept me up in the tide. "Okay sure." I laughed.

Abraham City was relatively safe, run by a gangster, but still safe in comparison to the violence that raged unchecked outside its limits. Especially at night. As we crossed through the checkpoint, we were in a no-man's land between Abraham City and Frank Murphy's turf, an area left largely unpatrolled by the police. I could immediately taste the anger and aggression, bitter and acidic in my mouth. Dark, grimy streets hinted at dangers, hidden and deadly.

UFC was held in an old gym and the building had seen better days. The corrugated walls were dented and rusty. Bullet holes formed bizarre patterns like a child's dot paintings. Stepping inside was walking into another world. It reeked of sweat and blood. There were the squelching sounds of flesh hitting flesh from the fighters, and the roar of crowd approval. The fighting was a mix of full-contact combat, martial arts, and wrestling. The UFC cage was an octagonal structure, contained within a metal chain-link fence. Foam padding covered the top. Two entry-exit gates stood opposite each other. It looked almost medieval, and I checked to see if there were bloody heads on pikes. We sat on the plastic seats.

"They have banned biting and eye-gouging, hair pulling, head-butting, groin strikes, throat strikes and fish-hooking." Jackson clarified with enthusiasm.

"Well, that's good." My sarcasm went over his head.

The men fought in shorts, no shirt, no shoes. The women wore crop tops. In the first fight, the winner had his opponent on the canvas seconds into the bout. He landed a few strikes to the head of his grounded opponent, and the referee stopped the match. The audience cheered wildly. The second fight ended with a knockout.

As I absorbed the emotional climate, I felt like a volcano, with hot, boiling magma almost ready to blow. It was the excitement, the fear, and the anger. And just like a volcanic eruption, the aggression in these fighters could kill. That possibility was all around me. The risk of a fatal injury was very real every time a fighter entered the cage. It was primitive. It was instinctive. It was bloodthirsty. I was nauseous.

By the end of the night, I felt like I had been continually poked with a hot branding iron. We had the birthday cake, but I was depleted and only managed some quiet conversation. Jackson on the other hand was still keyed up with excitement. He and Luca were practically dancing around the apartment and could not stop talking about UFC.

"It may be brutal, but it's also brilliant."

"Did you see that guy who kept jabbing with his right, then he fired a cross with his left and a fast head kick? It completely stuffed the other guy's rhythm."

Sage and I were quiet. I knew she didn't like fighting, but the excitement in the atmosphere had reached her as well. The violence we had witnessed hardly seemed unusual anymore.

Finn turned up again the following night. He was jumping out of his skin with excitement. UFC was on again and it was time for the *Justice League* juniors to have their first fight. That meant Jackson and Luca. Finn, Jet and Rayna would fight another night. Swayer once again decided to stay home, worried his presence would put Abraham on alert. Finn wanted to find out more about Abraham's recruitment methods.

Finn's blue eyes turned on me apologetically, while the boys raced to get ready.

I shrugged. "So, the first rule of fight club is that you never know about it until the last minute."

Finn laughed, but Sage grunted in acknowledgement.

Like last time, I felt like I was in a gladiator's arena. The gym was a chamber of toxic testosterone. Brutality and blood, to the sounds of applause. Jackson and Luca went out the back to get ready.

"Good luck," Sage and I called after them.

I felt the tension and concern in her tone, reflecting my own fear.

"Finn, keep them safe please," I implored quietly.

"Nova, they're both good fighters. They'll be fine."

I nodded, only slightly reassured. Finn and Jet were the corner-men, and I knew they could signal defeat for their own fighters if they believed it was unsafe to continue. I perched on the edge of the uncomfortable plastic chair and felt the butterflies in my stomach crippled over in pain.

Jackson was up first. He was cold and focused and I couldn't sense any fear, just adrenaline. He flexed his hands, adjusting to his open-fingered padded gloves. A mouthguard turned his smile into a snarl. My jaw tightened as I clenched my teeth.

All too quickly the battle began. A fist slammed into Jackson's face while he sunk a punch into his opponent's stomach. Blood pooled in his mouth. He spat, crimson on the canvas, while I gagged. They stumbled apart, briefly, catching their breath, before diving back at each other. Jackson threw himself forward with a growl, changing direction at the last minute. I felt his determination as he leapt and kicked high, straight to the nose. There was a blunt crack and blood leaked from both nostrils of his opponent. Pain and anger erupted as he repaid the kick by punching Jackson's jaw. His full body weight was behind the blow, and I felt it, like being hit by a train. The battering continued until Jackson fell to the floor. His chest rose and sank, struggling with each shallow breath. A wild cheer rose from the audience. My tongue felt like it was soaked in blood. The referee called the match. His opponent had won.

Jackson, bruised and winded, struggled into the corner. I felt like a steamroller had flattened me, but the relief was palpable.

"I could have kept going." I sensed Jackson's disappointment and shook my head in disbelief.

"It's your first fight," Jet said. "It's a good result."

"Maybe the ref wants to make sure you come back for a second." Finn patted Jackson's shoulder.

Luca was up next, and Sage's anxiety was a crippling onslaught to my senses. One elbow in the wrong place could prove fatal, a kick could snap a neck. Luca faced repeated jabs; his opponent's extended arm was a battering ram. He countered with overhand punches, like baseball pitches. Pivoting, he thrust his hip forward, kicking with maximum force. It was a powerful strike to the stomach. His opponent recovered. He moved forward, clasped his hands behind Luca's thighs and brought him down. The fight ended in a technical knockout, when the referee decided Luca could not continue. He was as disappointed as Jackson.

We were waiting on the boys to return from the change rooms, when Abraham appeared out of the dim light and sat next to me.

"Nova, it's time for the female junior bouts. Your turn. I've waited to see you."

"I can't fight." I shrank into myself, horrified at the idea.

"Anyone can fight. Your friends did. Theo, bring out Rob's girl. Nova is getting in the ring." Abraham spoke to one of his followers.

"She hasn't had any training." Rayna was firm but polite, aware of Abraham's status. "It would be better if she had some coaching first. Let me work with her for a few weeks."

"Nonsense. Let's just make this a virgin bout."

"I really can't fight." The dismay was clear in my voice.

"You can and you will."

I shook my head, just one movement. Abraham's eyes narrowed.

"Well then, it seems we need to negotiate." He loaded the last word with sarcasm. "Your friends are extremely interested in joining my followers. They have been asking a lot of questions. I have them out the back. I just might recruit them after all. They handled themselves well in the ring."

Finn appeared, flanked by some of Abraham's followers. He came to my side and nodded gravely, confirming that Abraham was indeed holding Luca and Jackson out the back. Jet was probably with them, but I knew that Abraham had absolute power over his gang, and I did not want to test his authority. Cold shivers ran down my spine, my stomach twisted and pitched.

"Just say you'll fight, and I'll let them come out." Abraham's face was hard, but his voice was oily with manipulation.

Every word burned me. It was like being doused slowly with petrol and waiting to be set alight. I watched my knuckles turn white as I clenched my fists, and I took a deep breath. Anger pulsed through me, at Abraham, and at the boys for asking too many questions, not being more careful. I let the aggression in the air around me fuel my resolve and pushed away my fear. I would fight. I had to. There was no other choice. Although, I did not think Sawyer would allow Abraham to recruit Jackson and Luca, I did not want him to even consider it.

"I'll fight." My voice wavered at first, but I drew on every ounce of my strength. "Let them go. Now."

My last word was an order and Abraham raised his eyebrows. But he nodded to Theo, who headed out the back.

Abraham turned to Finn. "You have five minutes to get her ready."

I borrowed shorts, gloves, and a mouthguard, and listened to Finn's advice.

"Watch for a punch or a kick and step to the side. Follow the momentum to push her down. Protect your face. Keep your feet apart and your knees a little bent. Move from your hips. Put your thumb on the outside, between your first and second knuckles, when you make a fist. We'll throw in the towel if you go down."

I couldn't take in any of his instructions; they came too fast, and my fear blocked them out. But I nodded.

"You don't have to do this, Nova." Jackson appeared at my side, gripping my arm, holding me back.

He was furious and filled with a crippling anxiety at the same time. It soaked through me. I hung on to the fury and pushed the anxiety away. His overwhelming urge to protect me was debilitating and I needed to find my own strength for this. I searched for anger in others close by and claimed it as my own. It made me feel stronger.

"Let me go, Jack." My voice was callous.

Jackson glared at me, but reluctantly released my arm. I clenched my teeth, as if this would stop my determination from escaping through my mouth and I climbed into the ring.

"Please don't get hurt." There was a desperation in his tone, but I shrugged it off.

I focused on being strong, in control.

I will not be afraid. I repeated the silent mantra I used when with Abraham.

My opponent was of similar build, a little taller, a stern face and penetrating dark eyes. Her hair was tied in a long single plait down her back. A moment before we started, I saw the girl's eyes flick between Abraham and me and I realised she was just as nervous as I was. I took a breath and let my body fill with warmth, imagining an invisible thread between us, an alliance. Her expression changed to confusion and then the corners of her mouth lifted in a tentative smile. I glanced at Abraham but was surprised to find no pleasure in his face. Instead, he looked annoyed.

She came at me, with a wrestling grip, her hands on my shoulders, her legs trying to trip mine. I pushed her back. A sudden rush of pain tore through my face as her fist struck my jaw. Making a pretence of bravado, I staggered back, pulled out my mouth guard and spat out the blood. I held up my arms as a shield against her volley of punches. It hurt, a lot, but I had the impression she was holding back. My legs were weakening, as was my resolve, and I stumbled. She dropped her arms and I shot out with the heel of my palm, connecting with her nose. It made a squelching noise as the blood gushed out.

"I'm so sorry." I was horrified, hoping it was not broken.

Her hands reached for her nose, trying to stop the flow of blood. I moved to help her, but she shook her head. Her eyes darted around nervously, as if she was looking for someone. Then a flying back kick hit me in the chest, knocking the air from my lungs and sending a spear of pain through my whole body. I crumpled to the floor and lay there gasping.

Finn called it, and I nodded at him gratefully. It was over.

Abraham was nowhere to be seen.

Jackson held out his hand to me. His expression was grim. I took his hand and let him pull me to my feet and into his embrace. My head was pounding. My knees wobbled. I felt like all my teeth were loose. It hurt to breathe.

"You didn't have to do it," Jackson said, and pride shone in his eyes. "You weren't terrible."

"I did. But thanks. Dad taught me some self-defence. The only other move I know is a knee to the groin." I tried to laugh but it hurt too much.

"You continue to amaze me, Nova."

I gave him a feeble smile, the best I could manage.

In the change rooms, I vomited repeatedly, until my stomach was empty, but it still convulsed. I was trying to get rid of the anger and violence that had been mine.

My opponent watched me warily while she changed. "Are you okay?"

I nodded. "I'll be fine."

"Sorry about that. You don't look like a fighter, though the nose jab was pretty nasty." She touched her nose carefully, which was still red though the blood had been cleaned up. "I've only been training a few months."

"I'm not a fighter. It was just luck. I hope that's not too sore."

"My dad trains me. He trains some of Abe's men too." She looked around nervously as though she expected Abraham to appear. "Abe scares me to death."

"Me too." I smiled at her and felt the bond between us, over a shared fear.

By the time we got home, my head was throbbing with confusion. Emotions piled up in a chaotic mess and I was too tired to sort them out. My mouth was dry, my jaw ached, and my body had been wrung out like an old towel. I clasped my hands tightly to stop them shaking, not sure if it was from fear or anger.

"Jack, I can't do this," I said.

"What do you mean? Can't do what?" I sensed his weariness, a match to my own.

"UFC. I feel like I'm swept along in an avalanche. The anger and violence pull me under, into a darkness, and I'm getting buried."

"Nova, I get it. You feel it more than most people." He frowned in concern. "But you are also stronger than most people."

"But how can you fight? How can you intentionally hurt someone?" My questions jabbed at him, like a sharp pencil.

He thought for a moment. "It's not like that, it's a sport. It's not personal. I respect the guy I'm fighting. And I'm good at it. I'm careful. You were good at it, too."

"You could die or seriously hurt someone else. It happens. No matter how good you are. And I'm not good at it. I don't want to hurt people; it makes me feel sick." My anger was dissipating, being replaced by a heaviness over my heart.

"What do you want me to do?" Jackson asked gently.

"I don't know. Not fight." My tears welled up and spilled over my cheeks.

"Come here, beautiful."

My face, screwed up, blotchy and bruised was far from beautiful, but he held me, until I had the energy to swallow the rest of my tears.

"Nova, I'm going to keep fighting. But I don't think you should come."

"So, instead I sit here, waiting, worrying. That's almost worse."

He shrugged, remaining obstinate, and then I felt a sudden shove of his frustration. "This isn't fair. I worry about you facing up with Abe every day. That is more dangerous and yet I would never tell you not to go. I know you can handle it. I believe in you."

I bit my bottom lip, unsure how to answer him. He was right.

"Yeah, fair point," I said, finally. "Okay. I can't tell you not to go. But promise me that you won't let the avalanche, the darkness, drag you under."

"I won't, and you won't let that happen. To me, or to any of us. Right?" His voice was gentle and kind.

"Right." I nodded sheepishly. "So then, where do you hurt?"

"Pretty much everywhere. You?" His smile was a grimace. "Same."

My whole face ached, not just my jaw. The ribs on one side sent ripples of pain when I stretched or turned. My arms, which had taken most of the battering, felt as heavy as lead. Still, I knew I was lucky, she had gone easy on me. I was sure of it.

"Do you hurt here?" I pointed at the cut above his eye.

He nodded solemnly. I kissed him on that spot. Jackson took his left fist from the ice pack that was wrapped around his hands and held it out, then his other fist, to be kissed.

"My cheek."

I kissed his cheek and the other where he pointed. He moved his finger to his jaw.

"Hang on, my jaw hurts too." I pouted.

He kissed my chin, a soft flutter of his lips. "Where else?"

"My arms. My ribs. My head."

Jackson covered me in silky caresses, only pausing when I put my hand on his mouth.

"Jack, are you sure we can keep ourselves out of the darkness?" My head still spun.

"Nova, you are strong, you know you are. And so am I. We will keep each other out of the darkness. I promise." His strength was a solid, supportive wall behind my back.

"I hope that's a promise you can keep, Jackson Lewis."

"Believe in me." He placed my hand on his heart. "And I'll promise you something else, Wilson. Coop might be your first love, but I will be your deepest."

I wondered if he was right. With our lives constantly in danger and so much loss, we were living in the present. I knew Jackson's feelings ran deep and I knew that when I fell in love, I went all in. Now, more than ever. After all, who knew what the future held.

32

With no further UFC for a while, I finally got my birthday celebration. It was almost curfew, and the streets were dead quiet. Our jeep pulled up at a small high rise. Our steps on the marble tiles echoed in the emptiness, as we moved through the lobby. The light from an ornate chandelier danced in rainbow colours. Electricity was still on. Embroidered silk sofas lined the walls. Nine months ago, the hotel had probably been packed with tourists and businesspeople. Now the building was asleep. Jackson led me to the staircase. I paused to listen. No lifts and not even the sound of an air-conditioning system. We climbed the six flights. The restaurant was on the top level, just as deserted as the rest, and the kitchens had been looted some time ago. Jackson pulled me up against his chest, his arms linked around my waist as we looked out into the void.

Beyond the window glass was a view of the city skyline. There were large dark shadows, the buildings that no longer had power, but there were just as many skyscrapers illuminated in brilliance, stretching up to the stars. A large moon hovered, lighting the world beneath. It was glorious and hopeful.

"Jack, it's beautiful."

"Wait, there's more." He pulled out a birthday cupcake, complete with a candle. "Happy birthday."

"Where did you get that?"

"The hospital kitchen."

His eyes were wide, and his face lit with a giant smile. The joy bounced between us like a children's ball.

"Nova, I love you."

And he did. It was evident in the tender way he spoke my name. It shone from his eyes and radiated from his heart.

"I know."

"You did not just use Han Solo on me." He looked at me with astonishment, admiration, and a good deal of amusement.

I shrugged and gave him a flirtatious wink. "I love you too, Jack."

"I know."

We grinned stupidly at each other.

Happiness cradled me, deep and profound. I felt optimistic for the first time in a while. With Jackson, it was all light. Emotionally, he was completely transparent to me, holding nothing back. There was no darkness.

Life went on.

While Sage, Jackson and Luca continued in their work-experience roles, I continued to split my time between Sawyer, the research laboratory, and the hospital. I accompanied Sawyer to his negotiations with Abraham and worked on strengthening my empathic influence.

"It's almost like you are reaching into a person. Look for any darkness, that's what I do. Flood them with calm compassion," Sawyer explained.

"Sometimes I feel like I find a trigger, do you get that?"

"No, but I keep telling you, you are stronger than me." Sawyer was encouraging. "Maybe it's the warrior gene you're sensing. Try and turn it off. It might not work on Abe but try it on his men."

Within the meeting room, it became easy for me to create an emotional climate of calm relaxation. Abraham had to repeatedly bark at his men to stand upright and pay attention. I did have a sense of darkness in the men, an emotional trigger, whether it was the warrior gene or some part of their past, I was not sure, but I tried to turn it down. Abraham was far more resistant. There were heavy pockets of black shadow within him.

Discussions focused more and more on Frank Murphy. DOVE was working with Abraham's followers, in conjunction with the police, to disrupt the criminal activities of Murphy. While Abraham was happy to assist in destroying Murphy's control, he was far more reluctant to relinquish his own power to legitimate government authority. Sawyer had to tread carefully. After a meeting with Abraham, I usually felt the need for a shower, to wash off the malicious hostility I had absorbed.

At the research laboratory, I pumped Sidney for information about my father. She knew very little about his research but suggested there might be information on his laptop at home. I made a mental note to check into it sometime. Although I was barely even a research assistant, I could tell that she enjoyed having me around. She chatted easily about the work they were doing. There were clear correlations between the warrior gene and the violent offenders they tested, but it did not really explain why the anger and violence had suddenly increased worldwide. Approximately a third of the population had always carried the warrior gene, it was not a new thing. Our laboratory, and others like it around the globe, had been able to create an artificial enzyme that stimulated anger and aggression, essentially replicating the warrior gene, but no-one knew how to turn it off. There were still no real answers, no solutions, and my frustration itched like a rash.

Jet, Finn, Luca, and Jackson continued to fight in the UFC. They noticed a pattern where the referee stopped fights earlier than necessary. These fighters disappeared for a health check but were not seen again. This added to the suspicion that Abraham was using UFC as a way of recruiting his followers. Finn suspected it was not entirely voluntary. Abraham's gang members were often there as security, but never competitors. Jet and Finn had never lost a bout, while Jack and Luca had each won one. Rayna had not bothered to attend again, and Sage and I didn't go. I did not want to be manipulated into fighting again. While they kept their debriefing to a minimum around us, the boys still brought home enough aggression to give me cramps.

To offset the anger, the fear, the brutality, that echoed through me day after day, I craved the release of exercise. I missed the beach, where going for a run was so much more pleasant than it was in the city. The streets of Melbourne were dingy and grey, often wet, and there were more people around. Jackson and I usually went out just before curfew because most people were already inside. This night we were nearly home, and we were weaving wildly on the footpath, laughing, and pushing each other, playing the childish game of not stepping on a crack. A police officer stepped out from behind a parked car and planted himself squarely in our way. Jackson and I stopped, suddenly wary, and breathing heavily.

"You're breaking curfew." The officer's voice was gruff and aggressive.

He was unshaven and his uniform looked creased and shabby, as if he had slept in it. A dark cloud overshadowed his authority, and I was very aware of the pistol in his gun belt. The bile rose in my throat.

"We still have 15 minutes, and we're not far from home." Jackson spoke politely but with an air of defiance.

"It's past curfew by my calculations. And you're drunk." He seemed to be staring at a point behind us rather than making eye contact.

"We haven't even been drinking." Jackson was getting annoyed.

My nostrils flared with the smell of alcohol, but it was not from us.

"Come on. I'm taking you in," the police officer said.

Jackson moved to the side, as if to go around the officer. When I noticed that he had stepped on a crack in the pavement, I had to choke down a hysterical giggle. Jackson looked at me in bewilderment.

"I said you're coming with me." The officer gave a gruff order.

My heart threatened to break through my chest, so I concentrated on breathing slowly, calmly, spreading vibes of cooperation. The officer reached out his hand as if to grab me, but it dropped back to his side. Jackson rolled his shoulders and sent me a glance. There was the unspoken acknowledgement between us that the policeman was unstable and hence, dangerous. Suddenly, the officer's fist shot out, glancing off the side of my face. The ground swam up towards me. I lost my concentration. Anger surged through me, a swarm of stinging wasps. Jackson took all of three heartbeats to size up the situation and then he and the police officer were head-to-head, shuffling in a violent wrestle. The officer was strong and angry, but Jackson was fast and more focused. When the police officer momentarily lost his balance, Jackson hooked his leg behind the officer's knees and brought him to the ground. The police officer lay awkwardly on the footpath, breathing heavily. When he fumbled for his sidearm, Jackson kicked it from his hand. The gun clattered into the gutter.

"Come on. Quick. Let's get out of here before we do break curfew." Jackson kept his voice low.

We left the police officer looking after us but making no effort to follow. I sensed his anger slowly draining away. My head was fuzzy, and my legs unsteady but Jackson pulled me along. I didn't worry about the cracks this time.

When we finally reached the stairs of our building, we stopped to catch our breath.

"Thank you. You were amazing." I gripped the railings, still puffing, while Jackson beamed with pride.

"You are very welcome. We make a good team, don't we?" His smile held a deep satisfaction. "I told you the fight training would pay off."

"Yeah, yeah. You were kind of magnificent, though."

"I was."

"Modest too."

Jackson laughed.

"You lost, by the way," I said.

"What?" Jackson eyed me with confusion.

"You stepped on a crack first." My giggle ended in a snort, then a groan.

I rubbed the side of my head where my laugh had brought back a dull throbbing.

He raised his eyebrows. "I think that blow caused you some serious damage."

With a cheeky smile, he kissed my forehead, then scooped me up into his strong arms and carried me up the stairs. It was past curfew now and I had never valued the safety of our apartment as much as that night.

It was the last week of October when Jackson received news that his older brother, Alexander, had been killed in a random beating. His mother had slipped into a severe depression. He was going home. Jackson said little but his eyes spoke volumes. They were dark brown pools that reflected his disbelief and sorrow. My heart was being chipped away piece by piece, with each person we lost, and each sliver hurt like hell.

While Jackson packed up his clothes, I felt him mentally sorting through his thoughts and tidying things up.

"So many people we know have died. Why them, why not me?" he asked.

"I don't know." I reached for his hand and let him feel my compassion and love.

We had come to know death and loss a little too personally over the last year.

I searched for something to say that would bring him back to our usual cheeky banter. "Maybe it's because you still have something important that you have to do."

"Oh yeah, like what?" His sarcasm was bitter.

"Stop the anger? Save the world?" I kept my voice light.

"Huh! Maybe."

"You better start soon though." I nudged him in the ribs.

He trembled with reluctant laughter and held me in a close hug. "Thanks for these last few months, Nova."

His voice had a strange tone, and my heart skipped a beat.

"You don't have to thank me. We are a team. Remember?"

He nodded, but his brow was furrowed. He pressed his lips together in a flat line.

"Nova, you need to be here, with DOVE. It's where you belong. But I need to be home and I'm not sure when, or if, I'll be back. I think it has to be over between us."

"Hang on. We can make it work." I felt like a loose end that he needed to clean up. "Maybe we can meet for weekends. Or I could come home …" I heard my voice trail off.

He shook his head. We both knew it was too dangerous to make weekend trips. And he was right, I did want to stay in Melbourne and continue working with Sawyer. I was just beginning to feel confident using my empathic influence.

"No, a distance thing will never work. Look how you fell into my arms when Coop wasn't here."

"That's not fair."

"Sorry. I'm kidding. Sort of." His smile was grim. "I don't think you're really over him though, not completely."

"You're a jerk."

"Look, I'm trying to be mature here. I know what I want. I want to be with you." Jackson took a deep breath. "Trouble is, I think Coop feels the same, in his own way. And I need you to just want me. I don't want to share your love with anyone, including my brother. I think you are in love with both of us, but I don't want that anymore. It has been okay, while Coop hasn't been here. But after this, when you come back home, there will be the both of us, wanting you. So, you need to make a decision."

I tried to swallow the huge lump that had formed in my throat. When I opened my mouth to say something, he held up his hand like a stop sign.

"I'm letting you go, setting you free, giving you time to think about what you want."

I was not completely blind-sided; I knew our conversations had often touched on my feelings for Cooper. Yet, I could still taste the bitterness of betrayal.

"Can I say something now?" My voice dripped sarcasm, and he nodded. "You make it sound like you're doing me a favour, but you're actually just breaking up with me."

Jackson shrugged and I felt the strength of his conviction. It had not been an easy decision, but he was standing by it.

"That's how I feel. You know where I'll be if it's me that you want. But you need to be sure."

I stood there, trying not to cry. There were no more words to be said. He had made up his mind. I felt the warmth of his love, but also a cold pang of regret. My heart was not just chipped now, it tore with a giant rift. While I sensed Jackson was on the verge of breaking down, he remained dry-eyed and strong. He studied my face, as if he were creating a mental photograph.

Finally, he kissed me as if we were the last people on earth. A goodbye kiss.

Sage, Luca, and I stayed in Melbourne. We kept going because that is what we do. Sawyer kept me away from Abraham, knowing I needed my emotional control at its best and strongest when dealing with him, and I was not at my best. I worked hard on being mentally calm so I wouldn't be a drain on the people around me. While I knew I needed the time to discover myself and what I wanted, it was hard to be alone. Sage was a windbreak for my whirling storm. She stayed solid and steady in her friendship.

"Sometimes I feel like I'm caught in a nightmare," I moaned, seeking sympathy.

"Tell me about it." It was an offhand response, but I knew she genuinely cared.

"I think I fall in love too hard, too fast. And I lose myself."

"I love that about you. You go all in." Her mouth curled in an affectionate smile.

"Yeah, but I lost myself with Cooper and he left. Then I lost myself with Jack and he left. And now I've come crashing down. Alone."

"Nova, Jack had to go home," Sage said gently.

"I know, but did he have to break up with me?"

"Well, that was harsh. He had his reasons, I guess. Are you over Cooper?"

"Yes. I think so. But I still don't want to hurt him." My head hurt from trying to work out how I felt.

"By trying not to hurt Coop, maybe you are hurting Jack."

"Oh, it's too hard. I care about them both. I don't ever want to be in love again."

I swung between moods, a fire in my blood gave way to a weight crushing against my heart. It was painful either way.

"I think, you love people fiercely. Love makes you vulnerable. And sometimes people leave. But just because you get hurt doesn't mean you should stop loving." Sage was wise and kind. "Maybe not a person with the surname Lewis next time though." She giggled.

I smiled weakly. "Stick together?"

"Like glue," Sage promised me.

November passed slowly. It should have been the end of our senior year. Graduation and parties. Instead, our senior jerseys hung in the wardrobe, rarely worn. Sage heard from Imogen that we would be issued with our school certificates, based on the work we had done so far. It all lacked finality. No formal, no graduation ceremony, no last day pranks, no hugging, no crying or getting drunk, no schoolies. There was no guidance about the future. We were just waiting until isolation ended, and all the while it got harder to remember our lives before all this.

The world was in turmoil. The uncertainty did not help my mood.

33

December was unseasonably hot. Our faces turned red with sunburn and our shirts were wet with perspiration. While the city was shrouded in a shimmering heat haze, the streets were ignited with a scorching crime spree of violence. With the courts and legal system straining under the sheer number of cases, Abraham took the credit for keeping the city safe. His gang delivered a quick, brutal street justice. Sawyer suspected him of creating incidents just so he would look good in resolving them.

Finn and I saw the street justice being delivered firsthand. It was another steaming afternoon, and we were stopped by a fist fight in the middle of the road. Two men pummelled each other. Their cars blocked the street, doors wide open, motors still running. Their rage was a dust storm that was searing the skin from my bones.

"Hey, hey, guys let's bring this down a notch or two." Finn was fearless.

He moved between the two men, a lion tamer separating alpha males. I stood back and focused on soothing emotions, laying down a blanket of peace. There was an immediate change in the men. My skills were getting much stronger. They moved apart, swayed on their feet, and dropped their fists. Finn stood in between, keeping them at arm's length, in case it started up again.

"What happened?" he asked.

"He cut me off," said one of them, but his voice was thick with embarrassment.

Now calm, they had realised this brawl to death was over nothing.

Another car pulled alongside us, and a huge man climbed out. He was the tallest person I had ever seen and solid muscle.

"I can look after this." His voice carried an authority born from his size.

On the side of his neck, he had a triangular letter *A*, a characteristic of many of Abraham's gang. I rubbed my own neck, hoping Finn would get the hint.

"It's okay, it's all sorted." Finn gestured for the two guys to return to their cars.

"Maybe someone needs to be held accountable." The big man's low voice was quietly threatening; he did not need to be loud.

Reaching for the fingers of one of the drivers, the big man peeled them backwards until he got a scream of pain. "We don't tolerate that kind of behaviour in Abraham City. Is that clear?"

There was a snap and another yelp. The driver cradled his fingers against his chest suppressing little sobs. I felt his pain and his terror.

"You need a lesson?" The tall man spoke to the other driver, who shook his head in horror. "Then get out of here, both of you."

They went, leaving a trail of fear and shame.

He turned to us. "Well?"

"Just going," I said quickly.

Finn watched the big man drive off before he started the car. "That was unnecessary. He was obviously one of Abe's gang and wanted to send a message."

The following day when I was helping at the research laboratory, I saw the big man again, sitting with a group of men in a waiting area. He was hard to miss.

"What are they here for?" I asked Sidney.

"I'm not sure." She hardly looked up. "I think they are here for clinical trials."

"Do you mean testing for the warrior gene? If anyone would have it, he would." I nudged her and inclined my head towards him.

Sidney gave a detached smile. "He certainly is a fine specimen. But no, it's not for genetic testing. They are doing some drug trials on medications that control aggression."

I started paying more attention to the people that came in for the clinical trials and noticed a lot of them had the triangle *A* tattoo. Finn had previously just dropped me off at the door, but he started coming inside and he recognised some of the UFC fighters as well. These were the people that were likely to have the warrior gene and so it made some sense that they were involved in a drug trial aimed at controlling aggression.

"They are volunteers. They are given either the medication or a placebo. They don't know which and then they are monitored. It's a normal drug trial." Sidney was puzzled by our interest.

"But where do the volunteers come from?" I asked.

"I don't know, I guess they answered an advertisement. That's how we usually do it."

But Finn and I agreed, too many of them seemed to have links with Abraham.

I was left with a sense of foreboding.

Christmas day dawned hot and steamy, a typical Australian Christmas. Of course, it was far from typical in every other aspect. There was none of the lead up we were used to. Santa was absent from the shopping centres, which were quiet and deserted. There were no carols and no church services. The councils did not bother with street decorations and there was hardly a house with Christmas lights. Neighbours did not meet for drinks, there was no backyard cricket, and children stayed inside.

It was a sombre morning for Sage, Luca, and me, as we reflected on the people that were not there. We grieved for my father and Sage's parents who would never share Christmas with us again. I knew my friends would all be feeling the same loss, staring at the empty spaces at the table for Christmas dinner. Too many of us had been forced to deal with tragedy. We managed to send and receive messages when the internet came up in the afternoon. Mia, Alice, and Ava sent warm wishes. I missed them.

Cooper's messages reflected his kindness and his steady nature. He was happy with the routine at home. Jackson's messages were cheeky and provoking, and showed he missed the adventure and the risk with us. I still was not sure how I felt and what I wanted. Sometimes the safety and consistency with Cooper held more appeal. But Jackson made me feel like I could make a difference in the world.

Although our Christmas day was tinged with sadness it was free from anger and darkness. There were no police sirens, no crime reports, no Abraham. The air felt lighter, cleaner. It was like the violence had a day off. Only one day though.

On Boxing Day, we went up to the hospital to share some Christmas cheer in the children's ward. There were toys to hand out, cake to eat and games to be played. It felt more like Christmas, surrounded by baubles, and twinkling lights. Sawyer wore a Santa suit, and Rayna was dressed in an elf costume. Finn had children hanging off him like decorations on a Christmas tree, while others hopped from foot-to-foot waiting on Jet to swing them high in the air. When these elite soldiers were playing with the children, the shadows I sensed inside them winked out, even if only temporarily.

With the development of my empathic skills had come a keen awareness of the secrets and violence that people hid deep. I did not always know what the secret was, just that there was something they wanted to stay buried, an inherent darkness. Sometimes, it meant something awful had happened to them and they carried a shame with it, like abuse or rape. I saw this in a lot of the children. For others, I knew that they had committed the act, they had hurt or even killed someone. It left a black scar. In some people where there was no regret, that left the worst stain of all. Finn carried a pocket of darkness, but it was not his by choice, and Jet was the same.

When I sensed a deep trauma in the children, I pushed at it with compassion and kindness, hoping to offer some healing. Within Ethan, one of the older children, there was a deep shadow. Thick hair hung across his face like a hood, and he kept his eyes on the floor. Even though he was distant emotionally, he followed me from bed to bed, hovering, and fidgeting. I had tried sending him comfort, but his darkness was strong. It was when I turned from Ethan to smile at another boy, that he pulled out a fork and stabbed it into the arm of the other child. The prongs met flesh, pink and soft, and sunk deep. His victim screamed. Ethan smirked. Pulling the fork out of the boy's arm, he raised it high, about to strike again. Before he was able to make a second jab, he was grabbed from behind by Sawyer and a nurse. The younger boy screamed while I struggled to hold him. He convulsed and trembled like a caged animal, the blood pouring from the punctures in his arm. Ethan's eyes were vacant, his expression was deadpan. There was no remorse, no guilt, just that inherent darkness.

"I should have sensed it coming," I said later when we were back at Sawyer's apartment for a drink.

My heart was heavy with responsibility.

"How could you? You can't actually read minds." Sage was kind and practical, as always.

"But I knew there was something hidden deep."

"He is a victim of abuse himself. And so, he acts out aggressively to get attention. It's what he knows," said Luca. "It's difficult to change that cycle."

"We can't always help everyone. We do what we can," Finn added.

I had the feeling he was talking of people and places beyond Ethan. Finn had seen more than his share of horror during his deployment.

"But why does it feel that we are not doing enough?" I asked.

Despondency settled on us like a pile of bricks.

"We can't save everyone," Sage said.

"You can try and stop people being angry, but you won't reach everyone," Sawyer agreed. "It doesn't mean you stop trying."

He too was looking beyond Ethan, although I knew he also felt responsible that he had not stopped it in time.

"How can we ever fix the world then?"

"Stop thinking global, maybe we just concentrate on our little part, and do our best."

"Is that good enough?"

"It has to be."

34

On New Year's Eve, Abraham sent for me. Sawyer had been called out to defuse some conflict at one of the checkpoints, so Finn took me in to meet with Abraham at his café. The darkness ran deep in Abraham, and I was particularly aware of it today. Shivers rolled down my spine.

"I hear you've been asking questions about my men around the university laboratory?" His eyes were cold and his tone aggressive. "What are you expecting to find out?"

Despite Abraham's threatening manner, I was relying on his need to keep Sawyer onside. Finn was sitting at a table out the front of the café. I could see his outline through the frosted glass window. Abraham and I were alone, except for one man, who stood behind the counter, wiping some glasses with a dishtowel.

"I've just noticed a lot of your men volunteering for the clinical trials. The drug trial is for medication that is supposed to calm aggression. I would have thought you preferred your people to be aggressive. I figured you would be looking for people that carry the warrior gene." I was aware that I was being a little reckless, but we needed to know what he was up to.

Abraham's gaze remained straight and unblinking, but I felt his irritation as pin pricks all over my skin.

"I know of several drug trials at that laboratory. I always encourage my men to do their civic duty and volunteer for a worthwhile cause. Surely if there is a drug that can stop this spree of violence in the world, we want the appropriate clinical testing completed as soon as possible, and trialled on as many different people as possible." Abraham's voice was steady and calm, but I knew that was when he was at his most deadly. "And, as for the men who ask to join my organisation, they need to have control. The warrior gene is not a requirement."

"Abe, all your men clearly have the warrior gene." I spoke sarcastically and indicated the men scattered around outside the café, with Finn.

All his followers stood erect, hands at their sides, feet spaced a little apart as if ready for action. The muscles on their torsos and arms bulged beneath the black T-shirts they wore.

"I don't need them to have the warrior gene," Abraham repeated. "I can turn them into warriors, myself." His tone was condescending now, and I sensed that he was tiring of this conversation already.

"Do you beat it into them?" I knew I was walking a thin line.

"Not at all. I have been running my own drug trials."

"So, you don't beat it into them, you drug them."

Abraham's eyes narrowed and I felt the anger pulsing through him. I was pushing his buttons and I knew I needed to back off. The darkness inside him frothed as I tried to reach in and find a lever, to calm it.

"Perhaps, it's time to see if we can turn you into a warrior, Nova."

I had a sense that he had snapped his fingers although he made no such action. He had reached a decision that he had been putting off.

"What do you mean? I am no warrior. You know I can't even fight."

Abraham spoke to his man behind the counter and gestured towards me. "Theo, bring her."

The room suddenly seemed to shrink, and I was pushing against a giant rouge wave that threatened to engulf me.

I turned to the front window. "I'll just get Finn."

But Theo grabbed my arm and pulled me in the opposite direction. He was taking me out through the back door. We crossed a small car park and entered another building. It was decked out as a gym with various fitness machines and an octagonal UFC ring in the centre. There were twelve men, all in grey tracksuit pants and black T-shirts. They were like clones. Strong, broad shoulders, biceps the size of grapefruits, muscles rippling across their chests. Two were in the ring, fighting, while the other ten cheered them on. They stopped and stood to attention as we entered. Like soldiers, or a firing squad.

"I have someone new for the ring." Abraham's laugh was sinister.

Theo pushed me through the opening. I sat on the mat in a position of submission. It seemed the safest alternative.

"Meet my warriors, Nova. Play nice." Abraham was goading me.

"What the hell is this, you psycho?" My words were far braver than I felt.

Abraham sat down on the edge of a weights bench, looking very much in control. In contrast, my heart thumped like a racehorse's. I could feel the warrior gene in these fighters, and their control hung by a thread. My breathing was fast and shallow, and I tried to slow it down. I felt the colour drain from my face. Perspiration soaked through my shirt. The warriors watched me, and while I sensed their confusion, I knew their loyalty to Abraham was absolute.

"Who's first?" Abraham asked in a soft voice, as if inviting children to play.

A young warrior stepped forward with a confident strut. I could feel his urge to fight, pushing at him, an addiction, but I was not sure whether it was instinctual, fuelled by a drug Abraham had given him, or just his need to impress Abraham.

"This isn't a contest, Abe. She's a girl." He winked at me, a quick, playful acknowledgement.

"Maybe not physically, Neo, but she will try and control your mind," Abraham warned.

The young warrior looked at me with interest and held out his hand to pull me to my feet. I could feel his hesitation, but the fear Abraham invoked overrode it. Neo rocked back on his heels, assessing me. Interlacing his fingers, he extended his arms, stretching until his knuckles cracked.

I did try to influence his feelings. There was a sadness beneath his anger, and I let my compassion flow into him. Where I sensed his darkness, I tried to extend some light. I focused on the people I loved, letting my feelings for them echo through the room, hoping to diminish the raw aggression surrounding me.

Neo seemed to barely move and yet his arm shot out like a lightning bolt, connecting with the side of my eye and then withdrew just as quickly. I instinctively knew that if he had been facing a man, his punch would have held a lot more force, but it was still the hardest I had ever been hit. I stumbled backward, gripping the padded fence for support, tears welling in both my eyes. For a second, I was too dazed to register anything except a light wetness on my cheek. Then pain flooded my head, my face. Raising my hand to my eye, I felt that it was already starting to close with swelling.

Job done; Neo stepped out of the ring with a cocky swagger. And yet, I sensed his shame underneath the confidence.

"Next!" Abraham called.

I will not be afraid. It was my mantra with Abraham. I repeated it to myself, forcing myself to believe it.

I was hit again, in the chest and then the stomach, until I doubled over, fighting to breathe. There must have been an unspoken agreement, one punch each. My knees threatened to give way, but I refused to let myself be defined by weakness or fear and so I struggled to muster the strength I needed to rise above this brutality. Every time I lifted my head, another warrior entered the ring. My tongue was thick, my stomach was on fire. I never got a chance to recover my breath. Any moves I made in my defence were about as effective as a mouse caught in a trap. Some of the warriors felt guilty about hitting me and their remorse tugged on my heart, but Abraham held their allegiance, and they didn't hesitate.

Pain slammed through my body as I was knocked to the floor and pulled back to my feet more times that I could count. My arms and legs became jelly, offering minimal support. Each breath was a ragged gasp, blood filled my mouth from my split lip, and my head throbbed as if filled with stinging bees. I had given up trying to exert any emotional control and I was powerless to stop the anger and aggression pouring into me. Eventually, I stayed on the mat, in a crumpled heap, and let myself dissociate so the violence could wash over me.

I only registered that Finn had come to my rescue, when I heard the thrashing that he was taking for me. The twelve of them still took turns but Finn received a lot more than one punch from each. There was no remorse this time as they beat him down, again and again. His courage shone, a brilliant light, strong and unyielding, but his agony tore through my numb body, a whip lashing my skin. Finn fought back. He was strong, and skilled, and brave, but they were relentless.

Alarm bells were blasting in my head, and I knew something bad was coming. I should have remembered that Abraham needed to have the limelight. As Finn's energy flagged, Abraham pushed his way into the middle of the fight, wielding a large machete. I could feel his rage, it was as cold as ice. The warriors held Finn's arms and legs in a tight lock and Abraham pulled back Finn's head to expose his throat.

Finn's eyes glared defiantly at Abraham and his mouth curled in mocking smile, despite the blood that smeared his lips and dripped from his nose.

With a glance at me to check he had my attention, Abraham sliced the large broad knife across Finn's throat. In one quick motion.

There was a scream, but it might have been from me. No sound came from Finn. They let his body slide to the floor, and watched as his blood oozed onto the cement, red staining the grey. Finn clutched at his throat momentarily, his fingers probing at the deep gash in his neck, poking at the wound, trying to make sense of it, covering his fingers in thick syrupy blood. A cold realisation swept across Finn's face as he realised his fate. It was the closest I had seen him to showing fear.

I tried to crawl forward, to help, but my arms and legs slithered as if I was floundering on a frozen pond. Icy cold shivers shook my body. My brain was numb, refusing to believe what my one good eye was seeing.

"Stay out of my business." Abraham's voice was cold and brash.

I felt a swirl of emotions coming from Finn. They swept through my body, a snowstorm obscuring my vision, clouding my comprehension, and then clearing again. There was anger, confusion, regret and finally acceptance.

Then nothing.

Finn's deep blue eyes turned dull, just staring.

I sucked in my stomach, ignoring the shooting pain from my ribs, and searched for his essence, his light. My heart froze over.

I fainted.

35

I came to in a small room. It felt like a prison cell. Four white walls, no window, and a closed door. An air conditioning vent pumped out cool air. I was lying on a single bed, just sheets and a pillow. A tight bandage wound around my ribcage. On a tiny wooden table was a water bottle, and there was one chair. Tentatively, I rolled to one side but realised how futile that was. A sharp ache stabbed through my head. My vision was blurred, and I reached up to feel that one of my eyes was heavy with swelling. Eventually, I simply had to get up to use the toilet. Each step was agony.

When I banged on the wooden door, the noise vibrated through my head, and an avalanche of pain echoed through my body. The door was swung open by one of Abraham's warriors. He looked sheepish and I could sense his apology.

"You're awake at last."

"Where am I?"

He shook his head but did not answer.

"Can I use the bathroom?"

It was across the hallway. Outside the door, I could hear him fidgeting as he waited. I rinsed my face, hardly recognising myself with the swelling and bruising. Then it hit me in a flood. Finn. I let out a strangled scream. Darkness surged through me. The warrior either heard or felt my grief because he came in and picked me up. He carried me back to my room, as easily as if I was a child.

I shut down, like a string of Christmas lights when a bulb is blown, and I stayed that way for several days. They brought me food, but I hardly ate. Every time I shut my eyes the image of Finn's final moments came up. It was a struggle to keep breathing. My body was heavy with exhaustion and the notion of doing anything was overwhelming.

Conversations scrolled through my head, providing small moments of light and hope.

"You need cheering up. What are you wearing?" Jackson's voice was distant, hazy.

"The most unattractive track pants ever!" I realised that someone must have changed my clothes.

"You could take them off for me. And then describe your body in specific detail."

"Oh yeah, and why would I do that?" I couldn't help encouraging him.

"So, I can tell you what I want to do to those body parts." Jackson's husky laugh soothed my pain.

"Jack!" I admonished him.

"What?" He was all innocence again. "I meant from a medical point of view. Tending to your cuts and bruises."

He was trying to make me laugh but laughing hurt too much. I felt lighter, until the image crashed through.

"Jack, it's Finn."

"I know. There was nothing you could have done."

"Because I'm weak. Abe said my friends make me weak."

"He is wrong. Your love and compassion make you stronger."

When I opened my eyes, I was still in my white cell. The conversation was not real.

Sometimes I spoke to Sage. "I'm broken, Sage."

"I know. But you'll get through this." Her voice warmed my heart.

"You've always saved me."

"And always will."

"You should get out of here. You and Luca. It's not safe anymore."

"I'm not going anywhere without you. Stick together?"

"Like glue."

I was still in my cell, probably going crazy.

Despite my despair, I knew my body was healing slowly, physically, and emotionally.

Neo was my jailer. He had been the first warrior in the ring with me. With a fighter's build, his physical strength was obvious, and he carried me easily from bed to bathroom and back. His black hair was crew cut short, only just longer than the black stubble on his chin and cheeks. A neck tattoo marked his gang membership, and he always wore blue jeans and a black T-shirt, a uniform of sorts.

"I'm sorry about punching you. I have never ever hit a girl before. It's just that if Abe commands it, I have to do it."

The cocky swagger he had shown in the ring was absent and I could sense that his regret was genuine, but my bruised body was a colourful reminder of what he had done, what they had done.

"Like Hitler."

"What? No, I'm not a Nazi."

He was hurt by the implication, but I just shrugged. If the cap fits.

"Abe said you get in people's heads."

I didn't answer. I put up a wall of indifference.

The next day he tried again. "I'm sorry you've been in so much pain."

I knew he wanted my forgiveness, but I stayed silent. It wasn't easy to get past the fact that he was one of Abraham's warriors.

"You seem a little better." Despite not getting a response, he continued to try and win me over. "Your bruises are fading. Your eye is open. Your split lip is healing. And your cracked ribs are strapped. You need to eat more. Get your strength back. I eat a lot. Especially after a fight. Mum always said I'd eat a whole horse."

"Where is your mum?" His easy-going chatter made it hard to stay quiet.

"Dead now. Drug-overdose."

"I'm sorry." I sensed a deep sadness in him, a darkness buried deep, different to the shadow created by his aggression.

I couldn't help but send him a wave of sympathy and compassion, and when I did, I felt my own heart spluttering back to life. It was a good feeling.

"Yeah," Neo said. "It was a while ago. And I never knew my dad. What about your parents?"

"Also, dead." The familiar lump formed in my throat when I thought of my father.

"That's a bummer." His kindness brushed against my crumbing wall of indifference.

The simple conversations helped pass the time.

"Do you have a boyfriend?" he asked.

I shook my head, reluctantly, and felt my heart thump as my thoughts flashed to Jackson. At least I was starting to feel things again.

"Do you have a partner?" I asked.

"I don't have much time for dating. I work long hours for Abe." Neo's cheeks flushed red as he looked at me from beneath lowered eyelashes.

"You've certainly been spending a lot of time here. Doesn't Abe mind?" I asked.

"I got first dibs, because I was first in the ring …" he stopped and looked at his feet. "I am sorry that I hit you."

I nodded and he looked relieved.

"Anyway, I like being here. I can even work out in the gym downstairs."

So, we were above the gym, where … Finn. My body convulsed with the memory.

Neo's eyes closed as he felt my jolt of pain. "Are you in my head now?"

"I can't get in your head." My tone reflected my impatience. I was tired of these inferences from Abraham and his men. "I'm just an emotional person and sometimes my emotions spill out."

He nodded. "It's better when you are thinking about good things. I can tell when that happens. It makes me feel happy too."

That meant I had been unintentionally influencing his emotions. I calmed my mind, thought of Sage, and let the warmth spread. Neo smiled.

"How are you today?" Neo asked.

"Below average."

"But getting better," he insisted "Are you hungry?"

He placed a tray of food on the table and sat on the chair.

I shook my head. "What's going to happen to me?"

He didn't answer. Maybe he didn't know. There had been no sign of Abraham. I assumed that no one knew where I was, and they were probably unaware of what had happened to Finn. Sawyer would have people searching though, and Sage would be frantic.

"How long have I been here?" I asked.

"Just over two weeks."

It must be mid-January. I wondered what Abraham was waiting for.

"Is Abe going to let me go?"

Neo shrugged. I felt like I had prickles in my shirt, scratching against my skin, and I realised it was from Neo's concern, he was dreading what Abraham might do to me. I knew he liked me, and I needed an ally.

"Do you fight in UFC?" I asked.

"I used to, but then Abe recruited me. That's where he gets his men. But only the ones who show control." Neo pushed his chest out. "We're not allowed to fight in UFC anymore, but we fight each other, and that's pretty tough competition. And most days there is a job or two, someone who needs disciplining." His voice rang with pride, but I knew he was talking about hurting people, dishing out Abraham's street justice.

"Did you join Abe's gang voluntarily?"

"You don't get a choice with Abe. Once he chooses you, you join or die." Neo looked at the door as if worried someone could be listening.

"So, is it Neo, like in Matrix?" I moved to a safer topic.

"Yeah." He blushed. "My real name is Nolan."

"Neo is cool."

He beamed with my approval. I couldn't help liking him despite his involvement with Abraham's gang.

At the end of the third week of my captivity, a doctor came to check me over. He was overweight, balding, and dishevelled. With the bedside manner of a corpse, he avoided eye contact and made minimal conversation. His cold hands moved over my ribs and the remaining yellowed bruises with a practiced expertise.

"You've healed well. Now just a shot to help your vitamin deficiency."

"No, I'm good, thanks."

"It's not a choice."

Neo moved to hold me, and I let my limbs fall loose. There was no point in resistance. I felt the sting as the doctor jabbed a needle into my arm. Neo flinched too.

Sometime through the night the injection took effect, and it was no vitamin.

I wanted to kill someone, or myself. Rage spread through my body like poison. It started slowly, but then accelerated until I was spinning and spinning, about to explode. The anger was a fire in my belly, burning hot within, threatening to consume me. I could feel my own fist smashing into my face as my screams tore through my throat. Although hyperfocused, I couldn't think clearly. I was all sensation. My body rocked with agony; my bones felt like they would burst from my skin.

Neo appeared from a fog. Strong, comforting arms wrapped around me, but the rage within was out of control. I struggled against him, while he wrapped me in a blanket, like a straitjacket.

Around midday the following day, my body was exhausted, and my struggles were feeble twitches. Emotionally, I felt hollow, wrung out. The gnawing pit in my stomach had twisted into a cold, ruthless nausea.

"Let me up." They were the first intelligent words I had uttered for hours.

Watching me warily, Neo loosened his hold and unwrapped my burrito blanket.

"Can I go to the bathroom?" I asked.

He nodded. When I tried to stand, I collapsed back against him. He scooped me up and carried me again. It was becoming an embarrassing habit.

"What happened to me? What did that doctor give me?"

Neo's eyes were sympathetic but cautious. "I don't know what it is, but we all get it before a fight."

"Does it make you feel angry?"

"Yeah, and fearless. It doesn't affect me like it did you though."

I searched through my fuzzy memories. Abraham had said he was making his own warriors and Sidney had mentioned there were artificial enzymes that imitated the warrior gene. That was what I had been given. I was sure of it. A cocktail of aggression.

"Where does Abe get it from?" I asked.

"The drug trials at the Uni lab. He funds them. It's to make us stronger." Neo was all innocence.

It seemed clear that Abraham's funding at the University allowed him special access to certain drug trials. He was creating his own warriors with a synthetic warrior gene. Yet, it didn't explain the bigger picture, the global pandemic of violence and anger. It couldn't have started with Abraham.

"Neo, you have to help me get out of here. I can't go through that again."

A hard shiver shook my body. I drew from deep inside and let my emotions pour into Neo, so he would feel my vulnerability and my fear.

"I can't." He shuddered too.

I knew his body was tired with my exhaustion, his heart hurt with my pain. He didn't want to go through it again, yet the loyalty Abraham commanded had been beaten into his followers until it was a part of them.

"Please. I'll die if I go through that again," I repeated.

"If I help you, I'll be killed." But I felt his mind turning, he wanted to help me.

I hoped he would find a way.

The doctor returned two days later. His medical examination was perfunctory. The injection loomed.

"Please, don't. I can't have it again." My plea was useless against Abraham's word.

"Hold her," the doctor instructed Neo.

"Neo, please, not again."

Neo wrapped his strong arms around me. He jerked and shook as my fear passed into him and he had to steady himself. The doctor paused, with a look of confusion, but then the needle pricked against my arm. As my body bucked in rebellion, my elbow came loose from Neo's grip and struck the doctor in the face. He stumbled backwards. I felt Neo's arms withdraw, and the doctor dropped to the floor at my feet. Behind him, Neo grinned at me. He had knocked the doctor out cold.

"Go, quickly, before I change my mind. Left down the hall, take the fire exit. When you reach the ground, run, and do not stop running. Abe will be coming for you."

"Thank you." I hugged him and let my gratitude flow.

He smiled and ducked his head in embarrassment. "Go. Now."

"Will you be ok?"

"I'll think of something."

I ran.

36

The sun was blinding after being inside for so long, and the deserted streets seemed exceptionally dirty after living in an all-white environment. My limbs were stiff from lack of exercise, but I kept running until I felt the enzymes take effect.

The all-consuming fire roared through me. I had no idea where I was, just that everything was hurting, and I needed to get it out of me. The only way to do that was to hurt someone else. I wrapped my arms tightly around my chest, a self-hug, but hurting myself, keeping myself restrained to avoid hurting others. There was screaming in my head, burning in my mouth. Ants crawled under my skin. I found a dark corner, the car park behind some abandoned restaurants. A derelict car, flat tyres. I smashed the window, enjoying the pain, the rush of adrenaline. Climbing in, I curled into a ball, behind the front seat, down on the floor. It was dark and dirty, but it was safe. More importantly I couldn't hurt anyone. I rocked against the seat while bad dreams and visions haunted me. I wasn't sure what was real, but I knew I was alive because the pain pulsed through my body, an electric current. Being dead couldn't hurt like this.

Cooper came to me. "Nova, I know I'm not very brave, but you make me want to be."

"You are brave, and strong, Coop."

"No, you are the strongest, bravest person I know."

He was soft, sweet, and caring. But it was not real.

Jackson came and challenged me.

"Nova, I set you free so you would come back to me."

"I don't know how to get back."

"You can do it. You are strong. Believe in yourself."

"I can't. The darkness is all around me."

"Then believe in me. I won't let the darkness take you."

His arms were around me, his breathing was regular, and the rise and fall of his chest was lulling. But it was not real.

Sage was there too.

"All you think about is boys."

"I'm a teenage girl, all I'm supposed to think about is boys."

"Then think about the good times, Nova."

"I can't do this, Sage. It's too hard."

"Suck it up, buttercup."

"Stick together?"

"Like glue."

She wasn't really there, either.

I saw Neo. He had been beaten but he was alive.

"I can show you the door. You have to walk through it."

He was misquoting movie lines at me. It wasn't real.

When I woke the blood had dried on my knuckles, and the skin was ragged, raw, and bruised. I was still in the car and still fighting the anger and aggression. The images in my dreams hung in my mind, while my stomach twisted in fear. I dragged air into my lungs, almost unwilling to continue breathing. The hatred was a toxic tide inside me. I wanted Abraham dead. All I could focus on was revenge. I wanted the man who killed my friend to see me coming and I wanted him to feel my loathing, to remember what he had done to Finn, before I cut his throat. After that, I didn't care what happened. Anger was my companion; it kept my heart beating and aggression pumped through my veins.

I was burning hot and knew my body was trying to reject the poison. I drifted in and out, not always sure what was real.

Someone found me, attracted by the broken glass. His hands moved over my clothes and I stiffened, but realised he was only looking for money or weapons. A teenager like me, grubby, skinny, living on the streets most likely. I hardly registered him being there.

Darkness fell, an old friend. I was not sure how long it had been since I escaped. For a moment, I felt good, I was alive and free. My thoughts turned to Finn again, and the familiar shockwaves passed through me, but this time I sat firmly, with clear eyes and steady hands.

The street kid had come back. He was asleep on the back seat.

"Hey, I'm Nova." I was attempting an introduction, but my voice was raspy and almost unintelligible.

He mumbled some words that ended with - "Bellamy."

"Are you from around here, Bellamy?"

His eyes narrowed in suspicion but then he nodded.

Another round of nausea hit me and stopped any further conversation. My body had rejected the artificial enzyme again, and Bellamy thought I was detoxing. I shook and shivered, headaches throbbed through my brain, and my arms and legs ached. Hardly able to move for hours, I was lethargic, but then restless when I tried to sleep. My stomach cramped when I ate, churning until I vomited. I rolled myself into a ball, rocking in time to a song in my head, staring at nothing at all. I felt Bellamy soaking up my strength, and it drained me. He had no energy to give in return. I was an empty shell.

With intermittent conversation, I slowly found out a little more about Bellamy. He was younger than I had thought, only fourteen. Tall and wiry, he had a maturity forced on him by rough living. His skin hid behind layers of grime and his blonde hair hung in a tangled mop. He knew how to stay hidden and survive. Any attention could mean trouble that he would rather avoid. We were in Richmond, his home ground. Even though the days were warm, Bellamy wore layers of clothing. Designer labels but looking a little tired and well worn. He got me some jeans and a jumper for the nights. They looked clean and new, and I suspected they had been stolen from a clothesline. He scrounged for food, looting through abandoned shops, or stealing. I didn't ask. We stayed in the car at night.

In some ways, it was easy being with Bellamy. He did not ask questions or make demands. There were no plans to be made other than sourcing some food each day. I had no money but nor did he. Bellamy knew which shelters provided meal programs and the best time to arrive. We went unnoticed. I had no phone. There was no way of tracing me. I needed to stay away from Abraham's gang.

The days passed while I regained some strength. I was still unsure on what to do, and worried about putting Sage and Luca in danger. Sawyer and the team might have given up looking for me by now.

Gradually, as Bellamy came to trust me, he talked.

"You can't stay at the shelters, or they try and find your parents. I'm not going back home. I'm not a child anymore. It used to be okay when I was little, but when my mum left it was shit with my dad. I had to leave, or he would have killed me."

I sensed one of those dark areas he had buried inside. Child abuse.

"It's better to just take the food and go. I lie about my age. They don't bother if they think I'm sixteen. I could be with a gang, and they don't want trouble. But I keep away from the gangs. I keep away from everyone. Except you."

I sensed his puzzlement. He was not sure why he felt safe around me.

"Bellamy, have you seen Abraham, the leader of the gang?"

"Yeah, I seen him. A nasty dude."

"Very nasty. I can't let him find me."

"Yeah. Okay."

The next day Bellamy got me a cap, to help keep my face hidden. It was time to get my life back.

"Bellamy, I need to get back to my friends. They will be worried about me. I have been gone a while. It will be a long walk though. Will you help me?"

He nodded and gave me one of his rare smiles. "Are they like you?"

"What do you mean?" I laughed.

He searched for words. "Nice."

"They are nice." I smiled, picturing Sage and Luca. "We can get you some food and clothes too if you want."

He shrugged; he did not need much.

The fog hung heavy, clinging to trees and buildings, but there was the promise of a sunny day when it lifted. Bellamy and I set out early. It was about a three-hour walk, mostly sticking to back streets, but I could not take a chance of being seen on public transport. We headed in what we thought was the general direction and looked for road signs.

I made for the hospital, in case Abraham was watching the apartment, and it offered a better chance of getting in unnoticed. Following Bellamy's lead, with my cap pulled down low, we shuffled in through the emergency department doors. From there, I knew my way to the children's ward. I sent Bellamy in, with a message for Sage and waited in the hospital toilet.

When Sage stepped through the door, before I could even draw breath, I was drawn into a tight bear-hug. There was disbelief in her eyes as if she thought I was part of a dream. I felt like I had been standing for weeks and had finally sat down. Her joy was a cloak around me while my body shook with sobs. I released the tension and fear I had been holding. Sage pulled back and wiped my tears with a gentle finger. Her light touch was a clear message of her relief and love.

"I knew you were still alive." Her mouth was a soft smile and she folded me into her arms again.

I just nodded, and blinked, and let her talk.

They had found Finn's body. Hearing his name still sent a jolt through my heart. Abraham had claimed it was a street brawl and his men had witnessed the whole thing. When asked about me, he denied any knowledge. I gave Sage an abbreviated version of what had really happened. Her emotions oscillated from disbelief to anger, to horror, and sympathy.

"Are they watching the apartment?" I asked.

"Maybe. Rayna is here. Luca too. She will take us back. Is the kid with you?"

I nodded. "Bellamy. I promised him some food and clothes. He's a good friend and kind of saved my life."

"Of course."

"Stick together?"

"Like glue."

I changed clothes with Sage. As I was taller than she was, her jeans only went to mid-calf, but I was even skinnier after my ordeal, so they fitted easily. Luca held my hand and the two of us followed Rayna to the car. I had kept the cap on, with my hair tucked up underneath. A close look would have easily given me away, but from a distance I could pass as Sage. We went around the block and did not seem to have a tail. When we came back to the hospital entrance, Bellamy and Sage were waiting.

Bellamy stayed silent, his eyes darting around nervously. He shifted uncomfortably in his seat. I was bombarded with questions from Rayna, who was clearly preparing a report for Sawyer. I told her all about the artificial warrior gene enzymes and the drug trials that Abraham was using to create his warriors. I confirmed that he did recruit from the UFC. Sage gripped my hand like she would never let it go. Luca kept turning from the front seat to look at me, eyes shining, mouth in a wide grin, and his sense of relief was unmistakable. I felt like a flower garden coming back to life after the winter.

At the apartment, I followed a similar procedure, pretending to be Sage. She and Bellamy came up the stairs a few minutes later. Rayna didn't think that anyone was watching us. She went to find Sawyer. The ugly yellow walls of the apartment were a welcoming smile after my time on the streets. It still had not been painted. The waft of Vietnamese food from below was soothing and familiar. I longed for a proper bed and felt the bedroom calling to me from down the hall.

"Nova, I love you and you would not believe how glad I am that you are home, but you stink. These clothes are putrid. You need to shower and change." Sage spoke quietly, and her nostrils flared delicately as she got a whiff of my odour.

I realised that she did not want Bellamy to hear her. I sniffed myself, but I was used to our smell. Luca had Bellamy in the kitchen, looking in the fridge. His eyes were as wide as saucers with the choice of food. He might want to shower and change into clean clothes if I set the example. I was hoping we might keep him with us, off the streets. Mind you, I was not sure what the next steps would be now. Probably not staying here. I needed to talk to Sawyer. After a shower.

37

Steam filled the bathroom and I let the water cleanse my mind as well as my body. If only the images of Finn could drain away with the dirt. In my own clothes, I was feeling like my old self, almost. My stomach rumbled to remind me of priorities, as the noise of cutlery and plates made a clatter on the table out in the dining room.

I was fighting a losing battle with the knots in my hair when the murmur of voices in the kitchen stopped. Fear slammed into me, a punch to the stomach.

I knew what it was before I even stepped out of the bathroom. There were five steps down the hallway to the lounge area. I clenched my teeth.

Abraham was there, casually leaning up against the couch. One hand was behind his back and I knew it would be resting on the gun he had tucked into his pants. His eyes narrowed when he saw me. I sensed his arrogance and pride, but there was not a glimmer of humanity or compassion. We had been stupid to think we could outsmart him. Luca and Bellamy were sitting at the dining table, adjoining the lounge, plates of sandwiches before them but no longer eating. Sage stood by the kitchen entrance, closest to me. There was a thick tension in the silent room. I could hear myself breathing.

"You seem to have nine lives." Abraham's smile was sinister.

"Abe." My voice was a squeak.

I will not be afraid. I replayed my mantra in my head.

Luca rose to his feet, brave and terrified at the same time. Bellamy seemed to fade into the background, a useful skill. I felt Sage digging deep for her courage.

"I just want Nova." Abraham's tone was one that was accustomed to being obeyed. "No one needs to get hurt."

Sage stepped out in front of me. She had a small pistol in her hand. It was something she must have acquired while I had been missing. Her hands were clumsy as she brought it up to aim.

"No." Her voice rang out, clear and defiant.

Abraham reacted instantly. Violently.

He shot her, two bullets, into her chest.

It sounded like a whip cracking, twice. Time does not move in slow motion when a bullet is coming for a person you love. There are no matrix moves to stop its progress. It happens in a millisecond. Two milliseconds.

Sage bent double then dropped to her knees. Her hands were clutched against her chest. There was so much blood. It pooled on the floor. I knelt beside her, gently easing her onto her back, so I could press my hands into the wounds. My thoughts were scattered but my instincts said that pressure would stop the bleeding. At least I hoped so. She had changed out of my clothes into a bright summer dress. It was ruined. Somehow that seemed important. I knew it was one of her favourites.

"It hurts," Sage said. "How bad is it?"

"It's fine. You're going to be fine." I was commanding it.

Luca was beside me now. I felt his confusion and fear, pulling me into a deep hole. He patted her hair, tiny dry sobs escaping from his mouth in gulps of air.

"We need an ambulance." I looked around the room searching for something, someone, to help but there was nothing and I turned back to Sage. "You're going to be okay."

"Stick together?" Sage's eyes found mine, and all she had was love.

"Like glue." I gave her the response we both needed to hear.

"Don't go to a dark place." Her voice was hushed. "Promise me."

I nodded.

"Say it. Promise me."

"I promise."

Sage turned to Luca.

"Luca, I love you."

Her emotions spilled into me. They were a whirlpool. I took them and cherished them, even as they spun me around. There was shock and disbelief, then sadness, worry and fear. And finally, there was hope and love. So much love. Her love was a life raft in the churning waters, it was the sunshine in the black storm. I clung to her.

There was a frozen second as the life left her eyes. The light was sucked from the room, from the world. We were all left in darkness.

Sage was dead.

Instead of me.

I searched for meaning, for understanding, for something to make sense, but there was nothing that did.

All I noticed were the small things. The shaving cut on Luca's chin. A fly that had landed on the tip of the knife next to a plate of sandwiches on the table. The distant drone of a car a few streets away. A smell of fresh mint floating up from the restaurant below.

And Abraham watching me, cold, cruel, and calculating.

A violent spasm ripped through my body. My throat was so tight I could hardly breathe. A powerful grief was growing deep within me. It was angry and desperate to be let out. I could not hold it in. It came out as a silent shock wave, the blast effect from a nuclear explosion. The effects ricocheted around the room. Luca cringed beside me, under its onslaught. I saw Abraham's knees buckle, and he grabbed at the chair to steady himself. His eyes finally registered some emotion. It was surprise.

I had taken Sage's pistol from her, and it felt cold and unfamiliar in my hand. There was a battle within my body, as rage fought against the anguish. My heart was a pounding hammer. My skin was on fire. Although it was hardly a conscious thought, I knew I had an opportunity, it was now or never.

I pulled the trigger, multiple shots in quick succession. These shots sounded more like gentle pops. They were no less deadly.

The irony was not lost on me. It was the residue of Abraham's synthetic warrior gene, that still swam through my body, that had given me the strength I needed to fire that gun.

Abraham slid down the back of the couch while still sitting upright, leaving a bloody smudge on the velvet. His eyes stared ahead, with no focus. I could tell he was dead because I felt nothing, nothing at all, from him.

Sawyer broke through the door, Jet and Rayna on his heels. The noise of the gunshots, probably. It took Sawyer seconds to take it in, but he was too late. Their shock and concern smothered me. From Luca there was an icy numbness. Bellamy slipped quietly out of the room. He knew how to disappear. Nothing mattered now. There was a low moaning sound and I realised it came from me.

"Get her out of here. I'll take care of this." Sawyer took the pistol from my hand.

I was not sure who he was talking to or who he was talking about. The floor was cold under my knees. Sage's blood was warm on my hands and in my lap, but there was no life force.

Sawyer spoke quietly, giving instructions. I let them float over my head.

Emotions crowded at me, including my own anger, which felt like a poison dripping down the back of my throat. I didn't have the energy to sort out what the others were feeling but I recognised the gentle calm wave lapping against all of us, which I knew came from Sawyer. I clung to it.

Luca had Sage in his arms. Silent tears ran down his face. Jet had a hand on Luca's shoulder and reached his other to me. I ignored it.

"Nova, we have to go. Now." Jet pressed a hand to my back.

Luca sat in the back seat of the jeep and Sage was wrapped in a blanket across his knees. I knew her body would still be warm to touch but when I probed for her usual lively spark, I felt only an emptiness which left me chilled. I sat in the front, with Rayna driving. We had changed our clothes, Luca and I like machines, Jet giving orders and moving our limbs for us. Rayna had documentation allowing us to take Sage home.

"Hold it together, guys. We need to get through the checkpoint." Rayna's voice was splintered with guilt, for not being there to protect us.

"We're fine," Luca said.

Luca was trying to be strong for me, yet his loss was just as significant. I knew I needed to be brave now, more than ever before. I straightened my back, focusing on the road ahead.

A darkness swirled deep inside me, settling into a crater. Abraham would no longer draw breath, his heart would no longer beat, all because of me.

38

Today

It was the first Tuesday in February. The day of Sage's funeral and exactly twelve months since we had started our senior year. It seemed like a lifetime ago.

Rayna had stayed to help Sage's sisters with the funeral arrangements. Yesterday, she had left for Melbourne to assist Sawyer and the team. They would be moving in on Abraham City. I had done them a favour.

We were back at Mia's house, after leaving the funeral home, having a few drinks to commemorate Sage's life. Mia came to refill my drink. Her eyes still held the grief of her father's death, and now brimmed with the added loss of Sage. Fatigue was etched on her face, but her natural smile sprang just as readily, if a little less bright.

"You okay?" she asked me, for the second time.

I nodded. "You?"

"Not really, but we'll get there."

"Yeah."

"Sage would be wondering why we haven't started drinking shots."

"Yeah." I plastered a smile on my face, but a dead weight pressed against my chest. "Maybe later."

Mia moved on, checking on people's drinks, making friendly conversation. Her heart was large enough to take care of us all.

Ava sat beside me. Her shoulders were hunched over, and her red curls hung lifeless and drab. There was a gaunt, haunted look to her eyes. The year had not been kind to any of us, but Ava's journey had been particularly difficult. Her painful memories, her nightmares, were still cutting deep. I sensed her courage though; it had just been buried. It was like new plant life pushing through regardless of the rocky inhospitable ground. That was hopeful. I silently vowed to help her, just not today. I didn't have the energy, today.

It had been three months since I had seen Jackson, and Cooper even longer. I watched Mia talking quietly with them, sharing a memory of Sage. Their sadness swelled but was intertwined with friendship and love. Jackson noticed my stare and sent me a wink and a grin. It was not his usual mischievous one, but it was affectionate and enquiring. I returned the smile I had been practising. I knew he saw through it when he started making his way over.

"We need to talk." Jackson's manner was curt but gentle at the same time.

I followed him out into the night. Mia's backyard was a miniature woodland of native shrubs and trees. Without someone tending to it, now that it was no longer safe to potter about outside, the neglect had set in. It was not without beauty though, and floodlights shone on the overgrown but blooming garden beds. I moved off the patio into the dark, where I knew it would be harder for Jackson to see my face. His eyes demanded my attention, but I kept my gaze lowered.

"You have got to let it out, Nova. You've put up a wall and locked us out. It's weird and uncomfortable." He came straight to the point as always, provoking me, hoping to get a response.

I shrugged, not game to let myself get angry at him.

"You can let yourself feel. In fact, you need to." He tried the gentle approach.

"I know, and I will. Just not today. I want to be strong for Luca."

"He's dealing with it. It's you I'm worried about."

Jackson paused, searching for the right words. I knew he was aching to hold me.

"You'll always have a safe place with me, if you want to let it all go." He was worried he had lost that special part of my heart.

"I know I do. Thanks. I'm worried I'll be a mess if I let go."

"I love it when you're a mess." Jackson chuckled.

"What if I let go and I can't bring myself back?" That was what I was worried about.

"Nova, I'll bring you back." He had turned serious again.

"What if you can't, Jack?"

"I can, I will. I promise I will."

The grief and the shadow inside, scared me. Especially when I had no Sage to help me recover. She was the glue that had held me together. I had no Sage, ever again.

"It wasn't me that flew too close to the sun. It was Sage," I said flatly.

He did not reply but he reached for my hand and flattened his palm against mine as we interlocked our fingers.

"Jack, Abe ..." The sentence hung in the air; I couldn't finish it.

Jackson nodded his understanding.

"Everything seems different now. It's like I know this is my body, my arms, my legs, my hands, but they don't feel the same. I don't feel the same," I tightened my grip on his hand.

"You are still you."

"But different. I have a darkness inside now." My voice quivered but I held onto my control.

"Nova, don't do that. It's grief, shock, mourning."

"Now you sound like Sage."

His face reflected the pain I would not let myself feel, at the sound of her name.

"Good. She was always right. There is no darkness in you. You had to do it, Nova."

"Did I? I'm not sure what it has done to me."

The pocket of blackness was there, and I knew it was permanent. It had settled, burrowed its way into me. I shuffled my feet, but still clung to Jackson's hand, like a lifeline.

"Nova, you are the best person I know." I felt his frustration at not being able to fix this for me. "I should have been there. I wish I had done it instead of you."

Although Jackson was fiercely protective, I wondered if he really could have done it.

"It was awful with Finn."

"It must have been." Jackson's voice cracked with pain and there was a glimmer of silver in his eyes.

It was his sorrow that tipped me over and I finally broke down.

It was a deluge. Grief poured out of me in blazing, blistering waves. I couldn't hold it in anymore. Jackson staggered as the tide hit him and he dropped my hand. He was in agony, but it was my anguish that he was feeling. Recognising what was happening, he took a deep breath and steadied himself.

His arms encircled me, holding tight, taking the brunt of it. It tested his strength too. We sank to our knees, still clinging together. Sobs rocked my body, and I could feel their echo in Jackson's. My mind jarred with each memory, the pain seared through my skin and took away every feeling of safety I had ever had. The sweet, good moments became an angry knife that slashed at my damaged heart.

Jackson did bring me back. I could feel his love for Sage, and for me, like a giant soft blanket. Slowly but persistently, it folded around my anguish. It did not extinguish the pain, but it soothed and protected me. It was some time before either of us could move or talk. We had been taken apart and then put back together, clumsily, and it felt a little unstable.

"I am a mess," I said.

"I told you I love you as a mess." His voice was croaky, like he needed a drink.

I tried a smile. It felt like the skin was peeling off my face.

"I miss her, so much."

"She knew you loved her."

"Yeah."

"Sawyer told me about Finn, but somehow I already knew. Sometimes, I thought you were talking to me, inside my head." He gave an embarrassed smile. "I was so worried when I heard you were missing but Sawyer wanted me to stay here, in case you came looking for me."

"I couldn't."

"I know."

"I think I was talking to you, in my dreams. Sage too."

The emotion welled up again, but it was softer. I didn't need to put the wall back up. Although I was still floundering, the sea was calmer, a gentler rocking. Jackson grinned at me; cheekiness restored.

"You are breathing properly again." His voice carried relief. "Before it was like you were permanently holding your breath."

People were starting to leave. It was almost curfew. Luca came to find me. I sensed he had something important to say. Jackson moved away to give us some privacy.

"It's not your fault, Nova. That's who Sage was." Luca's tone was gentle but firm.

I nodded and my eyes watered up again. "I don't know how I'll manage without her."

"You have to. We all do." His strength was inspiring, and I tried to echo it back to him. "Thanks for everything today. She would have liked it."

"Yeah. She would have." I rubbed my hand on his arm.

"I'll see you soon?" he asked.

"Definitely. Love you."

"Love you too."

We had not discussed what was happening next. It was too soon.

Imogen approached with a guy I had not met before. They were also getting ready to leave. She clung onto his arm, as if for support.

"Hi, Nova. Sorry I didn't get a chance to come over earlier." She hugged me. "I've missed you. This is my boyfriend, Charles."

I could feel her hesitancy. She didn't know if I'd forgiven her for Cooper, even though so much had happened since then.

"Hi, Charles." Charles and I smiled weakly at each other.

I sensed a kind and generous guy, and I was pleased for Imogen.

Cooper came over, as Imogen walked away. I guessed that he would have preferred to avoid talking with her. He studied me and I knew I must have looked terrible, with puffy eyes and a washed-out face.

"You know I have an available shoulder to cry on, if you need it?"

"Thanks, Coop."

He reached for my hands and held them in his. I had missed Cooper's warm hugs. Maybe his steady love could put me back together.

"Nova, I hate how I ruined things between us," he paused, "I'm sorry about everything before. I had some growing up to do."

"Have you done that now?" I smiled; it was happening more naturally now.

He and Jackson had turned nineteen while I had been held captive by Abraham. I wondered if nineteen qualified as being grown up.

"Yeah, I hope so." He grinned back at me.

"I'm still in love with you, Nova. I think I always will be."

"I'll always care about you too, Coop."

"Is it our time now? Are you staying here?" He was hopeful.

I looked down, twisting my hands together. The picture rose before my eyes. Cooper belonged here, in this town. Stable and secure. I could stay, be with him, get a job or start university, if they got that sorted. Helping the people of our town, staying close to my friends, having a normal life. Safe. Familiar. Comfortable.

"Coop, I'm just not sure."

I didn't know which question I was answering. He would not know either.

"We should talk. Just the two of us. I could take you out to the national park again." His voice was still wistful.

"I'd really love that."

Cooper looked over my shoulder and I followed his gaze to see Jackson watching us. When I turned back, Cooper pulled me into an embrace and kissed me, hard. As always, we melted into each other. I felt his love for me, pure and honest. A new level of maturity had joined his natural confidence and his kindness. He had grown up. The kiss had a sense of ownership though, and I did not know how I felt about that. I pulled back first.

He smiled. "It's still there, Nova."

My returning smile was non-committal.

"Can I call you tomorrow?" he asked.

"Sure."

Cooper walked away. Jackson replaced him at my side.

"Have you come to tell me off again?" My tone was light and joking.

"Only if you need it."

The air between us sizzled with tension. He did have something else to say.

"So, you've chosen Coop?" His voice was harsh.

I shrugged. These twins were doing my head in again. My brain was on low battery.

"It's okay. I want you both to be happy," Jackson said, more gently.

I still did not respond.

"Are you staying around for a while?"

"I'm really not sure."

"You're not giving much away."

We stood silently, each lost in our own thoughts. I felt him trying to give me space but at the same time wanting answers.

"If you go, when you go, I want to come with you. If you'll let me." His head tilted as he reached up to brush the hair from his face.

His eyes were searching, still trying to determine what I felt, while he shared his love without reservation. That was my other choice. Adventure, excitement, passion, love, Jackson at my side, wherever life took us. I could picture that too, and for the first time in over a week I felt my heart stutter as if coming alive again. My body tingled as adrenaline coursed through me. That is what I had wanted, once. But there would be no Sage this time. My heart lurched again. The darkness tugged at it.

Jackson must have felt the quick roller coaster of my emotions. His face clouded with confusion and doubt. Before he could probe some more, I changed the subject.

"Have you still got that bike?"

He looked at me carefully, wondering if I was serious. I grinned at him, feeling a lift of energy, and raised my eyebrows, waiting on his response.

"Yeah. But it's a risk to take it out. It still attracts all the crazies. And I have to go hard to get to the town limits before I get caught."

"I'm game if you're game."

I was taunting him, knowing that he couldn't resist a dare, knowing that it stopped him from asking questions and analysing me.

His responding grin was playful. "Always."

I could feel Jackson's love for me. It was different to Cooper's. Jackson loved like I did, deep and intense. This kind of love had scared Cooper. Jackson thrived on it. His love was a challenge, a thrill. It dared me to be better, to be more.

"Have you got a jacket for me?"

"I've still got yours."

I nodded, imagining the smell of the soft leather. It was a very fond memory.

"You'll have to hang on tight because I'll be going fast. Are you up for that?" Jackson taunted me now.

"Always." I fought against the smile that threatened.

It started as a chuckle, but like a stone dropped into a pond, the ripples radiated out until they became great waves of hilarity. It broke another barrier, another piece of the wall I had put up. We were two idiots laughing together, a little hysterical, after the worst day ever.

I looked deep into Jackson's dark brown eyes. They shone with his love and his desire. You did not have to be an empath to see it.

"There's one more thing, Lewis."

"What's that, Wilson?"

I reached for him and pulled him into a kiss. Jackson's lips locked onto mine. We burned. A slow scorch which warmed my heart and lit a fire deep inside. He returned my passion, the flames smouldering then flaring within him. When we paused for air, breathless, Jackson could not wipe the smile from his face.

He knew I had come back to him.

Epilogue

Theo was Abraham's second-in-command. A chill shivered through his body when he closed the coffin on his boss. He knew that Nova had killed Abraham, despite what the police said. It was the only thing that made sense. Abraham had told him that he was bringing her back and now he was dead. She had mind-controlled Neo and he still wore the bruises from the beating he had suffered as a result. Somehow, she had got to Abraham as well.

The blood surged through his veins, hungry for vengeance. The warrior gene enzymes fed his anger and aggression. He needed a plan, and it was not his forte. It might take some time, but he would get his revenge.

Acknowledgements

A small group of people gave me the courage to bring this book to life. They were my first proofreaders and unofficial editors. A huge thanks to my family – Graeme, Jordan, Brodie, Loueen and Mark, and to my close friends – Mandy, Maggie and Dean. Thanks guys, for your encouragement, support, all the suggestions, and for making the time to read and re-read my drafts.

I also want to acknowledge the 'young doctors', my high school friends, and especially Debbie, my lifelong best friend. Our adventures together provided me with some rich inspiration for my characters.

About the Author

Lyndal Hennell grew up in Melbourne, Victoria. At high school, her friends were nicknamed 'the young doctors' because their escapades were like a soapie drama.

Lyndal currently lives on the Sunshine Coast in Queensland. She loves cats, drinking hot chocolate and walking on the beach.

When she is not writing, Lyndal works as a registered psychologist, providing counselling support to young adults.

Flying Close to the Sun is her first novel.

www.ingramcontent.com/pod-product-compliance
Lightning Source LLC
Chambersburg PA
CBHW070537120726
47909CB00007B/2163